"YOU NEED CARNIVAL, JUSTIN. IT'S JUST WHAT THE DOCTOR ORDERED."

Bethany was only half joking. To let go and celebrate with few inhibitions was foreign to Justin, and somehow she knew that if he could learn to be less careful, his life would be happier.

"Analysis from the beautiful mask maker?" he asked.

"Before I can make the masks, I have to understand what goes on underneath them."

She held her breath as his mouth descended to hers. Justin's kiss was hungry, slowly devouring her with a steady aching pressure that threatened to eat into her very soul. Her hands tangled in his black hair, and she fingered the silky strands as he deepened the kiss.

"And what do you need?" he asked as he raised his head.

It was the perfect time to tell him she needed only him to make her life complete. But admitting that she still loved him was one confession too many to make.

"I think I need another kiss," she said, instead.

ABOUT THE AUTHOR

Now a resident of New Orleans, Emilie Richards and her husband, a minister, have lived in six different states. Emilie has a master's degree in family development, and in between raising her own four children, working in the social services field, traveling and pursuing her musical talents, she has found time to write four romance novels, including *The Unmasking*.

Emilie Richards

THE UNMASKING

Harlequin Books

TORONTO • NEW YORK • LONDON
AMSTERDAM • PARIS • SYDNEY • HAMBURG
STOCKHOLM • ATHENS • TOKYO • MILAN

Published July 1985

First printing May 1985

ISBN 0-373-70172-1

CHAPTER ONE

GRAY SKIES filled with billowing silver rain clouds melted into the distant jagged points of concrete-and-glass buildings. Dreary, bleak...these were not words normally used to describe the New Orleans French Quarter, but on this morning, the Quarter was the personification of the weather pervading the sleeping city. Slate-and-shingle roofs were slick and shiny with the previous night's storm, as were the charcoal-colored streets below them. No shafts of sunlight lit the historic old stores surrounding the French market, and the flea market, usually a lively, pulsating mass of color and humanity, was strangely subdued.

In the early-morning quiet, vendors were setting up their tables. Those who had reserved stalls under the covered walkway were cheerier than those who were setting up spaces in the parking lot. A proliferation of beach umbrellas and makeshift canvas shelters testified to the pessimism of the latter. A rainy day could spell disaster for vendors who ignored the warning signs and allowed their displays of leather goods, watches, paperback books, or countless other items to face ruin.

Under the covered walkway, two brilliant spots of color shone like beacons in the gloomy atmosphere. Hot-pink and scarlet ostrich feathers rode on top of the swirling dark hair of a young woman setting up one of the stalls. Next to her, a bright-eyed little imp wearing a woven satin headband of emerald-green satin and peacock plumes danced impatiently. "I want to do it. I'm big enough!"

At the same time that most young children were firmly ensconced in front of the television set in their pajamas, watching the Saturday-morning cartoons, Abby Walker was trying hard to help her mother unpack fragile feather masks and headpieces from a large wooden crate. Bethany Walker watched fondly as her daughter carefully unwrapped an intricate mask of Lady Amherst pheasant and laid it reverently on the black velvet spread draping the folding table.

Hopping first on one foot and then the other, the little girl finally arranged the mask to suit her taste. "Right there, mommy." Bethany bent over to land a quick kiss on her daughter's cheek as Abby giggled, "That tickles!"

Reaching to straighten the tiny headdress Abby was wearing, Bethany apologized with a wink. "I forgot I was wearing my mask. Tickling is the main problem with feathers."

"I can tickle, too." Abby lowered her head, flicking her mother's waistline with peacock tail feathers. "See?"

"I give up. You win." Bethany threw her hands above her head in mock defeat. "If you tickle me anymore, I won't be able to sell a single mask today."

Selling masks at the French market was not the way Bethany and Abby ordinarily spent Saturdays. Never a day of leisure, Saturday was always hectic and filled with work, but usually that work was done in the little shop, Life's Illusions, that Bethany owned with her friend Madeline Conroy. For the past six Saturdays, however, Bethany had chosen to display choice pieces from the shop inventory at the flea market in hopes that the added exposure would bring potential customers to the Royal Street store when they decided to purchase masks for Mardi Gras.

The fact that Bethany had no free weekends might have posed a serious problem if Abby were in school or if Bethany had a husband to coordinate schedules with. But Abby was only four and there was no man at home whose own work schedule had to be taken into consideration. Abby and Bethany could steal time to relax and to play without consulting anyone. This close to carnival, however, there were very few moments left to steal.

Standing erect, Bethany adjusted the mirror she had hung over her display so that potential customers could see themselves in the variety of masks she would try to sell that day. The mask she was wearing was one of her favorites and one of her own creations. In addition to the graceful, curled ostrich plumes that swept down over her hair to lay sensuously on her shoulder, there was an arc of smaller dyed feathers, curving in a solid sheet over one eye. Only an almond-shaped peephole allowed her to see from that side at all.

Although over one-third of her face was hidden from view, no one who knew Bethany would be fooled. The mask failed to hide enough of the milky-white skin, the large gray-blue eyes and the oval face with its decidedly pointed chin to keep her identity a secret. And secrecy had not been the point of this mask, anyway. Bethany had never felt comfortable withholding who she was from the world. Open and direct, she liked the scarlet-

and-pink mask because she could give the illusion of disguise without really hiding at all.

"I think that's it." After adjusting the mirror to her satisfaction, Bethany finished putting the last masks in the display case that held her most expensive creations. From the bottom of the packing crate she removed a small box of business cards. *Life's Illusions*, they stated in bold print. "We can't forget these, can we sweetheart?" After inserting a small sign into a lucite holder, she was finished setting up the table.

Abby had managed to exercise all the patience a four-year-old is capable of, but now that she knew her mother was finished, she tugged at her. "I'm hungry, mommy."

Bethany pulled a chair up behind the table and held out her arms. With Abby on her lap, she opened a paper bag filled with small square pastries covered with a cloud of confectioner's sugar.

"*Beignets.* And I've got a cup of hot chocolate for you and café au lait for me." Buying treats for her daughter was one way Bethany tried to make the long days spent behind the table at the flea market or the counter of the shop more fun for the little girl. It was not a bribe, but rather a thank-you gift for Abby's co-operation. Today they ate the puffy French doughnuts with gusto, taking care not to cover the black velvet spread with the powdered sugar.

"Abby, I think you just gained a pound." Bethany lifted the little girl onto the ground and they both dusted their hands over the sidewalk behind them.

"I like the flea market, mommy. I wish we could come every day."

"This is the last Saturday for a long time, I'm afraid,

sweetheart. Business at the shop will be picking up, now that Mardi Gras is getting closer, and we won't need the extra exposure.'' Bethany shook her head as Abby, ignoring her explanation, crossed the aisle to stare in admiration at a nearby table full of brightly painted wooden toys.

The flea market was beginning to come to life. Although it was only 8:00 A.M. and not all the spaces were filled, a few customers had begun to wander through the path between the tables. As she waited, Bethany exchanged pleasantries with Elvira Hastings, an old woman who was setting up handmade Raggedy Ann dolls at the table next to hers. Although Bethany was not a regular vendor at the flea market, she had sold there often enough to know most of the people who came to sell week in and week out. And on the shelf next to Abby's bed at home was a three-foot Raggedy Ann that Bethany had traded several weeks ago with Mrs. Hastings for a black-and-white ceramic mask of a clown.

''That baby is getting more grown-up and prettier every day, darlin'.'' Mrs. Hastings spoke with the accent Bethany had become accustomed to hearing from many people in the New Orleans area. Described by some as a Brooklyn accent with a Southern twang, it was as unique and delightful as New Orleans itself. ''She's gonna break some man's heart before ya know it.''

''Sometimes I can't believe she's already four,'' Bethany answered wistfully as she watched Abby investigate the tables of the other vendors. The little girl was happily trying on cloisonné bracelets at a stall down the row, and the vendor there was laughing and pushing more bracelets at her. "Do you believe that? I've seen him yell at potential customers just because they moved one of those bracelets an inch out of line."

"Everybody loves your little girl. Your husband must be a proud man." Mrs. Hastings shook her head slowly. "A proud man."

It was a natural mistake, and Mrs. Hastings was not the first to make it. "I'm not married," Bethany said so simply that her voice betrayed no emotion. "Abby and I live alone. And I'm proud enough of her to make up for anything."

There was no shock in the old woman's voice when she finally responded. "I'm sure it hasn't been easy, darlin', but the world wouldn't be as bright a place to live in if Abby Walker weren't in it.... Not nearly as bright."

The old woman's reassuring words made Bethany smile. "My world certainly wouldn't be as bright, Mrs. Hastings. Abby makes my life worth living."

The little girl *was* a bright flame, infusing everything around her with life and with warmth. Watching her daughter flutter from booth to booth, Bethany could almost forget that once, years before, she had been sure life would never be worth living again.

JUSTIN DUMONTIER SAT NURSING THE DRINK he'd bought an hour earlier to have with his breakfast. The mimosa, made with champagne and orange juice, had gone flat, but Justin couldn't have cared less. The morning had gone flat, too. Wining and dining the major clients in his father's firm was one of a hundred things he disliked about being involved in the private practice of law. Unconsciously he allowed his feelings to flicker across his face in an uncharacteristic display of emotion, but the man sitting across the breakfast table from him didn't even notice. His mimosas hadn't gone flat—they hadn't had time to.

Another lawyer in the firm, Paul Edwards, leaned over to murmur in Justin's direction, "I think we need some fresh air."

Privately Justin thought that his entire life needed some fresh air, but he only nodded tersely. "Let's go." Together the two men went around to help their client to his feet. "Mr. Perkins, we thought we'd show you the sights."

"I wanna go see Bourbon Street."

Visualizing a scenario of stops at every bar up and down the famous naughty thoroughfare, Justin shook his head decisively. "Not now, Mr. Perkins. Maybe a little later. Let's stroll around Jackson Square."

"I don't wanna see a square. I wanna see..."

Justin helped the older man with his coat. "We'll just walk this fine breakfast off for a little while, Mr. Perkins. Let's go."

Each lawyer gripping one of the inebriated man's elbows, they made their way out of the elegant restaurant and began to walk very carefully down the sidewalk. Turning at the corner, they headed toward the square, impeded by the shuffling gait of their charge. Paul began a rambling history lesson, pointing to the quaint old buildings and expounding on the Spanish origins of the iron filigreed balconies overhanging the sidewalks. Justin, tuning him out, felt the onslaught of a black cloud of depression that rivaled the day's gloomy weather.

In the distance he could see the familiar spires of St.

Louis Cathedral. It had been years since he had been to Jackson Square on a weekend, but he knew from experience how little changed in New Orleans. He was sure that when they got to the park he would hear the clamor of tourists exclaiming over the artists who had set up their stands, complete with paintings of celebrities and signs advertising the artist's availability to do likenesses. He was equally sure that at least one embarrassed teenage girl would have succumbed to the temptation and would pay a month's allowance to sit for a portrait. There would be flocks of pigeons, tour guides and 35mm cameras.

Jackson Square would be a festive place, and Justin felt anything but festive. In fact, in another moment of insight, he realized that it had been a long time since he had felt anything of the sort. During his years in the federal attorney's office in Chicago he had felt busy and productive. He had felt excitement and occasionally doubt, but he had never felt lighthearted or ready for merrymaking. And in exchange he had rarely allowed himself to feel depressed.

Lifting his strong, tapering fingers to his forehead, he pushed back his black hair. The movement revealed the clean angular lines of his face. Thick brows, large black eyes and an olive complexion testified to his Creole heritage. At Harvard his classmates had teased him about being well suited for the roll of a wealthy planter who would have to do nothing more than sit on the veranda of his antebellum mansion sipping mint juleps. Tall and slender with an athletic, muscular body, Justin Dumontier seemed to have been made to dance at a thousand balls, gamble on luxurious riverboats, or ride like the wind through fields of sugarcane or cotton or whatever it was that folks grew in that far-from-Harvard place called Louisiana.

Justin had taken the teasing good-naturedly and quietly gone on to graduate with honors, making a name for himself at the Harvard Law School. He had chosen Chicago as his home, turning his back on his native New Orleans and on the law firm of his father. Now he was home, but he counted the days until he could leave again. Once before he had felt his sense of desolation, of the purposelessness of life. Once before there had seemed no particular reason for existence. Once before he had felt empty, incomplete, drained of joy. Then he had been able to plunge himself into the work that exhausted him and gave him a peculiar sense of solace. Now there was nothing to help him forget.

"Don't you think so, Justin?" Paul's voice was falsely cheerful, as if he were making a supreme effort to keep up the chatter.

With a noncommittal nod, Justin helped guide Mr. Perkins over the curb and into the square. A quick glance told him that nothing had changed in all the years he had been away. Only Justin Dumontier was not the same.

"I KNOW YOU'RE TIRED of sitting here, honey. I wish I could take you to the square, but I've got to stay here until dinner time. Then Madeline will come and take over the stall for us." Bethany watched her daughter make horrible faces, and wished fleetingly she could capture some of those expressions in papier-mâché. They would be just right for Halloween.

The morning was wearing on and wearing thin for Abby. She had visited all the vendors, rearranged masks and eaten the last of the *beignets*. She had exclaimed over a six-inch rag doll given to her by Mrs. Hastings and taken the doll on fantasy trips everywhere a four-year-old could imagine. Usually a good-tempered little girl, even Abby had her limits. Sitting quietly at the flea market all day was one of them.

"You're always working, mommy."

The statement was unerring, Bethany thought. But there was food to buy, rent to pay, supplies for the shop that she had to purchase. And there was a large hospital bill with Abby's name on it from a bout with pneumonia the year before. "It must seem so sometimes."

"Why don't you just quit?" Abby's voice suggested that her mother was not too bright for failing to think of that solution herself.

"I love what I do, sweetheart. And I love it because you can be with me almost all the time. That makes it very special." With a twinge Bethany acknowledged to herself the reality of that statement. She and Abby were together primarily because of the flexibility of her profession. She shuddered when she thought of what the alternatives might have been.

Her reverie was interrupted by a booming voice rich with the lilting cadences of South Louisiana. "Sell me a mask, pretty lady?" The man standing above her was huge. Well over six foot, with a girth almost half as wide, the prepossessing body was softened by a broad grin barely visible beneath a straggly brown beard.

"Where would you put it, Lamar?" she said sweetly. "Your face is almost covered, anyway."

"Say the word, *cherie*, and I will shave it off, *tout de suite*." He pulled the beard with one hand, as if to be done with it.

"Don't make Lamar shave off his beard, mommy. I like it." Abby crawled under the table to jump into the crouching Lamar's arms. She buried her little face in his neck.

"A loyal fan. I guess we'll just have to dot the beard with sequins for Mardi Gras and forget the mask." Bethany laughed at the horrified look on Lamar's face. A native of the bayou country of southern Louisiana and a descendant of the Acadian—Cajun—exiles who emigrated from Nova Scotia two centuries earlier, Lamar Robicheaux had come to New Orleans with a small band of Cajun musicians to start a nightclub in the French Quarter. Luckily for Bethany, they had located around the corner from her shop and apartment, and she had learned to love their unique musical sounds and Lamar's unique personality.

Abby, who lived primarily in a woman's world, had taken to Lamar immediately. No one could play the fiddle like Lamar; no one could tell such outrageous tales of voodoo and pirates or tell them with a Cajun accent straight out of the nineteenth century; no one else let her ride on his shoulders as if she were completely weightless. Lamar, lonely for his family, had adopted Abby, and Bethany with her.

"What really brings you here?"

"Money. Me, I need some child labor." He tickled Abby, amid loud giggles. "I'm going over to Jackson Square to fiddle awhile, and I thought this *p'tit zozo* might like to come to pass the hat. Madeline told me where you were."

Bethany inspected Abby as she cuddled up to Lamar. In addition to her headdress, the little girl was dressed in a bright-blue running suit decorated with green plastic beads she had caught the year before at a carnival parade. With her dark hair and darker eyes, Abby would be appealing to the crowds in the square. Nevertheless Bethany knew that Lamar had really made the offer to give the little girl a break.

"It's a terrific idea. You'll have to watch her carefully, Lamar." She flashed a bright smile at his scowl. "Yes, I know you will. I'm sorry. Mothers are supposed to say those things."

"*Quoi y'a?* Do you think I'm going to let her run out in the street or dive off of Andrew Jackson's statue?"

"Of course not." Lamar was pretending to be offended, but Bethany knew it was an act. The big man was almost impossible to ruffle.

"Cajun men are very sensitive to children," he continued in the same offended tone, his accent thickening. "There was always plenty of little ones to practice on at home on the bayou." The way Lamar said it, "there" became "der," "the" became "de" and "bayou" became "bye."

"Teaching them to ride alligators bareback is not the same as watching them in crowds of people."

"Me, I feel safer with the alligators. I'll be careful."

"I know you will," she said leaning forward to plant a kiss on his cheek.

"I'll take care of *p'tit zozo* here and you take care of selling these masks. Take care of yourself, too. Maman Robicheaux would say that you've been working too hard." Effortlessly Lamar swung Abby around to ride piggyback on his broad shoulders.

"Thank you for being so thoughtful. Abby will have a better time with you than she would here." She watched them as they began to disappear into the crowd.

"Lamar!" He stopped to look back over the heads of the people surrounding him. "If it rains..."

"I'll take her back to the shop."

"She hasn't eaten any lunch yet."

"I'll buy her a po'boy," he called, referring to a New Orleans specialty sandwich served between two pieces of chewy French bread. Turning, he was gone.

The crowds in the flea market had picked up considerably since early morning, and Bethany found that she was busy enough for two people as the day wore on. Tangles of people wove in and out of the walkway, chatting, asking questions, tentatively trying on masks. In a few weeks, if her experience was reliable, the trying-on stage would almost always be followed by a sale. But Mardi Gras was five weeks away, and the crowds who were just browsing today knew they still had time to make up their minds.

The dark clouds continued to hover overhead, threatening but still withholding rain. A young couple approached her stall, admiring the colorful display. As Bethany watched them choose matching masks made from a simple form covered with sequins and silk flowers, she felt a small tremor pass through her body. She remembered a time in her own life when she, like the young girl in front of her, had used every opportunity she could find to touch the man she adored. Watching the young lovers, she stood rigid with longing, wishing incoherently that her own fingers were tracing the lines of the delicate mask, dipping to linger on the cheeks and the earlobes below the mask's boundaries.

Their absorption in each other was not uncommon. New Orleans was nothing if not a city for lovers. The sultry days and nights seemed to hold passion suspended like tiny droplets of water in the heavy air. It was a difficult city to be alone in, to be unloved in. In her four years of living there, Bethany usually kept herself too busy to be bothered by her own enforced isolation. Today even hard work could not make her forget, and watching the young couple, loneliness weighed on her with the smothering pressure of the very air she breathed.

A clap of thunder brought her back to reality, and she silently wrapped the masks in tissue paper, made change and presented the man and woman with their new acquisitions. "Happy Mardi Gras," she whispered, her voice trailing off as they walked away, oblivious to anything except each other.

The rain followed the thunder by minutes only. Vendors in the parking lot consolidated merchandise under their shelters and some scurried to cars and vans, loaded down with armfuls of every item imaginable. Those customers who had been in the parking lot descended on the covered areas, and Bethany found herself inundated with people who were trying to keep dry. By the time the rain let up, she had sold three more masks.

As the crowd thinned out once again, she sank into her folding chair, grateful for the respite. A small box of masks that she had been unable to display because of lack of space lay under the table, and she searched through the box, trying to decide which masks she should use to replace the ones she had just sold.

Perhaps, she was to think later, if she had been standing up and alert to the sights and sounds around her, she would have realized that the man walking toward her stall was hazardous and out-of-control. As it was, the only inkling she had that anything was wrong was the loud thump and crack of the table above her.

"What in the blazes?" Pulling her head from under the table, she moved too quickly, slamming her forehead into the sharp metal edge when she struggled to stand. As she blinked several times to stop her head from swimming, she took in the unmistakable sight of an old man lying face down across the table, passed out cold. The worst news of all was that he had chosen to pass out cold on top of her most expensive mask. Without looking, she knew that crushed underneath his limp body was the creation of black and white Lady Amherst pheasant feathers that Abby had displayed so lovingly.

"Get off of there this minute," she said loudly to no one in particular, because the man was obviously past understanding and obeying. Helplessly she looked around, cold fury obliterating her common sense. "Get off of there."

"Wait a minute, please. I'll get him." A young pleasant-looking man in a brown suit stepped over to her table. "Justin," he called, "come here, we've got a problem."

Too upset to pay attention to him, Bethany took the heels of both hands and pushed the old man's shoulders, trying with all the force of her one-hundred-three-pound body to shove him off the table. The man was obviously drunk, and that fact alone was enough to send waves of rage crashing through her body. "Just a minute, lady. I promise, we'll have him off of there in just one minute. Justin!"

Justin looked up from a table where he had been examining calculators. Following the sound of Paul's voice, he hurried through the gathering crowd. With a rough groan he took in the sight of Mr. Perkins, sprawled and unconscious on a table filled with delicate feather masks. "Damn. I told you he was too drunk to walk through here." Silently he cursed the rain that had forced them inside a Decatur Street bar, giving Mr. Perkins yet another excuse to down several potent drinks.

Bending over the limp body, he missed the soft gasp of the young woman standing behind the table. The two lawyers lifted the dead weight that was Mr. Perkins and heaved him off the devastated mask and onto his feet. Miraculously the movement jarred the old man awake, and he stared bleary-eyed around him as if to ask what the fuss was all about.

"Get him walking again, and for God's sake, get him out of here. I'll catch up with you in a minute," Justin ordered.

For the first time since the beginning of the brief encounter, Justin looked directly at the woman whose merchandise his client had destroyed. His eyes widened in shock as he took in the pink-and-scarlet headdress, its slash of feathers partially covering one side of the heart-shaped face. But it was not the outrageous decorations she wore that was causing the pounding rush of blood through his veins. It was the sight of the once-familiar features: the rich dark hair, shorter now than when he had let it fall like rippling water through his fingers; the fragile bone structure that still gave form and substance to the translucent skin stretched tightly over it; the generous mouth that he had once felt trembling under his own. "Bethany."

As he watched, the dusky-rose cheeks drained of all color. Enormous blue eyes stared back at him, and lips, seemingly unable to form a greeting, lay softly parted. He saw her tongue flicker across their surface as though to moisten and offer encouragement. Reaching across the table, he carefully lifted the flamboyant headdress off the shining hair as if to assure himself that he was correct. He watched her fingers, spread wide apart, as she ran her hand slowly through the silky strands. The gesture was familiar and it, more than anything else, tore at his heart.

"Justin," she finally managed. "It's been a long time."

"Yes." There must be something more that could be said. His mind ran through the possibilities. Idle chatter was not a skill he had cultivated; pouring his heart out here in front of the curious vendors and milling customers was unthinkable. He waited for her to take charge.

"Five years." Bethany examined him carefully at the same time that she chastised herself for wanting to. The years had been good to Justin. He was still slim with an almost tangible aura of strength and magnetism surrounding him. The coal-black hair was not yet touched with gray, and the dark skin was creased with tiny lines giving his face a new and pleasing maturity. The taupe suit and crisp white shirt accented the appearance he made of being a competent, powerful professional. But more about Justin than his physical appearance cried out to be examined. The expression on his face revealed nothing except surprise, and she found herself searching for some clue to his feelings. It was a game she had played many times in the past and never won. She saw immediately that today would be no different.

Their silent investigations were interrupted by Paul's voice somewhere in the crowd beyond them. "Justin!"

"I have to go." He picked up the shattered mask and watched as the feathers drifted to the table below. "This should have been under your display case."

"Don't worry. I'm not going to sue." She wondered at the voice she heard. Could that bitter sound have come from her own throat?

A flicker of response shone in the nearly impenetrable black eyes. "We'll pay for it, of course." He reached in his pocket and withdrew a sleek, kidskin wallet. "Here's my card. Assess the damages, and send us the bill." He waited for her to answer, until it was apparent she was not going to. Paul's summons echoed through the crowd again. "Be sure you include everything," Justin ordered, turning to go.

Bethany watched him lose himself in the multitudes clustered around the tables. The hand that held his card was rigid with the shock of the chance meeting. Convulsively she clenched and unclenched her fingers around the small piece of paper, molding it like papier-mâché, until the decisive moment when she balled it up into a wad no larger than a teardrop. Palm down, she moved her thumb the fraction of an inch that was needed, and the card fell neatly into the box of trash beside her table. Like a sightless person, she felt carefully for the arms of her chair, collapsing backward as she felt the seat beneath her.

"Beth—" she heard Mrs. Hastings's voice "—put your head down on the table, darlin'. You look like you've seen a ghost."

Obeying the other woman, Bethany rested her head on the table as Mrs. Hastings clucked over her, cleaning up the remains of the mask. She felt the old woman's hand stroking her hair, and in a few minutes she had recovered enough to sit up again. "I must have hit my head harder than I thought," she said by way of apology.

A slight smile curved the old woman's lips, carving new wrinkles in her face. "I'm sorry, but I don't think so." She waited a second, as if deciding whether to mind her own business. Finally she sighed. "It was more likely seein' your old friend. Surprises can do that."

Bethany's hair swirled back and forth, tickling the back of her neck as she shook her head vehemently. "That man is not my friend," she said.

Mrs. Hastings patted her hand softly. "I'm sorry he's not," she said sadly. "Because it is apparent, darlin', what else he is to you."

Bethany lifted her eyes to read the old woman's face. "I'm not sure what you mean."

Mrs. Hastings nodded. "If you didn't think anyone could tell, I'm sorry to disappoint you. But that man is obviously your baby's father. They're as alike as any two people I've ever seen." She continued at Bethany's slight movement of denial. "And there's no way you'll ever be able to hide it. No way in the world."

A bone weariness suffused Bethany's body, replacing the lost color in her cheeks with a grayness that would stay with her for the rest of the day. "Right now, Mrs. Hastings, you and I are the only two people in the world who are aware of that fact." She paused, as if the next sentence were too exhausting to utter. Finally she continued so softly that Mrs. Hastings only saw her lips move. "And I intend to be sure that it stays that way."

CHAPTER TWO

CLOUDY SKIES, clouded memories, vision clouded by unshed tears—Bethany would never think of that gray New Orleans afternoon again without the imagery of ever-changing cumulus masses. There had been a popular song about the time she reached adolescence that explored the different ways of looking at clouds, at life and at love. Gazing at the sky beyond the walkway, she tried to remember the words. Although she was only able to isolate a word or two, the song's message emerged crystal clear from her memory. Clouds had been compared to angel's hair and to ice cream castles. But there had been another observation, too. Clouds could block and twist reality, making an observer oblivious to their darker side.

Bethany remembered now that Madeline had got the name for their shop from the same song. Life, too, had its illusions sometimes making the truth difficult to grasp. *All along,* she thought sadly. *All along it's been my theme song.* And the memories she had tried so hard for five years to obscure behind a cloud of denial came forward into focus as clearly defined images.

She had been twenty-one years old, and unlike most of the other students that attended Florida State University in Tallahassee, she had stayed in the small capital city that summer after her junior year to take a job to help supplement the art scholarship she would be receiving in the fall. There had been other possibilities for jobs, and since she did not have a family to go home to, she had considered them all, free to make her own decisions. Some of the other art students had secured positions as waitresses and busboys at posh resorts in the Smokies or farther south on Florida's own Gold Coast. Bethany had been invited to join them for a summer of flirtation, swimming and generous tips, but the almost-hedonistic appeal of that much fun was foreign to her, and she had resisted.

When a friend from high school had invited her to become a counselor at a camp for handicapped children in the Adirondacks, Bethany had been sorely tempted. But the decision to stay in Tallahassee had been made when she had been unable to sublease the little efficiency apartment she rented six blocks from campus. The apartment spelled home to Bethany and leaving it, not to return to its safe confines in the fall, seemed too great a wrench. The apartment was nothing special; it was one of several in a square concrete-block building, with no adornments to give it character. But it was hers. She had lived there for nine full months, as long as she had lived almost anywhere, and she was reluctant to lose it.

Tallahassee without its full complement of exuberant students was a quiet town. And even in the first days of summer it was a town characterized by scorching temperatures. Bethany came home each day from job hunting to sit in front of her window fan until she had the energy to fix herself a snack. Evenings she spent at the campus library or student union, seeking relief from the relentless heat in the air-conditioned buildings.

After a depressing week of being turned down as a
sales clerk and waitress everywhere she applied, she was
called to an interview for a summer position as recep-
tionist at the FSU law school. Her warm competent
manner made a positive impression on the pregnant and
ready-to-deliver woman she was to replace for the summer months and she was hired on the spot.

"Don't get involved with the law students," the other
woman had warned her as she cleaned her personal
items out of the desk that was to be Bethany's. "Fifty
percent of them are already married, and the other fifty
percent claim they won't ever make that trip up the
aisle." She had examined Bethany with humor, taking
in the heavily fringed blue eyes, waist-length dark hair
and milk-and-roses complexion. "But I'll bet I don't
have to tell you how to handle men. I'm sure you had to
learn pretty quick."

Bethany, who had always handled men by not handling them at all, just smiled. She was certain that this
summer would be no different from what the rest of her
life up to that point had been: busy, productive and a bit
lonely. She was not in the market for a boyfriend. She
had found most of the young men on campus to be
amazingly shallow. Appalled by the drinking that accompanied fraternity parties, she had attended only
one, refusing thereafter to go out with fraternity men.
Afraid of ruining potential friendships, she had made a
firm rule not to date the other art students. Professors
were off limits for obvious reasons, and graduate students in other fields rarely crossed her path. She had
drifted through her three years on campus as friend to
many, special squeeze to no one.

But the FSU law students she came in contact with

that summer seemed committed to proving to her that her life could change. Her predecessor's warning rang clearly through her mind each time a different fresh-faced young law student tried to convince her their destinies were inextricably entwined. She became humorously aware that somewhere during the course of the unbearably hot month of July she had gained the nickname "Snow White," as much, she was sure, for her virginal refusals as for her unique coloring.

In late summer all pretensions of appearing business-like in the blazing heat vanished, and she took to setting the hearts of the young law students pounding by wearing a particularly cool ruby-red sundress with thin straps and a revealing cleavage. Hair coiled high on her head, emphasizing her graceful neck and fragile bone structure, she found herself holding court at her desk.

Actually the students at her desk had long since given up any attempts to date Bethany. But she was friendly and warm—up to a point—and she had always made her refusals tactfully. In spite of her lack of cooperation with their plans for her, she was still well thought of. It was into this circle of admiring and mildly annoying young men that Justin Dumontier walked one day in late August. She had raised her sky-blue eyes to gaze into his midnight-black ones, and she had experienced the uncomfortable feeling that her life was never going to be the same again.

There should be music playing somewhere, she had thought. Something terribly corny with a subtle crescendo that reached its climax about now. "May I help you?" was all that she said.

"I'm looking for Craig Williams. Is he here?" The dark eyes examined her casually, seeming to enjoy the subtle curves under the skimpy sundress.

"He's gone home for the day," she answered. "Will anyone else do?"

"You might," he intoned in a husky voice. "In fact, you might do very well."

"We've been outclassed," one of the perpetual decorations at her desk sighed, and she smiled ruefully at the parade that filed out her door.

"Are you a friend of Mr. Williams?" she asked in an attempt to keep the stranger at her desk a little longer. She, who almost never paid attention to a man's appearance, was busy memorizing this one's features. She liked the height and strength in the lithe muscular body, the dark skin and black hair and eyes, the way his nose shot down in a straight line to shadow the well-sculptured lips. When he smiled at her, revealing strong, even white teeth, the picture was complete. And it was with a trace of amusement at her own vulnerability that she recognized that her stomach was doing flip-flops.

"I'm Justin Dumontier. Craig and I went to Harvard law together, and I promised him I'd conduct some seminars for his students while I'm in town. I just arrived." His dark eyes were obviously conducting the same tour of her features that she had given his, and she hoped irrationally that she was passing with flying colors.

"He mentioned the possibility of your coming in, Mr. Dumontier, but I think he was really expecting you tomorrow."

"I caught an earlier flight."

"Let me call him at home. He'll want to pick you up right away," she said, lifting the receiver to dial the telephone.

His hand covered hers as he replaced the receiver.

"Are you married, engaged, or otherwise committed for the evening?"

"Are you always so quick to cut through the formalities?" she asked, wondering why the touch of his hand was sending tantalizing signals to the rest of her body.

"Only when it's important."

She liked his voice. It was husky and musical with the touch of a Southern accent, and it sent a shiver rolling down her spine. "No, I'm not committed in any way," she surprised herself by saying. "And you?"

"For dinner with you, if you'll accept my invitation."

They ate at an Italian restaurant within walking distance of the campus. Unlike the pizza joints she had often gone to with crowds of other students, the little restaurant had clean tablecloths and soft music. At least when she thought about it later, that was how she remembered it. More important, she remembered Justin's soft resonant voice and his carefully chosen words. And she remembered the new feeling of wishing the evening could last forever.

He was glad to find she was twenty-one and starting her senior year, and she realized he had serious qualms about robbing the cradle. She was delighted to find he was twenty-seven, with a thoughtful maturity that had been missing in the men she was acquainted with.

"You'll be here for a month, then?" she asked as she finished up the last bite of a huge plate of spaghetti.

He nodded, watching her in amusement. "When was the last time you ate?"

"When the temperature dropped below ninety. I think it was early spring sometime," she said, laughing at his expression. "No, I snack all the time, but I guess being with you has made me unbearably hungry." The implications of her words washed over her at the same moment that a delicate rose blush colored each visible inch of her white skin.

Justin sat back, a slow grin lighting his dark features. "If it's any consolation, Bethany, I feel hungrier than I have in a very long time myself."

Later they walked, hand in hand, over the graceful sprawling campus as Bethany identified the softly tinted brick buildings by name. Not because he needed to know, but because it gave them an excuse to be together. Pausing to rest on Landis Green, a tree-shaded oasis in the center of campus, they sat on a stone bench beneath a fragrant mimosa tree, and Justin, his arm casually resting on her shoulder, turned her face to his.

"You feel it, too, don't you?" he asked simply.

"This is a magic place," she said with a sigh. "Inch for inch, more kisses have been exchanged, more vows of undying love have been made here than in any spot in the state of Florida."

"I have always believed in helping statistics," he said as he bent the tiny distance to cover her mouth with his.

It was not that she had never been kissed. She had. She had been kissed by experienced and not so experienced men of different shapes and sizes and coloring. But nothing had prepared her for Justin's kiss. It was not like kisses that came later, not a burning thrusting kiss that melted her inner core so that she could receive the glorious molten essence of him into her soul. It was a gentle kiss, full of promise and patience, and it unnerved her completely.

When he drew back, her eyes were lifted to his, holding back none of the wealth of feeling he had uncovered. Somehow she had always known that it would happen this way for her, that when she fell, it would be sudden and complete. That knowledge must have shone brightly in her blue eyes, for he shook his head with a frown.

"Proceed with caution," he warned her. "I'm only here for a month."

A month would not be long enough; a lifetime would not be long enough. But with the abandon of the artist who gives herself completely to the muse, Bethany put his words out of her head. Now was enough...for now.

Justin had come to Tallahassee to do research for a case pending in Chicago. Although he based his temporary home in the capital city, he was gone intermittently on side trips throughout the state and back to Illinois. When he was in town, he spent every second of his free time with Bethany.

Bethany threw herself into her job at the law school, depending on hard work to get her through the moments they weren't together. When she was with Justin, she thought of nothing except him and her intensifying feelings. He was fast becoming the center of her universe, the key to the empty space inside her that she had been only peripherally aware of before.

They spent time together exploring Tallahassee. They prowled through the National Forest, swam deep in the woods in icy deserted sinkholes, watched Canada geese fly across the sunset over Lake Jackson. Often they spent quiet evenings in Bethany's little apartment, Justin working on his research, Bethany unobtrusively researching him. Their times together were almost idyllic. Except for one thing.

"Justin," she said one night in early September as he

lay on her sofa, head pillowed in her lap. "I have to ask you something."

"Mmm..." was his reply.

Glad that he couldn't see her face, she stroked the shiny black hair from his forehead. "Do you find me attractive?" It was as forward a question as she had ever asked, and she was sure he could feel the slight trembling of her fingers.

"There is probably not a male this side of eighty-five who doesn't find you attractive, Snow White."

She winced at the nickname, pinching his ear between her fingertips. "I just wondered."

His laughter rumbled over her lap, causing tantalizing vibrations. "What's the question behind the question, Bethany?"

That question she was not forward enough to ask, and she murmured, "I was just curious."

He sat up, pulling her close beside him. "It's time we talked," he said seriously. "I've been putting it off, too."

Suddenly she was sorry she had brought it up, and she pulled away to stand before him. "Let's not get serious tonight. I'll make you some coffee so you can get some more work done."

In a split second she was back in his arms, this time on his lap, held securely against him. "You want to know why I haven't tried to get you into that monstrous bed in the corner?"

The bed, a simple double bed with a simple double bedspread covering it, did loom like a monster in the tiny one-room apartment. She felt the heat of embarrassment and something else spreading over her body, threatening to encompass her. "All of a sudden," she said faintly, "I don't think I want to know."

"It's because," he said his mouth close to her ear, his warm breath sending signals to each separate nerve cushioned under her soft skin, "I'm afraid that once I've made love to you, I might never be able to stop."

It was as much of a declaration of commitment as she needed. Turning to him, the only sound she could make was a whimper at the glorious sensations flooding her willing body. Without a word he lifted her like a weightless spirit and carried her to the bed. When he pulled the knitted camisole from her unresisting body, he groaned with the sound of a man who sees his future. "God, I knew you'd look like this."

His mouth sought the valley between her breasts, sending warm nips and kisses to ease his way to the firm rosy flesh of her nipples. When he covered them with his lips and then with his teeth, she cried out in agony at the warring sensations inside her. Inexperienced to an unusual degree, she had no idea what to do, except enjoy what he was doing to her, what he was giving to her. "Justin" was all she could say.

Then his shirt was off and the taut tips of her breasts were caught in an exquisite friction against the dark hair of his chest. Still his mouth found new ways to send shuddering waves of feeling through her. His tongue traced the outline of her lips, compelling her to open to him, which she did with abandon. She felt he would swallow her, make her a part of him so totally that she would never find herself again, and then she was afraid he wouldn't.

His hands were dark velvet on white silk, seeking out the sensitive places of her body she had not even known were there. The thin cotton shorts she was wearing were off and his hand was on the elastic of the lacy bikini pants she wore. And then they were undressed somehow, and he lay almost covering her body, exploring her further with his tongue and his fingers.

So much pleasure was hers she became frightened that somehow she was not giving him enough in return. "Tell me what you want," she gasped.

"Only you," he said as he slid between her legs with his strong muscular thighs and slowly, carefully, entered the one part of her that was still unexplored.

It was a perfect moment for her. She was so intent on giving him pleasure, on making him her own, that the brief flash of pain went almost unheeded. Not so for Justin, whose strong body went rigid with surprise. That surprise was communicated to her as he attempted to withdraw from the silken warmth inside her.

"No!" she protested, clasping him to her. "Please."

"You should have told me," he said tautly, still rigid against her. "I had no idea."

"It doesn't matter. Please...it doesn't matter." Afraid that she was losing him, that the incredible pleasure he was giving her would be gone forever, she began to move slowly under him. "Please, Justin."

It was an ageless dance, the need of a woman for the man she loves, and Bethany knew by instinct he would not resist. He didn't. "I'll make it good for you," he promised her, and the cascading sensations born of the two of them together gradually overtook all conscious thought. Later as they lay satiated, she only knew that no verbal promise could begin to touch on the truth of the miracle that had occurred.

"What am I going to do with you?" he said finally as he played with the long dark hair lying across his chest.

"You can stop calling me 'Snow White,' " she teased.

"That should have been a clue," he admitted.

"Is it so awful to have been the first, Justin? Was my inexperience so awkward as to give you no pleasure?"

He pressed tiny kisses along the cushioned softness of her shoulder. "Were you protected?" he asked finally.

From what, she thought? From falling in love, from needing him more than before, from wanting him always? " 'Protected'?"

"You didn't know that what we did can result in a nine-month bonus package? Do you really live in a fairy tale, Snow White?"

Pregnancy had not occurred to her. Being prepared had not occurred to her. It was a major oversight, and she was humiliated at her own foolish innocence. "I will be protected next time. I'm sorry. I just didn't think about it this time."

"And if you're pregnant already?"

"Then I hope the baby looks like you." She felt him stiffen beside her, and she knew her teasing had gone too far. "I'm sorry, Justin. But I'm sure I'm not pregnant. It's the wrong time of the month for that. I'm at least sophisticated enough to know that much."

He relaxed again, pulling her closer. "Are you sure? Because in that case. . . ."

"Absolutely sure." She sighed, melting into him.

But she wasn't sure. She had lied about their timing. Honest almost to a fault, she had lied to keep him from worrying and regretting their private miracle. Telling herself that one slip up would not be too great a risk, she put the thought of pregnancy out of her head until the next day, when she and the drugstore could deal with it constructively.

And she did deal with it. Never again did she take any chances. With an almost superstitious fanaticism she took elaborate precautions, feeling that if she was extra-careful her one mistake might go unnoticed. There were other things to be concerned with, too.

Justin's time in Tallahassee was drawing to a close, even though he had managed to extend his stay a week. The remaining weeks coincided with the end of her job at the law school and the beginning of her final year at the university. Although no words of commitment were spoken, she sensed that he, too, realized how difficult parting would be. No longer did he return to his motel room after an evening together. Quietly, without either of them bringing up the subject, he began to stay overnight with her, finally moving his suitcases to her apartment.

Bethany rushed home every afternoon when classes were finished to fix dinner and wait for him to arrive. They shared details of their day like the good friends they had become, and later, after dinner, they shared their bodies, engaging in exquisite, soul-quenching love-making.

"Justin," she ventured one night as she lay locked in his arms. "You're getting close to being done here, aren't you?"

His hand was lightly brushing her stomach, finding the ridges of her rib cage and connecting them with invisible lines, using the tips of his fingers. He stopped at her question. "I'm due to leave on Wednesday."

She counted days…and nights. She could count on only four more of each. "It will not be the same without you."

"I'll miss you," he responded, his hand beginning to wander over her body again.

It was the most revealing comment he would make before he left her. Bethany, ever the optimist, was not concerned, however. Early in her relationship with Justin she had realized that this man was not given to expressing his feelings. Polite, kind, with a trace of sophisticated formality bred of his upper-class background, he kept his thoughts to himself. In fact, she was aware that her own generous warmth overwhelmed and often dismayed him. Where she was open and giving, he was cautious and closed.

She had fallen in love with abandon, and she had not tried to hide it from him. When he brought her to the peak of sensual delight and crushing waves swept over her body, it was words of love that she cried, thanking him for what he gave to her. In hundreds of ways she showed him what he meant to her, none being more obvious, however, than the joyous emotion that shone brightly from her warm blue eyes.

Justin said nothing. Obviously he desired her—his need for her was insatiable and unending. He seemed to find her amusing and fun to be with. She knew that he was genuinely fond of her. The rest she had to surmise for herself.

On Tuesday, standing with her arms buried up to her elbows in wet clay in a ceramics class, she began to count the little things he had done to show her that he, too, was in love. She remembered the way his fingers stroked the long strands of hair that he smoothed over his chest and the sweet words he would often whisper after their lovemaking. There were the times he would surprise her with presents, small tokens that reminded him of her; the mornings he woke her with breakfast cooked and the kitchen cleaned; the concern he showed over her hectic schedule; his admiration for her talent; his insistence that she give him a sketch she had made of herself for one of her drawing classes.

And there had been the time she had seen him looking at the small charcoal sketch, tracing the lines of her face in the air with his index finger, as if he were trying to memorize each feature. Justin Dumontier might not be able to say he loved her, he might not even be sure, but when Bethany washed the clay from her hands she consciously washed away her concerns, too. He needed time. He was a cautious person caught up in a whirlwind love affair and he needed time to catch up with himself.

Since Tuesday night was their last night together, Bethany skipped her final class of the day and went home early to prepare a special dinner. Justin had been very silent about his New Orleans background, leaving her with the impression that it was something he needed to put behind him. But she had noticed that he loved seafood, and as a surprise she cooked a spicy batch of shrimp jambalaya. The sausage, shrimp and rice casserole was just coming out of the oven when he arrived home, and she was rewarded for her thoughtfulness by having the casserole returned to the oven to stay warm while Justin took her promptly to bed.

It was with a hint of desperation that he made love to her that night. He could not be satisfied, as if he were storing up memories to last through the months ahead. Bethany was not frightened by his attitude, but instead it further convinced her that he was struggling with himself and only needed time to reach the obvious conclusion: that he was in love with her.

Perhaps her patience with him also hid a hint of desperation. The smell of the shrimp jambalaya in the small apartment was creating a fine queasiness in her digestive system. It was added evidence to prove a suspicion she had been trying to ignore. She, who was invariably on time with her monthly periods, was a week late. She, who was steady and stable, found herself wanting to cry over everything.

But it was early, and all the symptoms could be explained by the emotional turmoil she felt at Justin's leaving. She was to think later that if he had stayed with her several weeks more, she would have told him of her suspicions. But it was too early to worry him, too early to force him to make a decision about their relationship.

"Bethany," he murmured that night as they were falling asleep in each other's arms. "You haven't had your menstrual cycle in the time I've been here."

She started, pulling herself sharply from the drugged lethargy she had let steal over her. "You're just lucky," she said finally. "I'm not due for a few more days."

"Are you sure?" His voice was fading into sleep.

"Absolutely. I'm sure I'm not pregnant."

And somehow, without knowing how she knew, she was completely certain that she was lying to him. A part of her, that ancient tribal woman of her prehistoric past, in tune with the cycles of the moon and the tides, was sure without a doubt that she was carrying Justin's child.

CHAPTER THREE

"ARE YOU ALL RIGHT, Beth?" It was five o'clock, and Madeline's usual no-nonsense voice was filled with concern. "If possible, you look paler than normal."

Bethany sought every particle of strength inside her to smile as though nothing were wrong. "I'm fine. Just a little tired, maybe." She hurried on before the disbelieving look in Madeline's eyes became another inquiry. "We sold eight masks today, and there's a man who will probably come back to buy the coque-feather mask in the display case." She gestured at a black, iridescent shape under the glass. "He'll probably try to talk you down, but don't let him. That one is rock bottom already."

"Wasn't Abby with you?" Madeline's pleasantly lined face was still marked with concern. Tousled, permed hair stuck out from under a wide-brimmed straw hat. Her brows were drawn together in question, but with the help of the hat, she gave the appearance of a beachcomber squinting into the sun. No matter what the occasion, Madeline always looked like the Florida native that she was.

"She went to the square with Lamar. I'm going to go by there on my way back to the shop, but I'll bet he's taken her off exploring somewhere." Bethany shook her head at the question she saw forming on Madeline's lips. The two women had become such close friends that it was impossible to hide their feelings from each other. "No more now. You're right, something has happened. But I'm not ready to talk about it."

"I'm here if you decide to." Madeline's strong square hand patted Bethany's shoulder. "Valerie is minding the shop until you get back, and then she's going to finish a mask she's working on. Send her home if she stays too late."

With a wave to Madeline and a murmured goodbye to Mrs. Hastings, who was also preparing to leave, Bethany began the long walk back to Royal Street. The sights and sounds of the streets she trudged along went unnoticed. She did not stop to buy Abby sugarcane at the French-market vegetable stands; nor did she stop to tap her toe to the music of the piano player who sat amid wrought-iron tables, playing for tips. The gaudy window displays of Decatur Street held no attraction, and the artists in Jackson Square received no more than a passing glance.

Searching the square for Lamar and her daughter, she decided that he had indeed taken Abby on an exploration, and she continued toward home. Along the flagstone sidewalks, under the brightly colored flags flying from the roofs of brick hotels, stopping only to step aside to allow others to pass, she trudged on, and the past flashed in front of her eyes like a demonic slide show.

Justin had been gone for three weeks when Bethany finally dragged her tired body to the campus infirmary to receive the positive result on her pregnancy test. The test results did not surprise her. The infirmary doctor, overworked and hardened to the plight of young girls who should know better, made only a halfhearted attempt to offer her guidance. She refused even that, walking across the campus to an afternoon psychology class and taking notes on the lecture as though nothing had happened.

Convinced that Justin loved her and would be back for her, she somehow managed to put the implications of her condition out of her mind. Yes, she was pregnant. And no, she was not married. Not yet, anyhow. But she remembered the way that Justin had looked at her, his concern and his insatiable hunger for her body and her company. The tale of Snow White and the handsome prince would have a happy ending.

Six weeks passed, and Bethany divided her time equally between attending classes, hanging her head over the basin in the bathroom and waiting for Justin's letters. At first they came fairly frequently. They were casual letters, telling her what he could about the case he had been working on in Tallahassee, giving her unimportant details about the weather and life in Chicago. The letters were invariably signed, "Love, Justin," and for a long time she clung to that tiny piece of trivia as the only thing he had written that was important.

She wrote similar letters to him, telling him funny stories about her classes and about people he had known during his stay. Once after a particularly difficult day of trying to handle her nausea and her classes, too, she wrote him a sentimental note telling him how much she missed him and how empty her apartment seemed. He never responded directly to the letter, but the next week she received her only phone call from him.

After Bethany hung up the phone she tried to tell herself that Justin had called because he cared about her. The sound of his husky accented voice had caused her hands to tremble so violently that holding the phone had been a problem. He had kept the phone call friendly and casual, only deviating once.

"Bethany," he had said in a voice with no discernible emotion. "I've been concerned that you might be pregnant."

And so, for the third time, she lied to him.

"No, Justin. I'm not pregnant. You can stop worrying." And it was at that point that she began to worry herself.

Two more months passed, and Bethany's body, always slender and fine boned, began to blossom. Knowing that her secret could not be kept much longer, she began to consider the possibilities of a life without Justin. His letters still arrived, but with less frequency and even less information. He had taken to having his secretary type them, and they were stultifyingly formal.

She told herself he was working on a case that was probably taking all his time. She told herself he needed more distance and was backing off to take a better look at what they had together. On the day she realized that it had been three weeks since she had got his last note and that it had been signed simply, "Justin," she told herself she was a fool.

The months following her revelation were a nightmare. Distraught and unable to think clearly, she had done first what most young women in her situation do. She had sought the comfort of home. For Bethany, home was a father in the navy who was more often at sea than on land. For once, however, he was back at the naval base in Jacksonville, Florida, waiting for his next assignment, and at first he was reasonably glad to see her. When she told him about her predicament, he responded by demanding that she get an abortion. With fatherly concern he offered to pay for it.

Appalled and furious, Bethany refused, and found herself out on the street with the one suitcase she had not yet unpacked. On the verge of collapse, she called a high-school friend who was a student at George Washington University, and with her last bit of savings, Bethany bought a ticket to Washington, D.C.

With her friend's help she found a room in an elderly woman's house, cooking and cleaning in exchange for board. During the day she took a job with a temporary secretarial agency to pay for her other expenses. Making just enough money to survive, between assignments she sat in crowded waiting rooms at a maternal-health clinic, watching young mothers on welfare with their children. The realization began to settle over her that she could not keep her child.

Sometimes at night she would awaken, crying and holding on to the pillow beneath her, whispering, "Please don't take my baby." Sometimes at night, when she could not sleep, she would walk down the hall to the telephone and pick up the receiver, dialing Justin's number in the air above. But as terrible as the thought of giving up the baby was, worse was the thought of bringing the child into a loveless marriage. She could not be responsible for that. Justin would insist on marriage. She could not bear the thought of lying beside a man who resented her presence and the evidence of their mistake in judgment.

In the last month of her pregnancy, Bethany found that her need for emotional support was devastating. On a whim she wrote Madeline Conroy, a high-school art teacher who had gone the extra mile with the adolescent Bethany and given her encouragement and support. Bethany's scholarship at FSU had been largely due to Madeline's efforts on her behalf, and the two women had stayed in touch. Rereading the letter, Bethany revised it twice, both times toning down the nature of the crisis she was undergoing. But the story lay between the lines for the sensitive Madeline to read, and Bethany received a phone call the night the letter arrived in New Orleans.

Madeline had quit her teaching job and moved to New Orleans a year after Bethany had left the high school in Jacksonville where they had met. There she began making masks to sell in the "City That Care Forgot." Soon she had done so well that she had been able to rent a shop in the colorful French Quarter to display her masks and the masks of other New Orleans artists. Successful and overextended, she had been thinking of trying to find an assistant to help her run the shop. Bethany's letter solidified that resolve. She wanted Bethany for the job.

Most important to the tearfully grateful young woman was the fact that Madeline wanted her baby, too. "There's an apartment for you above the shop, Bethany," Madeline told her. "And it's big enough for you and your little one. You can keep the baby with you when you're working."

A month later Bethany held her squalling baby daughter in her arms. The seven-pound-four-ounce bundle given to her resembled nothing as much as a tiny creature from a friendly planet. But even though she was far from being the beautiful baby she would turn into in a few short weeks' time, Bethany knew that her daughter was going to look just like the father she would never know. And because she could not offer her Justin's last name, she named the baby Abigail Justine, as a small compensation.

The trip to New Orleans was brief, with Abby cuddled close to her mother's breast. Madeline greeted them with delight, immediately proving herself to be the baby's official slave. Bethany threw herself into the shop, and later into designing and making masks herself. The years flew by, and the charm of the enchanting Southern city ingrained itself in Bethany's heart.

Perhaps the one flaw in her life was that Bethany often, at first, found herself looking over her shoulder for Justin. She knew he did not like the city of his birth and would never live there again. But she also knew that his parents still lived in New Orleans, and she worried about running into him if he came back to visit. When her concerns remained unfounded, she gradually relaxed, accepting the fact that she needn't worry. Justin Dumontier became a painful memory, a shadow of her past.

Had it not been for the chance encounter at the flea market on that rainy Saturday five weeks before Mardi Gras, Justin might have remained a memory forever. But Bethany knew that the day's events were ordained to bring about a catastrophic change in her life. As she walked toward the little shop she was frozen with dread. The peace of mind that she had tried so hard to win was destroyed like the pheasant mask that had lain in tatters at her feet. And she had no idea how to go about picking up the pieces.

BLOCKS AWAY from Jackson Square she turned in at the door of a shop with a colorful mask painted on the window. A lovely young girl with skin the color of rich chocolate looked up to greet her.

"Did Lamar bring Abby back, Valerie?"

The young black girl smiled an extraordinary smile, changing her almost-average face into a display of rare beauty. Bethany was reminded, as always, of a peacock spreading its tail feathers. "No, not yet. He's probably got her off somewhere telling her about Jean Lafitte."

"She knows all those stories by heart, but that won't stop either of them." Gesturing toward the back of the shop, Bethany continued. "Madeline said you wanted to finish a mask. I'll take over down here." She watched the girl's face light up again. "Do you think you could teach me to smile like that?"

"Somebody ought to teach you to smile, girl. You look like you need a smiling lesson or a good cry."

"Hard day." Bethany managed to turn one corner of her mouth up. "Better?"

"Not much. You better practice while I'm gone. Pretend you're that dude over there." She pointed to one of a series of papier-mâché masks hanging on the wall. The particular mask she singled out was a clown with an ear-to-ear grin.

Bethany watched Valerie slip through the door in the back of the shop that led to a brick courtyard with stairs to Bethany's apartment and workshop. Valerie had been hired the year before to work behind the counters on weekends and after school. At the time, no one had realized the bonanza of talent packed into the girl's slim fingers.

One day for fun, she had helped Abby model a tiny doll's mask from papier-mâché, and soon there had been no limits to her creativity. Now she was working on a series of African tribal masks to display in the shop window, taking Life's Illusions into a delightfully new and different direction. Upon her graduation from the

New Orleans Center for Creative Arts, a high-school program for talented teenagers, Bethany and Madeline were hoping to offer Valerie a share in the shop.

With Valerie gone and no customers in the store, Bethany pulled a high stool to the U-shaped display case and rested her head on her arms. She had gone over and over the events of the day, either wishing that she had let Madeline man the flea-market booth or wishing that she had worn a mask that had covered her face completely, or wishing that she had never met Justin Dumontier. But the damage had been done. Now was the time to decide how to handle it.

She numbered her concerns. The first and foremost was that Justin would discover he had a daughter and would demand his legal rights to her. The second was that he might try to reestablish his relationship with Bethany, not realizing that Abby was his child. The third was that he might not even care enough to do anything.

This last thought sent a wave of dismay washing through her rigid body. What was she thinking of? She was done with Justin Dumontier. The worst thing that could happen to her would be to have him step back into her life. She had given him love once before. In return he had left her alone to carry the result of that love. She needed Justin as much as a magnolia needed a snowstorm. He could be her ultimate downfall.

Finally she came to the conclusion that she was wasting her time. By dinnertime Justin probably wouldn't even remember that he had seen her today. Her first order of business was to try to put the chance encounter out of her head. If by accident she saw him again, she would be casual, politely distant. And she would keep

Abby out of the Uptown area, where she was sure Justin's parents lived.

The thought of having to actually hide her daughter from Justin was almost more than she could handle. As a child she had often had to make up stories to protect her alcoholic mother from the disapproving scrutiny of others. When she had become an adult, she had made a conscious decision not to live that way anymore. But realizing the fact of her pregnancy, she had lied so that Justin would not feel compelled to marry her. At the time she had felt that he would want her, anyway. "How wrong could one person be?" she whispered softly.

The sound of footsteps alerted her to the presence of someone in the shop. Lost in her thoughts, she had not even heard the doorbell tinkle. Sitting up quickly, she ran her fingers self-consciously through her hair. Standing in front of her, his face impassive, was Justin Dumontier.

"Bethany."

How like him, she thought. Not "Hello, Bethany," or "How are you, Bethany," just "Bethany," as if those three syllables could say it all.

"Justin." Two could play this game. She would take her cues from him. She waited.

His eyes flickered over her face, falling to take in the sweet curves lying beneath the pastel turtleneck she wore. Her body was more mature than when he had last held her in his arms. Gone were the sharper angles, replaced by a flattering softness. Her hair was different, too, no longer waist length and free flowing, but short now, grazing the nape of her neck and swinging to hide her face when she moved. "When did you cut your hair?"

She had cut it the night she realized Justin would not be coming back to her. The memory brought with it a flash of pain as she saw the young, naive girl she had been, standing in front of the bathroom mirror, severing lock after lock of shining hair and sobbing as it fell in a dark puddle on the white tile floor. Cutting it had not exorcised the memories of Justin running his hands through the long lengths, murmuring how beautiful it was. But she had kept it very short for a long time, and only recently had she even allowed it to grow long enough to touch her collar.

"About the time I left Tallahassee," she answered.

"And when was that?" Again his dark eyes were impenetrable.

"A long time ago," she said with a sigh. Giving up the hope that he would quickly get to the point, she ventured, "What can I do for you?"

"I came to pay you for the mask. I went back to the flea market, but the woman at your stall said you had come here."

I should have told Madeline, she thought. *Now he knows where to find me.* "That was kind of you, Justin." She turned, rummaging for the notebook in which each mask was listed. "That mask was priced at seventy-five dollars, but we would be happy to get seventy for it."

"That's fair enough." He pulled out his wallet, selecting several large bills, and handed them to her. "There's some extra there for the trouble my client caused."

You will never know the truth of that statement, the persistent voice in her head screamed. She turned to the cash register, making change. "No, thank you. Paying for the mask is all I would expect."

He watched her back stiffen and her charming pointed chin lift an extra inch in the air. He reached for the money, swallowing his desire to insist. She was waiting for him to leave.

"Was there something else?" Bethany stole a quick glance at the clock over the shop door. Where were Abby and Lamar? Why didn't Justin leave? The situation was taking on the ramifications of a nightmare.

"It's been such a long time since I last saw you. Tell me, why did you decide to come to New Orleans?" It was his longest speech yet, necessitating a polite lengthy reply. The seconds ticked by as once more she glanced over the door.

"A friend, the woman you met at the flea market, offered me a job in this shop. It was an opportunity I couldn't turn down."

"And you came here from Florida?"

She shrugged, trying to hide her anxiety. "Just about." Apparently he was in no hurry. "And you, Justin? How did you find your way back to the Crescent City?"

"My father died last month. I'm here trying to put his law firm back in order."

"Oh, I'm so sorry." The genuine warmth in her voice surprised them both. This was the Bethany he remembered. Loving, giving, concerned about others. The resurrection of that memory flooded his body with hope.

"Thank you." He recognized the thawing of his own frozen responses. "It was unexpected, but he died quickly with little pain. Just the way he would have wanted."

She nodded, preparing to respond, when the shop bell tinkled again. "Mommy, I'm back." A four-year-old bundle of energy hurtled through the door and behind the counter, throwing herself into Bethany's arms. "We went to the wax museum and I ate a whole po'boy and some red beans, too."

Dear God, Bethany thought. She turned Abby so that the little girl's back was to Justin, holding her tightly against her own chest. "I'm glad you had such a good time, sweetheart. Why don't you run upstairs and see Valerie while I finish up here. Then I'll come up and you can tell me all about it." Walking sideways, she deposited Abby facing the door as she opened it. "There you go. I'll see you in a few minutes."

The doorbell tinkled again as Lamar came into the shop. "Where is she? Me, I told her I'd beat her down the block, but I almost destroyed two lovely ladies trying to run faster than that little imp."

"She's upstairs, Lamar. She told me about your adventures. A po'boy and red beans? What else?" Bethany was struggling to keep her voice light, but she hadn't looked at Justin since the ill-timed arrival of their daughter.

Lamar waved his hand nonchalantly. "Some popcorn, one praline, a lemon ice."

"I won't have to feed her for a week. Thanks a lot." She stuck out her cheek as Lamar bent to casually kiss her. "And thanks for taking her today. It helped a lot."

"You don't have to thank me. She's my special girl." He bent to kiss Bethany's other cheek. "You will come see me tonight? It's the debut of the new set I've been telling you about."

"I'm not sure." She sneaked a quick glance at Justin, who seemed to be taking in the interaction. "I'll have to see." She waved goodbye as Lamar strolled from the shop.

"I'm sorry, Justin. Where were we?" She didn't strangle on the words; in fact, an innocent bystander might have thought she was really as relaxed as she was pretending to be. Inside, however, her heart was pounding hard enough to qualify as aerobic exercise.

"The little girl is yours?"

"Yes." Surprisingly the expression on Justin's face changed for a moment, but he covered it up so quickly she could not tell what it had signified. Hoping to head him off, she inquired in a polite voice, "And you, Justin? Do you have children now?"

He shook his head. "I'm not married. No children."

Little do you know, she thought. "It's quite an experience," she said noncommittally.

"Is she your only child?"

Yes, she thought, *you see her father hasn't been available to father anymore.* "One is enough for right now," she answered.

"She's quite a big girl."

Bethany forced herself to keep her hands on the counter in front of her. "Her father is a big man."

Justin slipped his hands in his pockets. There was nothing left to say. But a part of him wanted her to know what he had thought of her, even if it was only a tiny piece of the truth. "Your husband is a lucky man," he said finally.

She could nod. It would be a simple lie, a lie of omission. She could pull her chin up and down a few inches, and she would never have to worry about Justin interfering in her life or Abby's life. But her head would not move the infinitesimal distance it needed to participate in this fourth lie to Justin Dumontier. She could feel the misty glaze of tears forming behind her eyelids. She shook her head softly. "I'm not married."

"Then your daughter's father is a fool."

"My daughter's father is many things, but he has

never been a fool," she replied. She had not lied to him, but she had not told him the truth, either. Looking directly at Justin for the first time since Abby had entered the shop, she realized he still had no inkling of her daughter's parentage. Even Justin would not be able to hide such a revelation.

"I guess I'd better go," he said finally. "I've wondered about you during these past years. I'm glad I've seen you again."

It was as personal a response as a "Wish you were here," on a postcard. "Thank you, Justin. It's been good to see you, too." She realized that now she had told her fourth lie to this man. It hadn't been good to see him. The meeting would haunt her for years to come.

Justin was turning to go, when the door in the back of the shop flew open. Valerie poked the side of her shining Afro through the opening. "Abigail Justine Walker," the teenager yelled up the stairs in a loud voice, "don't you dare come down those steps without your shoes on." Valerie swiveled to face Bethany. "Abby wants a piece of king cake. Do you care?"

Bethany shut her eyes, shaking her head. "No, go ahead."

The door shut, and Bethany opened her eyes to see Justin moving closer once again. His face was no longer a mask of formality, but the vulnerable, mobile face of a person in shock.

"Abigail Justine? Your daughter's middle name is Justine?"

Bethany nodded tiredly.

"Are you divorced or widowed?"

"Are you cross-examining me, counselor?"

He stepped closer, leaning on the glass counter, eyes

riveted to her face. "Are you divorced or widowed?" His voice was softer, and she recognized the habit he had of becoming more controlled when he felt great emotion. When she failed to respond he grasped her wrist.

"Let go of me, Justin." She refused to struggle, although everything inside her wanted to pull away from the strong, sure touch of this man. She was infused with memories.

"Tell me."

"No, I am not divorced. Nor am I a widow. I am a single woman raising my daughter alone."

"And your daughter? Where is Abigail Justine's father?"

She cast about for a way out of the trap his questions were weaving around her. Finally she said, "Her father didn't want us. He no longer exists for either of us."

She recognized the look stealing over his features. It was agony, pure and simple, and she dropped her eyes to avoid the lines of pain she saw etched in his face. "My God, Bethany. Did you give her father a chance to make that choice?"

"Choices are made in different ways. Her father made me aware of his choice when he decided he didn't want me anymore." But the hard words were softened by a catch, like a sob, in her voice. She clamped her lips shut to stem the tears that wanted to fall.

Silence fell inside the little room, broken only by the sound of laughter and traffic in the street. Minutes passed.

"Abby is my daughter," he said finally.

Bethany remained silent, lips clamped tightly shut.

"Tell me," he persisted.

The seconds crept by. She tried to pull her arm from his imprisoning fingers, only to find that they had tightened. He was hurting her. "Abby is my daughter. She belongs to no one but me. She has no father," Bethany flung at him.

The look in Justin's eyes had turned to dislike, revulsion, perhaps. With distaste he dropped her wrist. "Get your purse," he ordered her softly.

"I'm not going anywhere with you."

"We will go somewhere and talk about this now, or you will find yourself in court discussing it."

"You have no proof of anything. Your name is not on the birth certificate."

He regarded her with the same look of distaste. "And whose is?" He waited for her to answer. "Come on, Bethany. I can have a copy of that birth certificate on my desk tomorrow morning."

"No one's." The image of the kindly hospital clerk who had tried to get her to name Abby's father came to mind. The same shame flooded her body as it had when she had told the woman she did not know which of several men was the baby's father, thereby cutting off the discussion. The humiliating lie had eaten away at her since that day.

"If you tangle with me in court, Bethany, you will lose." His eyes were unwavering, and his voice, one level above a whisper. "Now do we go somewhere to discuss this, or do you wait for a summons?"

First round to you, Justin, she thought. Her wide-spreading fingers raked through the tumbled dark hair falling around her face. "I will see if Valerie can stay with Abby for a little while. But only for a little while, Justin."

"You owe me that much, don't you think?"

She shrugged, turning without a word to find her way up the stairs.

CHAPTER FOUR

IF BETHANY HAD BEEN OBLIVIOUS to the charm of the French Quarter on her previous walk through it that day, it was nothing compared to her lack of interest now. She sprinted along beside Justin with her chin in the air, trying to match his long stride. But her heart pounded harder than the moderate exercise could possibly warrant. Anxiety increasing with every step, she began to wish they would find a place to sit down and have their discussion before she was overcome completely. Still, when Justin motioned her through the door of a smoky little bar several blocks off Royal Street, she would have given anything just to continue walking.

"Would you like something?" he asked. The words were polite, but the tone was stiffly formal, lacking in any feeling at all. Had she ordered a cardboard sandwich she was sure he would not have batted an eye.

"Yes, I would," she countered. Trying to appear relaxed, she searched the one-page menu. "I haven't eaten anything substantial today. I'll have a cup of the seafood gumbo and some French bread."

"So the mother of my child doesn't take very good care of herself," he snapped after the waiter vanished behind the bar.

"You know, Justin," she said after a pause, "I think

of myself many ways. I'm an artist, a person, Abby's mother, a responsible citizen— I could go on. But nowhere on the list would appear the title, 'Mother of Justin Dumontier's child.' "

"Well, then, it seems that denial is your stock in trade. I'll tell you, though, I'd like to see you break the habit. Let me hear the truth from your lips just once. Tell me she's my daughter."

Bethany clenched her hands in her lap beneath the red-checked tablecloth. She shook her head slightly, but found that she couldn't meet his eyes.

Justin leaned back in his chair, barely tilting it on its hind legs. "Then tell me she's not."

Like the spider who tangles itself in its own web, she was caught. She could refuse to answer, but that response, too, would be an admission of guilt. She put her head on her hands, arms propped on the table. Another in the series of silences that had occurred since their meeting hours before passed slowly by.

The words when they came were wrenched from her, as if each one were torn from her against her will. "All right, Justin. I'll tell you. Yes, she is your daughter." She straightened and met his cold gaze. "But let me tell you something else. I'm prepared to lie, to deny it until I have no breath left in my body if you ever try to take her away from me."

"I could prove it if I wanted," he said after another charged silence. "There are blood tests, affidavits from friends who knew we were dating each other at the time she was conceived. And you named her after me, too. I think that would be enough to prove it to any court." His voice was liquid steel, a cold river of words meant to encase her in their rationality.

"Blood tests would only show that you could be her father, not that you are. And if you push me, I will find someone else who is willing to say that he could be Abby's father, too. As for the name, it is common enough to be a coincidence, nothing more. It proves nothing." Beads of perspiration were forming on her brow and at the nape of her neck, although the room was comfortably cool.

"You would go that far?" He searched her eyes, his face now a cynical mask. "You would completely destroy your reputation to keep me from my daughter?"

"I would go to hell and back. She is mine, Justin... mine. One brief moment of passion, one tiny sperm does not make you a father. I'm the one who gave birth to her, who got up twice a night for months unending to nurse and comfort her. I'm the one who sat beside her bed in the hospital last year when she struggled with pneumonia. I'm the one whose life changed completely the day the doctor said the pregnancy test was positive."

"And I'm the one who's been cheated out of the first four years of my daughter's life." For a moment the cynicism faded, to be replaced with disbelief. "How could you have done this to me?"

"With a lot of difficulty," she said finally. Clenching her spoon, she began methodically to choke down the gumbo the waiter had placed in front of her.

"You owe me your version of the story," he said, ignoring the ham sandwich at his place. "Start at the beginning."

"In the beginning I made a mistake that lots of foolish young women make," she said, exhaustion creeping into her voice. "I had sex with a man and got pregnant. He left and I was alone."

"'Had sex'? Isn't that rather crude? What happened to the old-fashioned term 'made love'?" His voice cut sharply into her monologue.

"I made love, Justin. You had sex. Of course, I didn't know that at the time. But remember, I was young and foolish. Anyhow—" she waved off his response "—I was caught with no place to go, and too ashamed to stay put." She pushed the bowl to one side, half-finished.

"And then?"

"I went home, where my father tried to shove an abortion down my throat. Instead I hopped a bus to Washington, D.C., where a friend helped me find a job. I worked through the rest of the pregnancy, and after Abby was born, I came to New Orleans to live with Madeline and work in her shop."

"Did it ever occur to you that I ought to be told? My God, I remember asking you if you were pregnant, and you said no." His fist hitting the table was the only display of emotion. His face was blank.

The hard thing to accept, she thought, watching his clenched fist in disconcerted fascination, was that he was right. Not telling him had been a selfish act of revenge and false pride. She was older now, a different person from the immature girl she had been. She could see clearly how much damage her silence had caused them all. But the wheels had been set in motion. Abby was hers and hers alone now. She would not be parted from her.

"I made a mistake, Justin. I've known that for some time. But I was hurt and I was proud. The two aren't a good combination in a crisis. We will all suffer for it."

"And yet...and yet you still didn't tell me until the truth was dragged kicking and screaming from you."

"I had too much to lose," she said truthfully. "It was no longer only my pride. It was Abby."

"And now?"

"I told you. If you try to take her from me I will fight you with every weapon I can think of."

He gazed at her from heavy-lidded eyes, taking in the false bravado. In spite of himself, something inside him was touched by her fiercely protective speech. She was like a mother lion defending her cub from attack. His fingers tingled with the desire to reach across the table and smooth her hair from her forehead, whispering words of consolation. But she had stolen his daughter. Without a word she had kidnapped the unborn child still nestled in her body and left him alone and oblivious. He hardened his heart. "I don't know what I will do, Bethany. But I will do something. You can count on that."

"Why can't you just leave it, Justin? It's not like she's a real person to you. You've never really even seen her."

"I'm aware of how well you spirited her past me in the shop. Would her parentage have been so easy to tell?" He stopped at the stricken look on Bethany's face. "She looks that much like me?"

"It's a matter of opinion," she started, and then gave up the pretense. "Yes. It's extraordinary."

"I'll see for myself. You'll introduce us tonight."

She shook her head firmly. "Not a chance."

"Have you forgotten that I'm a lawyer? I can insist."

"Justin, please..." She choked on her words, waiting to gain control before she continued. "Please don't do anything that will hurt us all. Go home. Think about it. I promise that I will, too. Call me in a week, and we can talk about it then."

"I want to see my daughter."

"And what will you say to her? She'll know that something is wrong. We're both overwrought right now. Please wait." Bethany instinctively reached out to touch his arm in a pleading gesture, but the hostile look on Justin's face made the movement seem ludicrous, and she withdrew her hand sharply, as if she had been burned.

He stood, throwing a bill on the table, narrowly avoiding the bowl of thick soup. "If you try to take her and leave town, I swear I'll find you and get custody so fast your devious little head will spin for a decade." Turning, he was out the door and down the sidewalk before she could take in his words.

The thought of leaving town had not occurred to her. Indeed, she had not had time to think at all since Justin had reentered her life. For a moment she felt a burgeoning sense of hope. Perhaps leaving was the solution. But the hope died quickly as she began to try to think of possible places to reestablish a life with her daughter.

There were no more Madelines or friends from her past to call on, no supportive acquaintances who would take on the burdens of helping her settle and begin a new career. There was not a vast market for mask makers in the world. Even here in New Orleans it was sometimes touch and go, except during carnival season. And even if she found a place where she could practice her craft, Justin would be sure to trace her. She had no doubt that he meant what he had said. Whether he could get custody remained to be seen, but in a strange place without the friends and supports of her present life, it would be easier for him to prove his case.

And there was something more. Now that the secret

was out and Justin knew about his child, she felt an obligation to see the situation to its conclusion. She had made the error of disappearing once before, and she could not in good conscience do it again. Justin would have to be allowed to assume a place in his daughter's life. All she could do was wait to see what that place would be.

Round two to Justin Dumontier. Wearily she pushed back her chair and started for the door.

THERE ARE one hundred sixty-eight hours in a week. Bethany discovered that fact the hard way. Each time the phone rang, the shop bell chimed, the clock moved closer to its one hundred-sixty-eight-hour deadline, Bethany became more and more anxious. Justin, for his part, seemed to have the patience of Job; he made no attempt to contact her during the long week. At first she was grateful for the respite, but as the tension built, she wondered how he was using this time. In his typical lawyer fashion was he building up a case against her— checking with neighbors and acquaintances to see if she was a fit mother, searching for Abby's birth records to see if she had told him the truth?

There was something more, too. When she was not overcome with the terror that Justin might try to take her daughter, she found herself thinking of him in another way. The long-buried potent attraction she had once felt for him was trying to reassert itself. Her traitorous body, long dormant, was remembering the feel of his hands, his lips. The images of him that had grown fuzzy over the years had been resharpened by this renewed contact.

She could remember how it felt to trace a line with her

index finger between the thick eyebrows, ending with a teasing circle around his earlobe. The way her mouth felt, molded to his, was familiar. His strong hard body enveloping her softer one was a memory that left a terrible longing in its wake. That she could still have those thoughts about him seemed like the ultimate absurdity. She was no longer the naive innocent she had been when Justin had entered her life, but her body did not seem to have received that message.

What was it about a particular arrangement of molecules, a random pattern of genes, that had such an intense effect on her? Why was Justin Dumontier different from the countless other men who had tried to interest her in their own uniqueness? When Saturday morning dawned bright and warm with the promise of spring in the air, Bethany was still no closer to the answer than she had ever been.

Madeline had invited Abby to spend the day at her small shotgun house near City Park. Abby loved to play at Madeline's in the interesting little house, called a "shotgun" because of its unique arrangement of rooms, one placed directly behind the other. The theory was that a shotgun could be fired through the front door, with the pellets exiting the back door, and nothing in between would be harmed in the slightest. Abby was fascinated by the bright-green gingerbread trim on the lemon-yellow dwelling and the vibrant colors used inside to highlight the sunny little rooms. Going to Madeline's held some of the same fascination that Hansel and Gretel must have felt upon spying the witch's candy cottage for the first time.

Bethany watched Abby drive off in Madeline's little Datsun with relief. Her time was up, and she knew that

Justin would be in touch that day. Hoping they could reach an agreement before Abby was brought into the picture, she had been greatly relieved at Madeline's offer. With some last-minute instructions to Valerie, who was at the shop counter for the day, she walked into the little brick courtyard in the back of the shop and climbed the steps to her tiny apartment.

Two of the three little rooms were littered with Abby's toys, and with a shake of her head, Bethany stopped to gather them up. Unceremoniously she dumped them on a low wooden shelf for Abby to straighten later. The apartment was crowded even for just one adult and a child, but it was flooded with light from floor-to-ceiling windows that wrapped around the two sides of the building featuring narrow metal balconies fenced off with intricate patterns of cast iron. With the sheer curtains thrown open, Bethany and Abby felt they had the entire world to live in.

In addition to the kitchenette-living room combination there was a bedroom and a workroom that Bethany planned to convert into a bedroom for Abby as soon as Life's Illusions could afford to rent a studio near the shop. In the meantime, Abby slept happily on the sofa bed, or in her mother's bed if Bethany needed the living room. The overly cozy arrangement was a necessary inconvenience.

Flicking on the bright overhead light in the workroom, Bethany flopped down on her beloved but hopelessly frayed desk chair and contemplated the mask in front of her on the wooden workroom table. She was pleased by the overall shape of the plaster-and-gauze form. With her hot-glue gun in hand, she began to overlap layers of orange and turquoise feathers to cover it.

The feathers were small and soft, dyed those brilliant hues by one of Bethany's suppliers. She worked cautiously, stopping only to rise and reach for some longer feathers, dyed silver pheasant, that were hanging in flamboyant cascades from hooks on the walls. As she cut the threads binding them, they drifted slowly to the floor like exotic lazy birds coming in for a landing.

It was almost noon and she was finished with the preliminary stages of the feather gluing, when the knock sounded at her door. Wiping her hands on the denim smock she had thrown on over blue jeans and a faded T-shirt, she hesitated, wishing she could pretend she wasn't there. But Valerie had obviously sent someone up to see her. And without peeking through the window, Bethany took a deep breath and opened the door to Justin's familiar figure. He was dressed casually, at least for Justin it was casual, with an ice-blue shirt opened at the neck and conservative dark pants. He carried a leather jacket that looked as soft as a down pillow.

There had been a week to prepare, seven days to get ready for this meeting, but Bethany felt much like she had when she had looked up from her ruined pheasant mask to see Justin standing there. *I wish,* she thought, *he were old and fat. I wish I could hate him.*

"May I come in?"

"Of course." Staring at him was not the way to start this encounter. "May I get you something?" she asked when he was inside the little room.

To his eternal credit, she thought later, he did not answer, "Yes. My daughter." Instead he murmured politely, "No, thank you. But I know I'm here at lunchtime. Go ahead and eat if you haven't already."

She shook her head and ran her fingers slowly through her hair. "Please sit down."

They sat on the small sofa bed, which was the only piece of sittable furniture in the room, since Bethany tried to keep the area clear so that Abby would have more space to play. She watched Justin take in his surroundings, a feat that could be accomplished in less than twenty seconds. "Do you both live here?"

"Of course," she answered. "It's small, but we manage quite well."

"Where does she play?" His voice was matter-of-fact and his face was expressionless, but Bethany had the chilling feeling she was on the witness stand.

"Anywhere she can."

Light reflected from the surface of his opaque dark eyes as though it too could not penetrate the depths of this man. "I noticed that there's no yard."

"Justin, you know enough about the French Quarter to understand that it was built with enclosed courtyards, not yards surrounding the houses. Abby rides her tricycle in the courtyard you walked through to get here. She plays with the neighbor's cat there and climbs the little tree in the middle. When the weather's nice she makes tents on the iron benches, and when it's very hot, we stop up the bottom of the old fountain and she wades in it."

"And you think it's safe for her to be out there?"

Bethany fought to control her voice, which was threatening to rise in anger. "She is always supervised, as any four-year-old should be, if that's what you are getting at."

"Tell me, Bethany." He stood up and wandered to the window, taking in the view of slate roofs and colorful narrow buildings. "Do you think that the French Quarter is a good place to raise our daughter?"

"I think that anywhere that I am is a good place to raise her. It's not the place but the love she receives that is important." She took in the erect stance and the disdainful stare out the window. She was getting nowhere.

"Do you know the crime statistics here?"

"Get to the point, Justin."

He turned and hooked his thumbs in his pockets. "I don't want her living like this."

"That's too bad, because this is our home, whether you approve of it or not." Her voice and temper were rising.

"I'm not here to get into a shouting match with you over this. I've come to make you a proposition," he said formally.

"The last time I took you up on one of your propositions, Justin, I became a mother," she said, trying for a lighter touch. The remark rang out like a nervous giggle at a funeral. It was an inappropriate response to a deeply felt emotion, and she was instantly ashamed.

"I'm serious, Bethany." His darkly handsome face was, if possible, more stern than it had been. "I've thought about nothing else for the past week. It's on my mind when I go to sleep at night and when I awaken each morning." He turned to stare out the window again. "I've asked myself a thousand times how this happened and how much of the fault was my own."

"But that doesn't really matter now, does it?" she said as she watched his shoulders straighten a millimeter.

"No, I guess it doesn't. What's important is that we find some rational way to deal with the situation as it stands."

"Abby is a child, not a 'situation,'" she interrupted with the sharp edge in her voice again. "I won't have her 'dealt with' like she was a bad case of the flu."

"Bethany, please let me finish." It was the familiar Justin whisper, the voice he used when he bucked no resistance. She swallowed the rest of her speech. "Of course Abby is not a 'situation,' but there is a situation surrounding her. It goes something like this. A small child living alone with her mother in a section of town that is not desirable for children has a father who wants to make her life better. Mix that up with a mother who is unreasonable in her demands that the father stay away from his daughter and a father who is fast losing patience with the mother, and you have our . . . situation."

She stared at him, two spots of color high on her pale cheeks. "Well?"

"I won't beat around the bush, since it isn't getting us anywhere." He walked to the sofa, sitting so they were looking directly at each other. "The obvious solution to this problem is for us to get married."

She shut her eyes, as if by doing so she could wish this man to another planet. Finally she said, eyes still closed, "That's an interesting way to look at marriage. A solution to a problem. I wonder if that's where everyone else has been going wrong. Maybe the divorce rate would be cut in half if everyone were as cold-blooded as you are. Someone ought to tell Elizabeth Taylor, and Zsa Zsa—"

"Dammit, Bethany. Stop it. Do you think it was easy for me to come here and propose to you?"

"'Propose'? You call that a proposal?" *I'm getting hysterical,* she thought with the small part of her that was still at least a little rational.

"Under the circumstances, I thought that a dozen roses, champagne and me on bended knee would be ludicrous. But it is a proposal nevertheless. I want you to marry me. Immediately. And next month, after I've finished straightening out my business here, I want you and Abby to come to Chicago with me to start a life together."

If I open my mouth I'm going to babble, she thought. She sat carefully counting the panes of glass in the windows of the room. When she was finished, she counted them again, this time backward. Having always prided herself on being a kind, tactful person, she was shocked at the cruel things she wanted to say to Justin, and it was several minutes before she was able to trust the sound of her own voice. "No."

She wondered if Justin was also counting panes of glass, because the silence stretched interminably. "You don't have to answer now," he said finally. "I can see this surprised you."

"No. I said no. That won't change."

"You are being unreasonable." His face was carved out of granite, and his voice, as hers had been, was expressionless.

"Perhaps. But when I marry, it will be for love."

The only answer she received was a further tightening of his already-immobile face. As she waited for him to break the silence, she sat thinking about his offer. To marry him now was unthinkable, and the proposal confirmed what she had known about him at the time of her pregnancy. Had she gone to Justin with the facts, he would have insisted on marriage. As the much more insecure person that she had been then, she would not have had the strength to refuse him.

One short letter, one brief phone call would have sent her life down a completely different path. She would now be Mrs. Justin Dumontier. Her daughter would live in a suburban Chicago house, play with expensive toys, attend a posh private school and have the cocker spaniel she longed for. Bethany would do volunteer work for the local art museum, attend club meetings and have a weekly bridge night. The life, even as stereotyped as she imagined it, was not the problem. Woven throughout the fantasy was the unsmiling face of the man who sat next to her.

Perhaps with Abby he would have let down his guard and given her the love she deserved, but Bethany was sure that her relationship with Justin, built only on "doing the right thing" would have been loveless and barren. How long would it have been before the sexual attraction he had felt for her turned to nothing more than a casual kiss on the cheek each morning before he left for a long day at his office? That kind of marriage had been unthinkable to her then. Now it was absolutely abhorrent.

"I don't want to threaten you, Bethany, but you leave me no choice. I will not be kept from my daughter. If you won't marry me I will have to find another way, and it may be more unacceptable to you than marrying me."

Here it was again, the threat that Justin would try to gain custody. "Is this a new version of the melodrama where the landlord threatens some dire harm if the sweet young thing refuses to marry him? Are you waiting for me to say, 'No, no, a thousand times no'?" *Why am I being flip,* she thought despairingly. *What am I letting him do to me?*

"You've changed a lot in the past five years, haven't you? I don't remember ever hearing you resort to sarcasm before."

"But, then, neither of us has ever been in this situation before, have we?" she answered wearily. "I guess I don't really know how to behave in these circumstances. I only know that I wish you'd leave."

Justin rose and walked to the window once more. "I won't have my daughter raised here like some kind of an ill-bred bohemian. She deserves a real life, one without a massive exposure to the crazies who sometimes frequent this place." His hand swept the scene before him. "And she deserves full-time consideration of her needs."

"That does it, counselor. Get out!" Bethany jumped up, marching to the door to fling it wide open, gesturing with her other hand. "I will not sit here and listen to you insult my ability to raise my daughter. Abby is a bright and charming little girl with better manners than her father. She is happy here. She is now and always has been my first priority. The day that I think this environment is going to damage her I will pack and move immediately. Until then, not you or anyone else will tell me where and how I should raise my little girl."

"Shut the door, Bethany," Justin responded icily. "I told you I wasn't here to participate in a shouting match."

"Get out," she repeated.

Justin marched toward her, his eyes blazing in an otherwise unreadable face. His fingers clamped firmly on her shoulders, thumbs pressing on the fragile collarbone beneath. She had the sudden premonition he was going to shake her the way Abby sometimes did her rag doll when she was angry. If he had intended to, he thought better of it. But his hands remained in place.

"Listen to me. You will stop trying to make this so difficult. Do you understand? I am tired of you taking everything I say and twisting it to make me into some kind of a monster."

She was sure the surprise she felt was reflected in her eyes. "What have I misunderstood?" she asked as calmly as she could manage. Justin angry was a Justin she didn't know. But more than his anger was unsettling. His proximity to her was startling; she felt overwhelmed by the heat from his body and his warm breath on her cheek.

"I am not accusing you of being a bad parent. I haven't even spoken to my daughter, and I have no way of judging how adequate her upbringing has been. But I can see where she is being raised, and I am very concerned about it."

"Not every child has to be raised in suburbia to emerge as a happy healthy human being."

"And I am concerned that you seem to have no intention of letting me into Abby's life," he said, ignoring her response. She noticed, without wanting to, how Justin said his daughter's name. It rolled off his tongue in the same way that a teenager said the name of his favorite rock star. There was a certain quality of wonder, of reverence in his voice.

What am I going to do, she agonized silently. It was so easy when she could cast Justin as the villain in this hopeless little melodrama. She could not let him into her heart. Not again.

"Bethany?" The pressure from his hands lessened, and finally they dropped to his side. "You've refused my offer. What's your proposed solution?"

She tried to dredge up her anger, reaching deep inside herself for anything she could find to spur it on. "I don't know, but I don't want to talk about it anymore right now. Please leave."

"You've had a week. I've been patient, but I'm not going to wait any longer."

"Are you afraid that a few more days will ruin your daughter completely?" she said acidly, but with little inner conviction that she was in the right.

"I know you're scared, and I'm sorry." The words were spaced evenly, but there was a quality of concern in them, and she shut her eyes to avoid responding to the softening in his.

"Please leave, Justin."

She felt rather than saw him go through the open door. When she opened her eyes a moment later she was alone. Alone with her doubts and her fear. Alone with the knowledge that she could not hold him off much longer. Alone with the startling thought that a part of her didn't want to hold him off at all.

CHAPTER FIVE

ON A WARM EVENING in New Orleans, windows and doors were invariably thrown open to catch the breeze stirring the heavy humid air. Later in the season, the loud hum of air conditioners would drown out the city noises, but this night, the light breeze was cooling enough. Bethany sat on her living-room sofa, windows wide open, listening to the distant sound of the blues drifting from the famous Bourbon Street jazz clubs only one block away.

Madeline had asked permission to keep Abby for the rest of the weekend, and Bethany, who had almost forgotten how to use that precious gift of a free moment, was alone. She had worked until ten o'clock, hoping she could fall exhausted into bed. But it was past midnight and there was no hope that sleep was going to come easily. She sat on the sofa, sipping a glass of iced tea as she looked out over the lights of the city.

It was at times like these that she loved the French Quarter the most. The haunting sound of the blues woven into the raucous blare of dixieland; warm air sometimes punctuated with the sweet smell of native flowers; remnants of a mauve-and-gold sunset laced across the sky with wispy clouds—all these had merged in a vivid jumble in her head to provide an image that she entitled "home."

She was not a complete romantic. She knew there were problems with her chosen place of abode. There was crime. There were oddballs who came into the Quarter looking for trouble. There was too much drinking for her to feel comfortable. And on Bourbon Street, side by side with the jazz clubs were strip shows of the sort that embarrassed her just to walk by.

No place was perfect, she had always reasoned, but New Orleans was far from being dull, which in Bethany's artist's soul was the greatest sin of all. Tonight, however, she found herself concentrating on all of the negative aspects of her chosen life-style.

What would Justin hear if he were with her on the sofa listening to the night noises? Would he hear the provocative drifting music that was weaving a sensuous spell around its admirers? Or would he hear the quarrel that had started in the street below between two drunks? Would he notice the steep roofs, sliding into nothingness over balconies so intricate they took her breath away? Or would he notice the trash collecting in the narrow alleys from the overflow crowd off Bourbon Street?

And what did Abby notice? Was she becoming so acclimated to life here amid the exotic sights and sounds that she thought this was normal? How much of the colorful atmosphere surrounding her was the little girl absorbing? Bethany rose and walked to the tall windows, slamming them shut. The noise and the breeze had become irritants, playing on her overwrought nervous system like chalk squeaking on a blackboard.

It was not the Quarter, the noise or the breeze that was causing her strange mood. Certainly Justin's disdain for her surroundings had affected her perception of them. But where she lived was only a small part of the problem. He had picked that particular issue because it probably was important to him, at least on some level. But she was sure that more important was the message behind it. Justin was telling her in no uncertain terms that he was laying claim to his daughter. He was going to be involved in her life, and he was going to have a say over what happened to her.

And it was time for Bethany to make a decision. For a week she had avoided dealing with Justin's presence. She had deluded herself into thinking he might just decide to forget that he was a father. By pretending to be courageous and sure of herself she had fooled no one, except possibly herself, and then only for a short time. Justin could prove that Abby was his daughter. What judge, when faced with the final evidence of the little girl's face, would decide otherwise? Bethany's decision, therefore, was fairly simple. She could go on pretending, try to call Justin's bluff and hope he would quickly grow tired of the struggle, or she could graciously consent to allow him to be a father to his own child.

There was one other vital aspect of the "situation," as Justin had called it. She, who prided herself on her openness and her honesty, had cheated this man of his most basic right. Now it was time to take the first step toward settling the matter fairly. Justin had tried, in his own way, to solve their impasse by offering marriage. She could not accept that alternative, but she could allow him unfettered access to their daughter.

Perhaps as difficult as sharing the little girl was the knowledge that she was now allowing Justin back into her own life. She would be exposed to him no matter how hard she tried not to be. When he came to visit or to take his daughter out, she would have to make small talk with him in order to help reassure Abby that this man, her father, was not a monster.

Justin would of necessity be involved in all decisions about Bethany's own life that might affect Abby. And she would have to discuss her plans for their daughter, report on her progress in school and in her daily life, consult him on any matters relating to Abby's welfare. They would be irrevocably entwined until Abby was an adult on her own. Even then they would have to share Abby and Abby's own family at some holiday celebrations and family events.

Bethany knew that she was losing part of her daughter. Almost as frightening was knowing that she was losing a part of herself, too: that safe, inviolate space inside her that was walled off from memories of this man. No longer could she bury her reminiscences. They would be with her now in Technicolor, and she tasted fear. The night stretched on, and even when she finally turned down the covers on the old-fashioned four-poster she was not able to sleep.

Justin sat at the table in the breakfast room off the sprawling French country kitchen of his mother's St. Charles Avenue home. He was alone except for the Sunday paper spread in untidy heaps around his plate.

When he had lived in Chicago, Sunday morning had taken on a ritual quality. Rising later than his weekday 7:00 a.m., he had thrown on weather-appropriate jogging clothes and run the eighteen blocks necessary to buy the sampling of out-of-town papers he always read. With papers under arm, he had jogged another seven blocks to a small restaurant, where he ordered coffee with lots of milk in it—a habit from his New Orleans childhood—and a ham omelet. There he had settled down to make his way through the front page of the *New York Times*. The rest of the day was spent in leisure activities, punctuated by spells of reading the half-dozen newspapers he had purchased.

The pattern had been unchanging. Sometimes he was joined for breakfast by a lovely companion who might spend the rest of the day with him; sometimes he spent the day alone. Always he had taken the time to comb the various papers, looking for a name, a picture; giving the arts section of each paper his special attention. He had told himself many times that the habit was nothing more than a slightly deranged compulsion. Yet in spite of that rational assessment he had been unable to stop.

Coincidences did occur. He believed strongly in them. There had been times in his professional life that a name dropped casually, a face seen unexpectedly in a crowd had made the difference between winning and losing a case. When he had made the decision not to have professionals search for Bethany after he discovered she had left Tallahassee, a part of him had not given up hope that somehow, somewhere he would stumble on her again.

And now he had. Not in the pages of a distant newspaper, but in the flesh, in his hometown. How ironic, he thought, that in all those years in Chicago he had never once thought to buy and read the *New Orleans Times-Picayune*. Now it lay scattered around him, partially read and totally unabsorbed.

"Justin?"

He lifted his eyes to meet the glance of his mother, who was standing in the doorway. Louise Dumontier was regarding her son with a concerned expression. At seven-thirty she was already dressed impeccably for the mass she would attend at ten o'clock. An attractive woman, with the particular well-kept look only available to the rich, Louise Dumontier exhibited none of her usual poise.

Justin stood, motioning to the chair beside him as he cleared off the table. "Sit down, mother."

She sat with regal grace, spoiled only by the watchful glance at her son. "You're up so early."

"I always get up early, mother."

"But today's Sunday. And you went to bed so late last night."

"I always go to bed late, mother."

She sighed as if to give up trying to tactfully coax information from him. "Justin, is something bothering you?"

Her answer was the tightening of the muscle visible in his jaw.

"I know it's probably none of my business—" she covered his hand with her own diamond laden one "—but can I help?"

He shook his head firmly. "No." The expression on her face was so heavy with disappointment that he relented. "Not now. Perhaps later, after I've had time to sort out everything."

His reward was the brightness of her smile. "Well, then, can I interest you in going to church with me today?"

"I'm going in to the office. I've got a lot to do there."

Mrs. Dumontier shook her head. "That's where your father took his problems, too. Whenever we quarreled he packed up and headed in to work. Sometimes I wouldn't see him for days."

Justin looked at his well-bred mother with surprise, and tried to remember a time when she had admitted that she and his father actually quarreled like normal people. "I don't remember that," he said finally.

"He was gone so much, anyway, that you probably wouldn't have noticed." She sighed.

Was her voice actually tinged with dissatisfaction? Justin turned his hand over to grasp hers and squeeze it. "Did that bother you?"

She seemed startled by the personal question, and hesitated, as if trying to figure how to turn the tide of the conversation. Finally she sighed again. "Yes, quite a lot. Justin. If you ever marry, I hope you'll be able to share yourself with someone. I think that in the greater scheme of things, sharing must be the thing that makes this life worth it all."

The room grew gradually lighter as they sat quietly. Finally he squeezed her hand again as he stood. "I hope that sometime I have the chance to find that out for myself," he said as he bent to kiss the top of her head. "I'll see you tonight."

Although the one remaining New Orleans streetcar ran directly in front of his house, Justin drove his car to work, parking it in the garage next to the office building housing his father's law office. He was teetering between giving Bethany more time to make a decision and forcing her to allow him to see his daughter. He wanted his car on hand in case he was able to make up his mind. The realization that he was unsure how to handle this situation gnawed at him, creating an internal tension that matched the tension of the situation itself. Yet he was no closer to knowing what was best than he had been during the sleepless night he had just spent.

When his private phone rang at eleven o'clock, he had just been able to settle down and concentrate on the brief in front of him. It was with annoyance that he answered it.

"Justin?"

He had forgotten how sweet her voice was on the telephone. He had often thought that even if he had never seen her, her voice alone would conjure up a body and a face no different from the real thing. He was swept by a wave of warmth. "Yes, Bethany."

"I got this number from someone at your house. . . I hope I'm not disturbing you."

You've never done anything except disturb me. "Of course not. Is anything wrong?"

She hesitated as if trying to figure out his meaning. "Do you mean with Abby? No, she's fine. She's spending the weekend with my business partner, Madeline." There was another short silence. "Justin, I'd. . . I'd like to see you today, if I could."

"When and where?"

She hesitated again. "Well, anytime is fine. Abby won't be home until five o'clock. I could come there, or you could come here. . . no, I guess that's not such a good idea," she said as if thinking aloud.

He winced at her soft words, aware of the damage his diatribe against the French Quarter had done. "I'd be glad to come there, Bethany. But better yet, why don't we meet on neutral ground. Have you had lunch yet?"

"No, I haven't eaten."

"I'll pick you up at noon and we can go out for lunch." The thought of their last meal together in the smoky bar off Royal Street made him change his mind.

"Better yet, wear something casual and we can drive out to the lake. I'll pick up some sandwiches."

"Are you sure you want to go to all that trouble, Justin?"

This time he paused. "You've always worried about causing me trouble, haven't you?" There was no answer and he said gently, "Noon, Bethany," before he replaced the receiver.

She had an hour to decide how to dress for her picnic with Justin. Finally settling on a grape gauze blouse with billowing sleeves and black form-fitting jeans tied with a colorful Mexican sash, she stood in front of the mirror in her bedroom, brushing her hair with a vengeance. She was satisfied with everything she saw except for the circles under her eyes. Justin would take one look at her and know about the turmoil she was undergoing.

When the buzzer sounded she pushed a button by her front door, leaving it depressed long enough to allow him to swing open the iron gate to the side of the courtyard. She let herself out the door, locking it securely behind her, and met him at the bottom of the stairs.

"You're the only woman I've ever known who never keeps me waiting," he said as he watched her walk toward him.

She smiled hesitantly, at a loss for words as she tried to quell the rush of attraction she felt for him. He was dressed in a white knitted shirt with a crawfish embroidered on the pocket, the New Orleans answer to the popular alligator or polo pony. He was also wearing crisp, dark-blue jeans. "Do you know," she said without thinking about how it sounded, "I've never seen you in blue jeans, Justin. You look terrific." The instant the words were uttered she felt foolish. She had called him to try to come to an understanding about their daughter, and here she was complimenting him on his pants.

He, too, seemed surprised by her comment. "I'm not quite the conservative gentleman you seem to think, Bethany. I've actually got more than one pair of jeans, and several running suits, too. I don't wear three-piece suits when I'm having fun."

She remembered exactly what he had worn five years before when they had been having fun. Nothing. The thought suffused her face with color, and she stammered, "I think your impression of my impression of you..." She gave up at the smile on his face. "Where's your car, Justin?"

"Six blocks away. This place is crowded even on Sundays."

They walked in silence to the car, although after the first block Justin steered her to the window of one shop, pointing out a display of masks on the wall. "Are any of these yours?"

"The big one on permanent display in the corner is." She pointed to a feathered mask done in Lady Amherst pheasant, similar to the one the old man had collapsed on. "It was one of the first feathered masks I ever did. It bought Abby and me enough groceries for three weeks, and I was very proud."

She looked up into his unsmiling eyes, and realized how her remark had sounded, but there was nothing to say in defense. They had been poor; there had been times when providing for Abby and herself had been difficult. She could not lie to him. She could not live those years over again. All she could do was tell him the truth. "Justin, if it had ever been really critical, if we had ever stood on the brink of starvation, I would have come to you."

"I wonder" was all he replied.

His car, when they reached it, was what she would have expected. It was a dark-blue Mercedes sedan, built to last forever. He opened her door and helped her in, dropping her arm at the first opportunity. She knew he was still angry.

Why am I so concerned about his feelings, she wondered as they sped toward Lake Ponchartrain. *Was he concerned about mine? When he left me, did he think about the damage he was doing to me? Did he ever care at all? Was I ever more than just a warm body to make love to?* But trying to whip herself into an angry frenzy was a useless gesture. Justin had every cause to be upset. Little by little over the past week she had begun to allow herself to understand some part of his feelings. Now, sitting in the car beside him, she felt the entire weight of them surround her. For the first time she was faced with the enormity of the mistake she had made.

Reaching out to him, she put her hand on his shoulder for a moment, surprising them both. "Justin, I'm so sorry," she whispered. "I don't know how I could have done such a terrible thing."

There was no answer from the driver's seat, but she took in the visible relaxing of his facial muscles. She was far from being forgiven, but the barriers between them seemed a little less impenetrable. Closing her eyes, she relaxed against the cushions.

"Do you always fall asleep instantly like that?"

Bethany awoke slowly. She was curled up snugly on the seat of a very comfortable car. An arousing male voice buzzed sensuously against her ear, and the man smelled the way she remembered Justin smelling. It was the smell of cleanliness, of expensive soap and male skin. She yawned and stretched, not wanting to look to the side and be disappointed. It was not the first dream that had ended that way.

"Bethany?"

She turned, wondering at the familiar voice. Only Justin called her by her full name. She was "Beth" to everyone else. "Justin?"

"Mmm..." His voice was relaxed and tinged with humor. "Do you know where you are?"

She sat up straight, shaking her head groggily. "But give me a minute, and I'm bound to figure it out."

"We're at Lake Ponchartrain, and although this may be hard to believe, you've only been asleep for about fifteen minutes."

"That's fifteen minutes more than I got last night," she said, stretching again. "At this rate I may get a full eight hours by the beginning of the next century."

He held out his hand and stood next to her, helping her from the car. The surprising thing was that he didn't drop her hand immediately. Instead he continued holding it as he reached to stroke the side of her face with his fingertips. "You looked like a little girl, asleep like that."

His caress made her feel less like a little girl than anything imaginable. For a moment she leaned toward him, her eyes closed again. When he stopped, her eyes flew open and she stepped backward, uncertain and astonished at her own behavior. "Well, I'm awake now," she said finally.

There was a faint smile on his beautifully chiseled mouth. "Let's find a place to eat."

The lakeside was alive with cruising cars and groups of people picnicking. The day was fairly warm, and the sun streamed down to highlight the white sails of the boats far out against the horizon. The lake itself was large enough to seem an endless expanse of sparkling blue water. Because there were only a few yards of land between the lake and the road running around it, they spread a blanket halfway up one of the banks of the levee, overlooking the water. The spot was also far enough away from blaring car radios and flying Frisbees to be comfortable.

"It's beautiful here, Justin. Thank you for bringing me."

He watched her with surprise as she took in the sights and sounds. "You haven't been here before today?"

She shook her head, breathing deeply of the air that was tinged with salt. "I don't have a car, so I'm dependent on the bus or my friends. I just didn't realize this was so special, or Abby and I would have made the trip across town." Shutting her eyes to enjoy the sunshine, she didn't notice the darkening of his eyes. His question came as a complete surprise.

"What do you do in emergencies?"

His formal tone caused her eyes to fly open. "I haven't had many."

"Aren't you in rather a precarious position without a car?"

Shrugging, she searched his eyes for an explanation. "Well, it can be awkward sometimes, but I've always managed."

"You know as well as I do that New Orleans' public transportation system is inadequate at best and sometimes even dangerous. What if Abby were suddenly ill?"

"Justin, I know it would be better—safer, maybe—if I had my own transportation. But there are taxis, ambulances, friends. I just can't afford my own car right now. The gas and insurance would ruin me financially."

A disapproving look similar to the one he had worn while criticizing her choice of housing was firmly rooted on his features. She had the sinking feeling that the afternoon was destined to go down in defeat before she could tell him why she had asked for this meeting.

"Look," she started, "let's eat, and I'll tell you why I called. Then if you still want to, I'll give you fifteen minutes to criticize my life-style. If that's not long enough, then we'll have to make arrangements to continue it another time. I'm not sure I can handle all your cold-blooded inquiries in one day."

Without a word he reached for the bag he had carried up the little hill. Inside were two sandwiches wrapped in white butcher's paper and a six-pack of beer. He handed her a sandwich. "An oyster po'boy? That's my favorite." She chewed the French bread and fried oyster combination as she watched him open a can of beer to pass her. "I'm surprised," she said honestly. "I never imagined you like this."

"Like what?" he said, lounging on the blanket as he opened his sandwich.

"Like this. Eating po'boys up on the levee. Wearing blue jeans and crawfish shirts. Acting like a real N'Awlins native."

"I am a real N'Awlins native."

"I thought you had rejected all this."

There was an explosion of feeling that flew across his face. She felt as though she were caught in a whirlwind, but she blinked, and when she opened her eyes, his ex-

pression was neutral again. They sat chewing thoughtfully, washing down the sandwiches with ice-cold Dixie,
New Orlean's only local beer.

"Why did you call?"

She swallowed the last of her sandwich nervously.
Now that the time had come, she wasn't sure how to
begin. "Justin, I've done nothing but think about
this since I saw you last Saturday." She cleared
her throat, willing the lump in it to subside. "I told you
in the car that I was sorry. I meant it. All these years
I've refused to think about how unfair I was being to
you."

"You never gave it a thought?"

"Sometimes I did. But you see, at first I had no idea
what an incredible experience having a child would be. I
knew I wanted to have the baby and raise it, but I just
had no idea what it could mean. I told myself that you
would be better off not having the burden of a child you
didn't plan for in your life."

"And later?"

Bethany stared out at the lake, watching the sailboats
dance against the sky. "Later, when I let myself think
about it, I realized what I was cheating you out of. But I
thought it was too late, and I was too proud." She
turned to him, eyes bright with unshed tears. "I can't
make up any of the years you've missed, but I can share
her remaining years. Abby is your daughter. She deserves to have you in her life."

Justin was reclining on one elbow, tracing patterns in
the blanket with his index finger. She watched him,
waiting for his answer. His black hair had fallen over
one eye, giving his face a boyish look that softened the
angular features. The bright sunlight gave his skin a

burnished polish, and she was suddenly aware of just how much of him was a part of their daughter.

"You will love her, Justin. And she will love you. The two of you are so much alike," she said impulsively.

He looked at her then, raising the dark eyes that were the original version of Abby's, to meet hers. "Tell me about her," he said simply.

How could she catch him up on four years? What could she say in a minute or an hour or a week that would adequately introduce him to his daughter? She began. "She's bright. Sometimes she scares me with how bright. She understands so much already. She senses what's going on around her better than most adults do. She's very pretty, but that's not the most noticeable thing about her. I think the first thing that people notice is how much energy she has. She wears me to a frazzle sometimes." She paused, trying to smile at him. "What else?"

"How is she going to react to having a father in her life?"

Bethany looked away, feeling for the right answer. "It's going to be hard for her to understand. When she's asked about you, Justin, I've told her that you had to go away before she was born and that you weren't able to come back."

"At least you didn't tell her I was dead."

"This may be hard to believe, under the circumstances," she said softly, "but I try not to lie if I can help it."

He sat up, grasping his knees with his hands. "How do you propose we work out custody?"

A small prickle of fear shot through her body. "I want custody, of course. But I'll be glad to let you see her almost anytime. After she gets to know you, then I'm sure you'll want to have her visit you in Chicago. And I'll let her, as long as the arrangements are suitable."

"So I get to play visiting father. I take her to Disney World, buy her ice-cream cones on Sunday afternoons and pay for her wedding. In the meantime you nurture her, watch her grow, hold her hand when her best friend fights with her or when her first boyfriend is caught kissing the class flirt." The bitterness in his voice was unmistakable.

"But you're not even going to be here, Justin. How can you expect to spend more time with her? Even if we had a joint-custody arrangement one of us would have her most of the time in these circumstances. She can't fly back and forth between New Orleans and Chicago every week."

"I want more than a casual acquaintance with my daughter, Bethany."

"I want that for you, too, Justin. I will do my best to help that to happen. What more can I say?"

"You can say you'll marry me, that you'll come to Chicago and the three of us will live as a family."

She bent her head, and her hair fell forward, covering her profile for a moment. She was grateful for the dark curtain, because she was sure the conflict his words were causing were visible in her face. And like a good lawyer, Justin would press his advantage. When she straightened, she swept her hair back over her ear and turned toward him.

"I can't marry you. Abby deserves better than two parents who only tolerate each other. Someday perhaps one of us will marry and provide her with the model of a marriage that she should have, but until then, I think it would be best if we don't try to pretend." The words cost her more pain than she had believed possible. Not only was she refusing to marry Justin, but she was giving him her permission—encouragement, even—to find another more suitable wife. Directly following the pain was the realization that she must still be tied emotionally to him; it would not hurt this bad otherwise. Was she still in love with this man?

"I didn't intend for us to pretend, Bethany. I'd want us to make a real commitment."

"Based on what, Justin? On the result of one ill-planned act of passion that occurred five years ago?" In horror she realized that her voice was becoming thick with unshed tears. She turned to look over the lake and compose herself.

The warmth of his arm encircling her shoulder was a surprise. He pulled her toward him to lean her head against his chest. Sitting quietly like that, she could not prevent the tears from slipping down her cheeks, and she mopped them with the napkin he provided.

"I've always had trouble taking what you offered me, Bethany." He turned her toward him so that their faces were only inches apart. He bent his head the infinitesimal distance to kiss her gently. His lips against hers were warm and firm. He applied no pressure, just held himself close to her for a moment and then moved away. "I accept your offer to become a part of Abby's life."

If he had reached out to slap her she would have been no more surprised. Buried memories of this gentle Justin began to surface in painful surges. She realized that she was staring at him and that she had no idea what he had said to her. "I'm sorry," she said shakily. "What did you say?"

"I'm willing to play the game by your rules. At least for a while. If I'm to become part of our daughter's life, I'd like to begin right away. Where do we start?" He smiled encouragingly.

"We'll have to introduce you," she said inanely.

"Yes. How do you suggest we accomplish that? It's bound to be a shock."

Bethany began to pleat the blanket with nervous fingers as she ran through possible scenarios in her mind. "Abby is an exceptionally charming child, but she can be very temperamental, too." She smiled at his quizzical look. "She obviously gets that from you."

"How long have you wanted to tell me that?" he said with a laugh.

Pleased by his response, she went on. "She tends to hold grudges for a very long time, but she also loves with abandon. I honestly can't say how meeting you will affect her. Perhaps we shouldn't tell her who you are at first." Before he could answer, she shook her head decisively. "No, she would know. She knows she was named for her father, and she's too smart not to notice the resemblance. She'll have to be told."

"Perhaps you should prepare her before I come to see her."

Bethany nodded. "That would be best. Then maybe you can take her out somewhere so that you can be alone together."

They both sat quietly, until Justin broke the silence. "It won't work. I don't know that much about little girls, but I can't imagine it working. She won't want to go anywhere with me. I may be her father, but she doesn't even know me."

"You're right, Justin," she said reluctantly. "I hate

to interfere with your first outing with her, but I think I'd better come along. It will make it less awkward. I'm sorry."

"I'm relieved. Until I learn to be a father, I would appreciate your help and support."

The statement was as close to a statement of needing her as anything he had ever said. It sent a spiraling joy echoing through her body, and without thinking, she covered his hand with hers. "You've got it. I'll do whatever I can."

"Then help me come up with a place and agree to have dinner with me tonight. You and our daughter."

She stood, brushing crumbs from her pants as she forced herself to assert control over her bubbling goodwill. The very closeness she felt to him should be warning enough, she thought. Once before she had allowed her feelings to take control, and the outcome had been disastrous. She was the mother of his child; perhaps they could establish a good working relationship. But the outrageous joy she felt when he touched her or made a simple request was totally inappropriate.

"That gives me very little time to prepare her, but maybe that's best," she said finally.

Justin gathered up the blanket, folding it to put in the trunk of his car, and they walked down the levee. The drive home was quiet, with each immersed in his own thoughts. As they pulled up in front of Bethany's apartment, Justin asked, "Where and when?"

"Six o'clock. Let me think about where. I'm afraid that eating out with a four-year-old is a unique experience."

"Anything goes," he answered.

"That's a terrific idea. I'm glad you thought of it."

"I think I've lost you."

"That's the name of a restaurant not too far from here. Anything Goes. I've heard it's a great place to take children. We can walk across the Quarter, and Abby can work off some energy first." She laughed at his look. "Come prepared to eat in a tepee."

Slamming the door, she waved goodbye as he drove away. The sidewalks were crowded as she watched his car slowly disappear into the traffic. Turning, she made her way to the iron gate. She had the rest of the afternoon to get her emotions under strict control and to decide how to tell Abby that her father had come back. Somehow even a lifetime didn't seem long enough.

CHAPTER SIX

BETHANY HELD HER ARMS OPEN WIDE as a whirlwind of pigtails and excited screams came running up the stairs toward her. "Abby, I'm so glad you're home."

"So am I," groaned the woman's voice at the bottom of the stairs, and Bethany laughed as Madeline climbed slowly to meet her. "I understand fully why God gives children to the young."

"Did you wear poor Madeline out, Abby?" Bethany asked, kissing the tip of the little girl's nose as she held her close.

"She likes it, mommy. What's for dinner?" The little girl ran excitedly around the apartment, checking each nook and cranny to be sure nothing important had changed since she'd been gone.

If she only knew, Bethany thought. Everything had changed. She turned to Madeline. "Make you a cup of tea?"

The older woman collapsed unceremoniously onto the sofa. "Please!"

"What's for dinner? Can I go down to the courtyard to see Bum?" Abby hopped from foot to foot waiting for an answer.

"We're going out for dinner, and yes, you can play with Bum while I talk to Madeline."

She watched the little girl scoot down the stairs, just

slowly enough to keep from falling head over heels. At the bottom Abby caught sight of the big yellow tomcat, named "Bum" in honor of the New Orleans Saints football coach. Bum the cat, like Bum the coach, had a large bulky body and short fuzzy hair that stood straight up all over his small head. Bum, as usual, wallowed shamelessly in the love freely given by the little girl.

Bethany whistled softly. "She's wound up like a top. Has she been this way all weekend?"

"Pretty nearly. She liked being at my house, but I think she worried about you, too. You haven't been yourself this past week." Madeline sat back with her arms folded. "Are you ready to tell me what's going on?"

Bethany filled a kettle with water, setting it on the burner to heat. She measured the tea and scalded the teapot with hot tap water as she thought about Madeline's words. It was not going to be easy to tell anyone about Justin.

"You make tea the way you do everything. You put so much of yourself into it. You're the only person I know on this side of the Atlantic Ocean who actually heats her teapot." Madeline was watching her.

"Abby's father is in town." The statement fell into empty space, and Bethany, not expecting a response yet, felt around for the right words. "I saw him at the flea market last Saturday. One thing led to another and he found out about Abby."

"'Found out' about her?"

"I never told him I was pregnant, Madeline. His name is Justin Dumontier. I was very much in love with him, and when I realized that he didn't love me, I decided not to tell him about the baby."

"I always wondered." The older woman waited for her to go on.

"I've agreed to let him assume a place in Abby's life. He's coming to take us out to dinner tonight."

"Both of you?" Madeline raised an eyebrow.

"Abby will feel more comfortable that way."

"And you. How will you feel?"

Bethany took the boiling water off the burner and slowly poured it over the tea leaves. "Confused. I've been hurt and angry for almost five years. Justin walks back into my life, and for a while today I actually found myself feeling glad to be with him."

"I can see why you're confused." Madeline patted the sofa next to her. "Come here."

Bethany moved to the sofa and sat facing the older woman. "Do you believe that I could still be so vulnerable?"

"Beth, just don't make any decisions right now. Realize you're vulnerable, that you're still hurting, and let time take care of the rest. You're a different person now from what you were five years ago. This Justin probably is, too."

Bethany shut her eyes and leaned her head against the cushions. "If I'm different it's because of you and what you've done for me."

Madeline's laughter rumbled around her. "You always give more than you get and you never realize it."

"Mommy, can Bum come up and have some milk?"

Bethany stood and walked to the steps, peering down at her daughter. "Only if he follows you—don't carry him." Like a tame housecat instead of the half-wild creature he was, the giant cat slunk up the stairs after the little girl.

"I'm going to skip the tea, Beth. I think you and Abby probably have some catching up to do."

"Thank you for this weekend, Madeline, and for listening."

"Entirely my pleasure." The older woman bent to give Abby a quick kiss. "Don't tell your mommy about the ice-cream cone you had for breakfast." She laughed as Bethany rolled her eyes. "I'll see you in the shop tomorrow."

Bethany held out her hand to Abby. "Well, sweetheart, come tell me about your day."

The little girl was kneeling beside Bum, watching in fascination as his rough tongue lapped the milk. "We played hide-and-go-seek over at City Park. They have big trees there, but Madeline always found me." She pouted slightly.

"What else?"

"Madeline let me help cut the kip for a new mask." Madeline specialized in making masks of leather, soaked and molded on hand-cast plaster forms. It was a technique developed centuries before and used originally for vessels and armor, as well as masks. "She says that if she sells the mask she'll give me a dollar."

"And what will you do with a dollar?"

"I'll buy Lamar a new hat to wear to Jackson Square. His old one has a hole in it and the money falls out." Bum finished the milk and took off down the stairs as if he were possessed. Abby bounced on the sofa next to her mother. "Are you going to marry Lamar, mommy?"

Bethany ruffled the little girl's hair. "No, I'm not. You know we're just good friends. Why do you keep asking me that?"

"I'd like him to be my daddy. Do you think he could be even if you don't marry him?"

It wasn't the first time Abby had expressed her desire for a daddy. But it was the first time Bethany had an answer. With a sigh she pulled the little girl onto her lap. "Abby, do you remember what I told you about your daddy?"

"He went away before I was born, but you said he would love me very much if he knew me."

"That's right, you do remember."

"I think it's silly. Daddys don't go away."

"It's hard to explain." Bethany sighed. "Your daddy didn't know you were going to be born. And after you were, I never saw him again."

"Daddys aren't s'posed to go away." Abby's lower lip dropped to her chin. "I don't like him!"

"Your daddy is a good man, Abby. You mustn't say that. And something exciting happened last week." Bethany tried to make her voice sound happy. "I saw your daddy again. I told him about you and he wants to meet you very much. He wants to be a real daddy to you." She realized suddenly that she was gripping the little girl tighter and tighter as she talked.

"Ouch, you're hurting me."

"I'm sorry, sweetheart." Relaxing her hold, she waited for the little girl to say something about the unexpected development in her search for a father. "What do you think?"

"Mommy, can we get a puppy? We could keep him in the courtyard and he could play with Bum."

"Abby, your daddy is coming to take us to dinner tonight." The expression on the little girl's face didn't change. "Abby?"

"He's a dumb daddy. I don't want to go with him."
Abby jumped off her mother's lap and ran to the door.
"Can I go see Bum?"

Bethany nodded, watching the child's features settle
into the impassive mask that was so like Justin at his
most maddening. "He's going to be here in a little
while. You go play with the cat, but you'll have to come
up and change in ten minutes. Understand?"

The dark eyes that met hers were not twinkling. "He's
a dumb daddy," she said as she turned and marched
down the stairs.

So much for tactfully setting the atmosphere, Bethany thought as she ran her fingers through her hair in
distraction. It was understandable that Abby would be
apprehensive about the forthcoming meeting. But she
was more than that. She was angry. The little girl per-
ceived her father as the man who had deserted her
before she was born, and she wanted no part of him.

Rising to empty the carefully brewed pot of tea down the
sink, she wrinkled her forehead in concern. Had she given
Abby that impression? Had she said things in such a way
that Abby had grown to dislike him so? She sincerely
hoped not, because that had never been her intention. She
wondered if she should warn Justin. Would he see her
phone call as an attempt to keep him from his daughter a
little longer? It was an impossible situation. Helplessly
she went into the bedroom to begin gathering suitable
clothing for what promised to be a difficult evening.

"ARE YOU GOING OUT TONIGHT, Justin?" Louise Dumontier was standing in the doorway of his room,
watching him knot his gray striped tie. "Shall I tell Mrs.
Waters that there'll only be one for dinner?"

Nodding, he watched his mother's curious reflection in the mirror. "I'm taking a friend out to dinner."

"I hope it's Danielle de Bessonet. I couldn't help noticing that she seemed to have her eye on you at the supper dance the other night. And she comes from such a nice family."

He shook his head tersely. "It's not Danielle tonight. It's a friend from Florida whom I haven't seen in several years."

"Did you meet her when you were in Miami on a case? I'll bet she's a friend of the Fraziers. They know such interesting people."

"No, I met her in Tallahassee." He turned to his mother, eyeing her warily. "What else do you want to know?"

Mrs. Dumontier shrugged helplessly. "It's just that you seem so alone, and there are dozens of girls from good New Orleans' families who would love to get to know you better."

He smiled, kissing her on the cheek as he walked past her and down the hall. "Well, I won't be alone tonight, mother. Don't wait up."

Sprinting down the stairs, he nodded to the old man who was polishing the chrome on the Mercedes, wincing slightly as the man took too long to stand up. "You shouldn't be working so hard, Homer. I could swear you polished the car earlier this week." The old man just smiled as he opened the car door for him. Justin drove slowly around the circular drive, barely seeing the Japanese magnolias showering the driveway of the stately Greek revival mansion with their creamy pink petals.

His mouth was set in a grim line as he turned the car

toward the French Quarter, maneuvering it through the light traffic. The encounters with his mother and with Homer had not helped to lighten the load of apprehension he carried with him. They had fussed over him as if he were a teenager on his first date, and like that teenager he found himself wondering what he could say and do to make the long evening ahead of him go well.

He had spent the afternoon trying to remember what he had been like at Abby's age. What kinds of things did you talk to a four-year-old girl about? Should he bring her a present, or would that seem as though he were trying to buy her affections?

And Bethany... Here his mind refused to form questions. They would be together for the evening with their daughter, almost like a family. She would be close enough to touch, to smile at, to laugh with, to— Consciously he broke off the dangerous train of thought. He was going to meet his daughter. One major complication in his life was all that he needed.

"HOLD STILL, ABBY. I'm almost done." Bethany held the long lock of black hair in one hand, gently teasing a snarl with a wide-toothed comb. "There, you look beautiful."

The little girl looked at herself in the full-length mirror and sniffed. Obviously she wasn't impressed with the vision staring petulantly back at her. With a trace of desperation Bethany had decided to dress Abby in a lavender dress with white puffed sleeves and belt. It was the little girl's favorite outfit, and usually, wearing it was reason enough for being in a good mood. Not tonight, however.

The dress brought to life Abby's vivid coloring: black

eyes and hair like her father, with his sweeping aristo-
cratic features. Only her alabaster complexion was like
her mother's. With a smile on her face Abby was a re-
markably beautiful child. Tonight there was no smile.

"Cheer up, Abby. You'll like the restaurant we're going to a lot. I'll bet your daddy will want to buy you a
big ice-cream sundae for dessert." There was no response.

Bethany put the finishing touches on her own outfit.
She knew it was ridiculous to be so concerned about
how they both looked, but she had stood in front of the
closet for ten full minutes, bemoaning the lack of
clothes to choose from. Finally she had settled on a simple turquoise blouse and gathered skirt. With them she
wore beaten-gold hoop earrings she had traded one of
her masks for with another craftsman. When the buzzer
sounded she took a deep breath, trying to calm the butterflies swarming in her stomach, and pushed the button
to release the lock on the iron gate.

She knelt in front of the little girl, silently willing her
to cooperate. "Abby, if nothing else, please be polite."

At Justin's knock she stood and walked to the door,
opening it wide. "Come in, please."

"Hello, Bethany." He stepped inside, eyes seeking
the figure of the little girl. She was standing with her
back to him, staring out one of the tall windows.
"Hello, Abby." There was no response.

"Abby," Bethany said firmly. "Come here and meet
your father."

"No," said the small voice. "I don't want to."

Faced with out and out rebellion, Bethany waited in-
decisively, wondering what to do. Justin solved the
problem for her by moving to stand beside the small

figure. "I'd like to see your face," he said quietly. The little girl turned her head a few inches, giving him a clearer view of her profile. "You're very pretty," he said slowly. "At least, I 'think' you are. But really, I can't see enough to tell."

It would have worked with almost any other child in the world. But not with Abby. She sniffed disdainfully and turned back to gaze out the window. Justin crouched beside her. "What do you see out this window?"

"Nothing."

"Would you like to go to dinner now?"

"No."

Bethany watched the interaction, the butterflies in her stomach flying convulsively from side to side. "Abby, either I can carry you out that door, or you can come quietly on your own. It will have to be up to you."

The little girl turned in the direction away from Justin to face her mother. "I don't wanna go."

Bethany sighed. "I know. But you're going, and that's that."

Justin stood, his face impenetrable. "It's chilly. You'll probably both need sweaters."

Bethany nodded. "I suspect it's no chillier outside than it is in here," she said ruefully.

He shrugged. "Shall we go?"

Bethany thought later that there must have been safe, comfortable topics of conversation to discuss on the long walk to the restaurant. All she could think of after several silent blocks, punctuated only by the complaints of Abby, who was marching ahead of them, was to ask Justin what he thought of his daughter.

"I think," he said, "that she has the idea that I'm some sort of an ogre."

"I'm sorry, Justin. I really haven't tried to make you into the bad guy. She's a very sensitive little girl, and I think she's hurting. When she has more exposure to you, she'll learn to love you."

"We'll see."

"Don't you think the resemblance is uncanny?" she tried again.

There was a slight softening of his features. "She looks exactly like my sister, Marie."

"I didn't know you had a sister. For some reason I thought you were an only child."

"Marie died when she was a child, only a little older than Abby. She was eight years younger than I was."

"Oh, Justin." She tried to imagine what it was like to lose a child. Even without having the actual experience, she was sure it must be the worst possible kind of hell. "That must have been terribly difficult for your family."

"It was. Marie had always had problems. Lots of colds, chronic asthma, pneumonia. Finally one particularly bad infection got the better of her. And there was nothing that all the money in the world could do about it."

Bethany shivered, pulling her sweater tighter around her. "So that's where Abby's problems come from."

Justin turned to search her face. "What do you mean?"

"She's always had more than her share of respiratory infections, and the doctor asked me if it ran in the family. It doesn't run in mine. Now I can tell him a little more."

"You mentioned pneumonia last week when we were talking," he said, staring straight ahead again.

"I did?"

He gave a harsh laugh. "Yes, something about how sitting by her bedside when she had pneumonia made you a true parent."

She shivered again. "She was in the hospital last year for ten days. She has recovered very well though, Justin. You don't need to worry. I watch her very carefully."

"Has she had any problems since?"

"Abigail Justine, wait for us. Don't you dare cross that street!" She turned to Justin. "I'm sorry, what?"

"Has she had any recurrences of the pneumonia?"

"No, nothing serious. Most of the time she's the picture of health. It's only occasionally that she has problems."

"What do her doctors say?"

She envisioned an entire fantasy staff of doctors crowded twenty-four hours a day around the bedside of the little girl. Actually, there had been only one doctor, an old general practitioner, whom she had used occasionally, and he had been conspicuously absent during most of the illness. Abby had got steadily better, and there had been no money for specialists, who weren't critical to her recovery. She hedged slightly. "The opinion was that there was nothing to worry about."

"I'm tired of walking. I wanna go home." The little girl's voice was high and shrill, steadily climbing the ladder that led to a temper tantrum. Bethany recognized the signs. Abby had probably got very little sleep at Madeline's over the weekend. Her schedule was thrown off, she was trying to cope with a strange man who claimed to be her loving father and she was exhausted. It added up to a child with almost no self-control. Without a word she scooped the little girl up in her arms and whispered comforting words.

Justin lifted an eyebrow. "Do you always give in so easily?"

Bethany's summer-sky eyes widened in astonishment at his criticism. "I do when I see her point."

He shrugged. "We're there now. Shall we?" He opened the door, ushering Bethany and the clinging child into the restaurant.

"Look, Abby!" She pointed to a huge stuffed gorilla in a cage by the door. The smiling woman behind the desk reached down and pushed a hidden button, and the gorilla rattled the bars.

"I wanna go home!"

Bethany smoothed back the little girl's hair. "It's all right, honey. He's not real. Justin, we'd better get her to a table."

In the middle of the restaurant was an Indian tepee. A waiter dressed as Winnie the Pooh led them to the table inside it, obviously trying not to notice the rigid expressions on the three faces. "Your Indian will be with you shortly," she quipped.

"All the waiters dress in costume here, Abby," Bethany tried to explain. "It's all pretend." There were different themes at each table. Under normal circumstances Abby would have been enthralled, but her tolerance for new situations was completely used up. Bethany cursed her own lack of judgment, but there was nothing to be done now except make the best of a bad situation.

A tall, bronzed Indian chief with enough war paint to challenge the entire Sioux nation stepped up to their table. "Paleface want drink?" he said in his best grade B movie voice.

For a minute Bethany thought Justin was going to leave. The incongruity of the entire situation was almost laughable. The restaurant would have been perfect to enjoy with a happy child, but with Abby sitting between them with a face like a thundercloud, it was too much. She heard Justin order himself a drink, and she shook her head as he cocked an eyebrow at her. "Abby, would you like a soft drink?" she asked softly in the little girl's ear.

Abby's only answer was to fold her arms and put her head on the table. Bethany shook her head at Justin.

Determined to carry the conversational ball, she tried to smile brightly. "Can you imagine this crazy place anywhere else? It started out as a Playboy club, and then they transformed it into this. Only the French Quarter could handle something like it."

Abby continued to hide her face, and Justin just stared at Bethany.

"Well, at least I didn't suggest Antoine's," she said finally, referring to one of New Orlean's most famous and dignified restaurants. There was no response, and she lapsed into an uncomfortable silence.

They managed to get through dinner. Wisely Bethany restrained Justin from ordering a meal for Abby. It was obvious that the little girl would refuse to eat anything. Although he was unfailingly polite to his daughter, making repeated attempts to draw her into conversation, he was coldly formal toward Bethany, refusing to bite at any of her conversational hooks. Abby, for her part, was rude to them both.

The reappearance of the Indian chief initiated a change in the evening's atmosphere. "Me want little squaw," the man said, arms folded across his naked chest.

Abby raised her head. "Do you mean me?" she said with the first flash of interest she had shown during the long evening's meal.

"You!" He pointed. "Come."

In the room beside theirs was a table being served by outer-space creatures for a satirical late-night television show. Dressed in outrageous costumes complete with tall pointed heads, the two creatures were encouraging patrons to play ring toss as they squatted on the floor acting as targets. The Indian chief held out his hand, and Abby, with the air of someone escaping a sinking ship, ran around the table and grabbed it. "Come on," she said.

Bethany sipped the coffee that had signaled the end of the torturous meal. "What a disaster this has been," she said tearing her eyes from the sight of her daughter battering the coneheads with her rings.

When Bethany met Justin's eyes she found him staring at her with the cold-blooded look that was beginning to seem natural. "Yes, hasn't it," he said.

"I'm sorry," she said impulsively. "I told you I just couldn't predict how she'd act. She can be pretty awful when she's upset."

"And of course you have nothing to do with her being so upset."

Puzzled at his words, she sat quietly for a few seconds before responding. "Well, of course it's my fault that she hasn't always known you. I've told you that was a mistake, and I know that forgiving me will take some time."

"That's not what I meant." He set down his coffee cup and reached for her wrist, causing her to spill drops of the hot liquid as the cup clattered out of her hand.

His fingertips sent icy messages of surprise to her brain. This was not the touch of a man who wanted to convey anything except his fury. "You set this up tonight, Bethany. That child would not be so angry at me if you hadn't filled her full of hate and distrust ahead of time."

She pulled her wrist from his encircling fingertips in horror. "Justin, that's not true!"

"I'm not a complete fool. You don't want me in Abby's life. You've told me so in no uncertain terms. I wouldn't leave you alone, so you found the only way you knew how."

Behind the anger was hurt. Bethany could see it straining to go unrecognized. Her heart went out to the proud man in front of her who had been cheated out of so much and feared he was being cheated of more. But she was hurt, too, and reaching out to him was terribly risky. As calmly as she could, she picked up her coffee cup, watching him from over the rim. "I would never do that to you," she said simply. "Never... And I would never do such a terrible thing to my daughter."

"Your daughter," he almost spat. "I'm beginning to wonder if you've told me the truth at all, Bethany. Did you get pregnant with that child on purpose? You needed love. Perhaps you felt that you needed a child to give it to you. I was going away, so I was a terrific candidate for fathering a baby for you. When I left there was no need to share her with anyone ever. It was very convenient. Neurotic as hell, but convenient."

The words lay between them with the finality of the iron curtain. That he could think her capable of such deceit severed all the tentative bonds they had begun to form. The hope of an amiable relationship based on their daughter's needs was extinguished. Without a word she stood, walking through the doorway into the next room, where Abby was engrossed in her game. "It's time to go, sweetheart."

The day's events had finally sapped all resistance from Abby's little body. Without a word, she held out her arms, and Bethany gathered her up. Thanking the Indian, Bethany made her down the stairway and through the door without looking in Justin's direction.

Outside the streetlamps were lit and the sky was darkening quickly. Bethany began to carry Abby in the direction of Royal Street, which would be more well traveled than most streets other than Bourbon. When darkness overtook the French Quarter it was best to play it safe. A block down Royal Street she heard footsteps closing in on her and she began to walk faster.

"I'll take her," Justin's voice sounded in her ear. "You'll wear yourself out carrying her all the way home."

"I can manage," she said tersely, walking even faster. "For all you know, I planned for the evening to end this way just so I could have the sheer joy of being this close to her."

"I'll take her," he said, planting himself directly in front of them.

"No," Abby cried. "I want my mommy. You're not my daddy. Mommy said you were, but I don't believe her."

"Why not, Abby?" Even the not quite hysterical child could hear the demand for an answer in his soft voice.

"Because real daddys stay with their kids. They don't leave them alone."

"Do you know why I haven't been able to be with you?"

"Because you didn't know about me." Bethany, watching Justin, saw a look of surprise cross his features, erasing the anger there.

"And who told you that?"

"Mommy did. She said it wasn't your fault. But I think you're dumb." She quickly hid her face against her mother's blouse, as if she were sure that lightning would strike her for saying something so rude to a grown-up.

Justin put his arms around the resistant body of the little girl and pulled her from Bethany's grasp. "I feel pretty dumb, Abby," he said with a catch in his voice. "Sometimes grown-ups do dumb things, say dumb things, just like kids do."

"I want mommy."

"Hush," he said quietly. "I know you don't want me to hold you, but your mommy is tired. Be a good girl and let me carry you home."

Bethany cast occasional sidelong glances at the two of them on the walk back to her apartment. At first Abby held herself away from her father, her body stiff and unyielding. But as they covered the long blocks home, Bethany saw the little girl gradually relaxing, until finally her head fell against Justin's jacket in sleep. That picture and the silent plea in his eyes sparked the gradual dissolution of the painful knot in Bethany's stomach.

Abby did not wake up when her father carried her up the stairs and into the apartment. "Where does she sleep?" he asked softly.

"Put her on my bed for now." She went ahead of him to turn back the covers. He watched as she undressed the sleeping child, leaving her to sleep comfortably in her slip, and pulled the covers around her.

In the living room they stood looking at each other. "Thank you for carrying her home," Bethany said formally.

"Very definitely my pleasure."

"I'm sure you'll want to see her again soon. Just let me know and I'll have her ready for you."

"I'm sorry."

The apology came as a surprise. Not because she didn't deserve it, but because of the concern in his voice.

"I know," she said finally.

"I was way out of line. I don't know how I could have said those things to you."

"I don't, either," she said honestly, "but until now, I've been the world's champ at overreacting when I'm hurt, so I should be able to accept a little of it from you."

He breached the distance between them, pulling her to rest against his chest, and for a moment, without thinking, she let her body nestle into his. This was Justin, the real thing, not a product of her imagination, not a fantasy being, but the living, breathing man. Warm currents of feeling filled each cell, and every place he touched she felt alive.

"You give and give and forgive. And even when you've been hurt yourself, you keep giving." His words were muffled in her hair, and his hands were stroking her shoulders as if the silky turquoise fabric were not there.

"Don't delude yourself, Justin," she said huskily. "I'm not a saint. I have needs, too."

His hand came up under her chin, lifting it so that

their eyes were locked, a meeting of bright afternoon and darkest midnight. "God knows, so do I." When his mouth came down on hers it was with the sweetness of remembered kisses and the passion of yet-to-be-discovered intimacy. It was a giving and a taking, and when his tongue traced a heated path around her lips she opened her mouth to allow him access.

This was Justin, the man she had loved, the man who knew what she needed and who desired to make her whole. And this was Justin, the man who had left her without a backward glance. "I think you'd better go," she moaned as she pushed him firmly away. "I don't think either of us is thinking clearly."

"I never thought that thinking clearly had any part in what we were just doing," he said with his arms around her still.

"Perhaps with a little more thought we wouldn't be in this situation." She broke away to turn and lean her cheek against the window.

"With a little more thought we probably wouldn't have gone for spaghetti together the first day we met," he said, stroking her hair. "I would have taken one look at you and realized that I was going to get involved. You would have taken one look at me and known I wasn't going to be good for your life."

"In spite of everything, that's not true," she said, letting her eyes drift shut as his stroking relaxed her. "I wouldn't want to forget any of it."

His answer was a surprise. "It was a very special time, and from it has come a very special child. Our child."

Her eyes opened again, and she stared at him without speaking. Finally he broke the silence. "Can you come down to the courtyard and sit with me for a while? We can leave your apartment door open in case Abby needs you."

She knew she shouldn't go, but telling herself that being outside would be less dangerous than remaining indoors with him, she let Justin take her hand.

The courtyard was cool, with moonlight silvering the worn bricks. Light from a streetlamp filtered in through the wrought-iron gate that led to Royal Street. They sat on a bench beside the silent fountain that had once been the showpiece of the gracefully designed patio.

"I remember spending a night very much like this one with you in Florida," Justin reminisced. "Do you remember the cove off of Lake Jackson where your friends had that little cabin?"

The cabin had been a renovated bait house that art-student friends of Bethany's rented during the school year. That summer they had paid the rent for the time they'd be away and told Bethany where to find a hidden key in case she could go out to check on the place.

"Yes, we'd take your rental car and park it at the top of the road. Then we'd walk down that steep clay path to avoid getting stuck if it rained."

"Do you remember the evening we went out and cooked hamburgers on a grill beside the lake?"

"I remember the hamburgers were too well-done."

"I remember why."

They had spread a blanket as close to the hyacinth-choked lake edge as they could and flopped down to watch the Canada geese fly across the sunset in their uncanny vee formations. Early September in Tallahassee was not cold, but the setting sun had caused a subtle change in temperature, and Justin and Bethany had huddled together in mock protest.

The cabin was surrounded by acres of pasture and cows on three sides and by acres of water and one tiny alligator sunning itself on the other. The privacy had been entirely too tempting for the two lovers, who completely forgot about dinner in their enjoyment of each other.

Bethany shivered at the memory, which like all memories of Justin she had attempted to suppress during the long years since. "We were oblivious to everything. I don't think either of us ever thought beyond the moment."

"Was that really true for you?" Justin sounded hurt. Bethany moved to see his face, but the shadowed darkness and his own rigid control kept her from reading his features.

"Well," she said carefully, "I certainly never thought it would turn out like this. Did you?"

He didn't answer directly. "How did you think it would turn out?"

"I lived in a fairy tale," she said quietly. "I believed in happy endings."

"What exactly did you want?"

Bethany stood and walked to the fountain, examining the widening cracks in its brick sides. "Do you realize that you suffer from an occupational hazard, Justin? Do you have any idea how upsetting it is to be interrogated like a devious witness in one of those trials you love so much?"

"What exactly did you want?"

"You're still doing it." She turned to face him, arms folded against the increasing chill of the night and the conversation. "Why don't you come right out and ask me what you want to know?"

"I thought I was."

"Then you have a lot to learn about questioning witnesses, and that's hard to believe."

Justin watched her standing there, the moonlight throwing shadows to accent the planes and hollows of her face. The delicate loveliness of her features was lost as the shadows melted together into a facade he could not penetrate. For a moment she was lost to him again. Fear shot through his body, spurring him to ask the question she had sensed. "Did you love me, Bethany?"

He saw her lift her hand to run her fingers through her hair. "With all my heart, Justin," she said finally. The shadows shifted subtly, and once again each of her features was distinct, accented by the unshed tears in her eyes. "I loved you more than I had known was possible."

He stood to join her, wrapping his arms around her body against the chill. She did not resist. They stood quietly, as if observing a prayerful moment of silence in tribute to something that would never be the same again. No matter what happened between them now, no matter what questions still lay unanswered, the innocent simplicity of that time, of that past love, deserved remembering.

"I thought maybe I had imagined so much of what happened between us," Justin said against her hair. "Memories can alter with time. It's easy to pretend that things were different from what they really were."

"And why does it matter to you now?" Bethany asked. "The present is still the same. We still have a child asleep in my bed upstairs. We still have visiting arrangements to work out."

"Doesn't it matter to you that you were in love with

Abby's father when she was conceived?" He wanted to say more, to reveal his own feelings, but he could sense that the time wasn't right, that Bethany wasn't ready to hear his revelations.

"Being in love with you made it more special and more painful. When you left and I finally realized that our fairy tale wasn't going to end happily, I had Abby to comfort me and to remind me of you. Obviously having her also made it more difficult to forget and go on with my life."

"I've never forgotten that time."

His words were comforting. Bethany knew that Justin was reassuring her that their weeks together had been important to him, too. How important, she didn't want to know...not yet, anyhow. There was still too much between them to be confused by more intimacy.

"I'm glad. I like knowing that what we had was special for you, too." She put her finger to his lips. "Shh. It's time for me to go inside now." She tried to step back, but he wouldn't let her.

"Do you remember how we'd say goodbye in Florida?" He kissed her on the forehead, his mouth making a warm circle down her cheek to her chin before he came up to her mouth. "We'd always end an evening together like this." He covered her mouth with his, pulling her closer, until he could feel her soft breasts pushing against his chest. It wasn't enough, just as it hadn't been enough those first weeks they had been together. He wove his fingers into her hair, tugging gently on her bottom lip with his teeth. He could feel the shudder pass through her body before she brought her hands to his chest and pushed.

"No more," she said, freeing herself. They stood slightly apart, staring at each other.

"Let me know when you want to see Abby again," she said, finally breaking the silence that threatened to extend forever.

"Wednesday night," he said after a brief hesitation. "I'll pick you both up after work. Does Abby like pizza?"

"You'd better take her without me. It might be easier."

"Bethany, please come with us."

The familiar melting feeling that always occurred when he expressed need for her began to course through her veins. "I could never say no to you, could I?"

"You're managing more nos than I want to hear. Please say yes this time." He was still so close she could feel his warm breath on her cheek.

"All right."

She turned, and her footsteps going up the stairs were the only audible sounds in the still night. She shut and locked the door, and then on an impulse, she opened one of the floor-to-ceiling windows and stepped out onto the balcony. Unobserved, she watched Justin walking down Royal Street. At the point where he should disappear down the next block he turned, raising his hand in farewell. Somehow he had known she was watching him all the time.

CHAPTER SEVEN

ABBY SAT with elbows propped on the table, resting her chin on folded hands. In front of her was a white ceramic vase holding four perfect pink rosebuds. Bethany watched her daughter as she stared morosely at the flowers, and wished she could say something to help. But there were no words comforting enough for what Abby was dealing with.

The roses had come the morning after their abortive dinner with Justin. With them had been a card identifying them as a gift to Abby from her father. The little girl was no longer outspoken in her anger, but subdued and clearly troubled. When Bethany had made overtures to her, expressing her willingness to listen, Abby had not responded.

"Hey, sweetheart, why don't you go find the cat and bring him back up here." Bethany's neighbor and proud owner of Bum the cat had conveniently gone away for a week and left Bum in their charge. As an enticement to cheer up Abby, Bethany had been keeping Bum in their apartment, when they could find him.

Abby sighed softly, rose and walked to the door as if it were a three-mile hike. "Okay."

Bethany listened to the plodding footsteps disappear down the stairs. Maybe some interaction with the four-footed creature would spark some of the life back into the little girl. Obviously Abby was struggling to make sense out of the changes in her life, and she was sure to be having ambivalent feelings about them. Bethany also suspected there was a healthy dose of guilt mixed in because of the way she had treated her father.

"Hey, Beth."

Lamar stood in the doorway, wearing a pair of faded jeans, a huge T-shirt with the logo Let's Fiddle A Round and a bright-purple baseball hat, turned backward. "Where's the *p'tit zozo*?"

"Didn't you see her in the courtyard?" Bethany walked to the landing and peered over the railing. "She's over there in the bushes on the other side of the fountain, petting that old tomcat."

"She didn't say anything," he said, plopping down on the sofa and resting his feet on the coffee table.

Bethany joined him, leaning her head on the sofa's back. "Lamar, she's hardly talking to anyone right now."

"*Pauvre 'tite bête.* It will just take her some time to get used to the idea of having a papa."

Lamar had come looking for them on Tuesday and Bethany had filled him in on the changes in their lives. Amazingly, she found that telling the story was getting easier and easier. Lamar reached around behind her and pulled her to rest against his large body. "And you, *cherie,* how are you doing?"

"As well as can be expected."

"And that means?"

"It means I'm adjusting."

"A three-syllable word meaning nothing." His fingers cut a quick flip in the air. Lamar spoke the unique Cajun French as his first language, followed by English liberally peppered with "Cajunisms" that he cultivated as part of his image. While the rest of his generation growing up in South Louisiana had tried to exorcise these unique expressions from their language, Lamar emphasized them. His very own version of sign language completed his extensive communication skills. The French was musical; the English was passable. But the sign language was exquisite.

Bethany yanked on his beard, which was very long and easy to grab. "Know it all," she teased.

"*Arrête,*" he said seriously. "You're upset by all this, too."

"Who wouldn't be?" Her shoulders hunched in the air flippantly.

"Me, I'm not fooled. What is it that this man is doing to upset you so?"

"It's not like that Lamar, so stop getting that steaming Cajun blood in an uproar. Justin has been very kind, considering everything I've done to him."

"So what takes the roses from your cheeks?" Lamar turned to her and ran his thumb down the side of her face.

"Hard work. I've been staying up late finishing masks. Mardi Gras is only three and a half weeks away."

"Can't sleep, you?"

"Can't sleep, me," she said giving up the pretense of nonchalance.

"Maman Robicheaux has a cure for that. Come home with me for the weekend, you, bring the *p'tit zozo* and let maman take care of you both."

Bethany shut her eyes, as if the idea of so much bliss was impossible to perceive. "And I would leave your bayou fatter, rosier and probably married off to one of your brothers. In fact, I would probably never leave your bayou at all.''

She could feel Lamar shrug beside her. "It could be worse, heh?''

"Much worse." She sighed, snuggling closer to him. "It's very tempting, but under the circumstances I think I need to stay in town. Justin needs time with Abby now. Perhaps later we could get away for a weekend.''

"Bethany.'' Opening her eyes slowly she looked to the doorway, where the image of Justin came into focus.

"I didn't hear you come up, Justin. Come in." She smiled, enjoying the sight of him in his crisply tailored duck pants and his navy knitted shirt. Pulling away from Lamar, she stood and stretched, walking to Justin to take his hand. "Come in and meet my good friend Lamar Robicheaux.''

Lamar stood, and the two men shook hands warily. "My pleasure," Justin said formally.

"Yes," answered Lamar. "Also mine.''

"Sit down," Bethany invited the two men, but Lamar shook his head. "*Mais jamais.* I've got a rehearsal. I want to spend some time with Abby before I have to go." He raised his hand in casual farewell to Justin, pulling Bethany close for a kiss on the forehead. "I'm going to take you home to the bayou unless I see roses soon.''

"I didn't expect you so early, Justin," she said, patting the sofa beside her after Lamar's departure. "When you said 'after work,' I was assuming you meant at least seven o'clock.''

"Well, I could see you weren't expecting me," he said dryly.

She looked down at the paint-spattered white overalls she was wearing. "My clothes?"

"Your visitor."

She laughed, shaking her head. "Lamar shows up any old time he pleases. I can never tell when he's going to come. He and Abby are an item." She stopped at the injured look on Justin's face. "But, then," she said contritely, "he has no past history to atone for, either. She can love him without any restrictions."

"Will she ever reach that point with me, I wonder."

She patted the sofa again and turned to him as he sat carefully beside her. "Did you see her before you came up? She's in the courtyard, hiding beside the fountain."

"I saw her. I spoke to her. We've graduated from one-word to two-word answers."

"I wish it were easier for both of you," she said. Justin's face was impassive, but beneath the carefully guarded expression was pain, and she wanted to reach out and soothe it away. With difficulty she restrained herself. "Abby has had a hard few days. How about you?"

The look he gave her spoke clearly of his need to unburden himself. "It hasn't been easy."

She waited, but nothing else was forthcoming. Even if Justin wanted to talk about his feelings, his natural reticence was making him wary. Finally sensing that "it hasn't been easy" was as close to a revelation as she was going to get, she stood, slowly running her fingers through her hair.

"I've got to change. Would you mind waiting while I take a quick shower?"

"Go ahead." He stood and restlessly began to pace the limited floor space available.

"Would you like to see where I make my masks?" she asked on a whim. Justin was acting like a man who needed something to do.

"All right."

She opened the door to her workroom and turned on the light, beckoning for him to follow. Her work table was cluttered with supplies. Feathers hung in long streamers from hooks on the wall, and masks of every shape and size covered one side of the room.

Justin whistled softly. "I feel like I'm in a mask museum. I didn't expect you to have so many on hand."

"Some of them have been commissioned specially. Some of them are for a show two weeks after Mardi Gras at a French Quarter gallery. And some of them I just haven't been able to part with yet. Like this one."

She held up a creation of snow-white feathers on a base that resembled the head of an owl. The tiny feathers covering the form graduated to larger ones sweeping in arcs over the side. In tufts on each side were floppy plumes outlined with tiny shining crystals. More crystals lined the mask's edges and the slanted peeping eye holes. The effect was a shimmering otherworldly mirage. "Someday when someone comes to me and tells me they want to be a snow queen for Mardi Gras, I'll have the perfect mask for them. And maybe by then I'll be tired of it and willing to sell."

"I'll bet this inventory cost a pretty penny," he said, unconsciously running his fingers down the feathered streamers.

"Believe it or not, I've got thousands invested in feathers alone. It's not a cheap art form. Sometimes I wish I weren't so enthralled by colorful plummage. If I liked papier-mâché like Valerie does, I'd need nothing more than Schwegmann bags, paint and glue.''

"'Schwegmann bags'?" Schwegmann's was a local grocery chain famous for their gigantic stores, some featuring as many as thirty check-out counters. "That's what happens to all those bags. They become Mardi Gras masks?"

"Can you imagine anything more exciting for a colorless paper bag than to be turned into a spectacular mask?" she teased. "It's amazing what wonders Mardi Gras can initiate."

Justin was busy examining more masks as she turned to leave him. "Will you check on Abby while I'm showering? She can't wander off with the gate closed, but I'd feel better if you'd look out occasionally."

He nodded, engrossed in his investigation.

Not until she was under the steaming water did she remember that she would either have to put on her dirty overalls to get back into her bedroom or wear a smile and a bath towel. Lathering generously with magnolia-scented soap from a French Quarter *parfumeur*, she reluctantly finished her shower and dried herself with a small hand towel. Cracking the door, she peered out, satisfying herself that Justin was still in her workroom. She wrapped the dry bath towel around her, tucking it in tightly over her water-pinkened breasts, and stepped out of the bathroom.

The sound of a door closing echoed like a cannon through the small apartment, and Bethany jumped in surprise. "You scared me to death, Justin," she said, turning to find him watching her from the doorway of her workroom.

"You surprised me, too," he murmured.

She looked self-consciously down at her scanty attire and felt a blush starting at the tips of her bare toes. "I'll just be a minute," she said, scampering toward the bedroom.

"Wait."

In the split second that she hesitated, Justin crossed the room to put his hands on her shoulders. "Let me look at you," he said in a husky voice, turning her to face him.

"I wasn't trying to put myself on display for you," she said faintly.

"Hush." His hands moved slowly up her neck, cupping the sides of her face as his thumbs stroked the silky skin under her chin. With his fingertips he explored the back of her neck, feeling the slight hollow space below her hairline. "I could never find this before. It was always hidden by all that glorious hair."

"Not anymore," she said shakily. "One of many changes."

"I like the change," he said slowly. "Your neck is so lovely. It was a shame to hide it."

His fingertips continued their search, like a blind man seeking images to remember always. At the base of her neck they fanned out to lightly stroke the pliable skin of her gently rounded shoulders. A quicksilver shiver whirled through her body, communicating itself immediately to Justin's wandering fingers. "Are you cold?" he asked softly.

"I've got to get dressed."

He ignored her words as if they had never been spoken. "Your body has changed. You're rounder, softer now. You were lovely then. You're lovelier now."

Another shiver echoed helplessly through her body.

His hands held a terrifying magic. She shut her eyes and waited for whatever the moment would bring. His hands went to her back, holding her fast as he moved closer to her. "You smell like magnolias," he whispered in her ear as his lips began to tease her earlobe. "Exactly like magnolias."

She could feel his hand gliding between her silky skin and the rough terry cloth of the bath towel, following the curve of her spine. There was a flame being kindled inside her that she thought had been extinguished, and the knowledge of that secret fire gladdened and terrified her.

"No one else feels like you do." His tongue was burning a trail of exquisite sensation, and she heard herself sigh with a sound that was very much like a surrender.

"Mommy!" Abby's voice came from the bottom of the stairs. "Bum won't come."

The child's voice shook them both from the trance they had fallen into. Bethany stepped backward, grasping the bath towel as Justin dropped his hands abruptly. "Justin, would you please tell her to come up and change. I'll be out in a minute." Without waiting to see if he could manage to get the little girl to do what he wanted, Bethany fled into the bedroom, closing the door behind her.

It had been almost five years since Justin had run his hands over her body with the same deliberately enticing touch. She had been given five years to empty her heart of memories and her body of responses to him. There had actually been days, weeks even, when she thought she had succeeded. And yet this man could walk back into her life and assume his place with no preliminaries and no promises. She was a fool ruled only by her gullibility and their chemistry together. Determined to show more pride in herself, she pulled out an amethyst jump suit and began to dress.

"THAT WAS a marvelous pizza, Justin. I've never had better." They were standing in the courtyard of Bethany's apartment, watching Abby search for the cat. "One of the best things about New Orleans is all those unassuming little restaurants tucked away in the middle of nowhere with some of the best food ever."

"That place has been there since I was a kid. I used to go there with school friends to hang out after classes."

"I can't imagine you ever hanging out. It's incongruous."

"Did you think I spent my afternoons at cotillions and teas?"

"Actually, I've never thought of you as a child or a teenager at all," she answered, trying to keep a straight face. "I guess I pictured you coming into the world as a twenty-seven-year-old federal attorney."

"And you came into the world as an innocently sexy twenty-one-year-old art student?"

"Something like that." She stopped at the loud screech of a cat. "Sounds like she's found Bum." She held her arms out to the determined little girl, who was half dragging the resisting cat. "Hand him over, sweetheart. I'll carry him up the stairs."

She started up with Abby close at her heels, until she realized that Justin was standing below, watching them. "Aren't you coming? I thought maybe you could read to Abby before she goes to bed."

"Well..."

"Come on, Justin. You're very welcome," she said with sincerity.

The evening had not been the disaster that their first dinner together had been. Abby had not been openly rude to her father, nor had she been particularly polite. But neutral was a giant step in the right direction, and Bethany could tell that Justin was feeling more hopeful. Although she still didn't direct any questions or statements to him, Abby at least responded when he spoke to her.

The shining moment of the dinner had come when Justin persuaded the little girl to play some of the arcade games lined up along one wall of the casually run pizza parlor. There had been one game he had chosen that had been easy enough for her to manipulate, and the two of them had fed quarter after quarter into the machine, enjoying the game and each other's company. Bethany, watching them together, could sense how the distraction allowed them both to relax and be themselves for a few priceless minutes. The tall virile man with the tiny little girl on the stool was a warming sight, and for the first time, she had been confident that the father-daughter relationship was going to work out.

"Abby, go put on your nightgown and your daddy will read to you when you're ready." Rebellion lit the little girl's eyes, but Bethany shook her head firmly. "Do as I say, sweetheart. No arguments."

"Come on, Bum," the little voice huffed as the bedroom door closed with a slam.

"Abby will never give in easily," Bethany said with a sigh. "The man who marries her is going to have a merry chase." She turned to Justin. "Can I make you some coffee?"

He nodded, going to stand by the windows. "You're doing a good job with her. Being a parent seems to come so naturally to you."

She was warmed by the compliment as she put the coffee on to drip in the automatic pot. Waiting for it to finish, she joined him at the window—in the tiny apartment there was no place else to go. "You were very good with her yourself tonight. Before all this, had you ever imagined yourself as a parent?"

He could tell it was a question asked in all innocence, but the real answer promised to reveal more than he wanted. "Once before," he said finally, watching her profile. "Once before I thought seriously about it."

Concern shone in her eyes. "And you decided against it?"

He shook his head. "Not exactly. But things don't always work out the way you want them to."

"You should have a houseful of little ones. They bring out the best in you," she said carefully, trying not to let the stab of jealousy that knifed through her alter her response. So there had been a woman he had wanted to share his life with, share his children with. After five years of knowing that he had never really cared for her, why imagining Justin with another woman should bother her was a mystery. But if the pain she felt was evidence, she was bothered more than a little.

"You'd be good with a houseful, too," he said noncommittally.

"I'm afraid that Abby is it for me." With surprise she felt his hand under her chin, turning her to face him.

"Why? Did something happen at her birth?"

It took her a moment before she realized what he meant. "Oh, no, nothing like that. I'm perfectly capable of bearing a dozen more, I'm sure. Abby's was an easy uncomplicated birth. It's just that a baby needs a father."

"I shouldn't think it would be too difficult to find someone willing to take on that job," he said, tracing a line along her cheek with his forefinger.

Offended by his words, she pulled away to stride back to the kitchen to pour their coffee. When she could trust her voice, she said matter-of-factly, "Regardless of what you think of me, Justin, not just any old man will do. I know I fell salivating at your feet five years ago, but I'm normally quite discriminating."

When she turned he was there, forcing her to put the hot coffee back on the counter. "I hurt you. I'm sorry."

"For which time, Justin?"

"For all the times. I've never intended to bring you pain."

"Sometimes," she said simply, "good intentions aren't enough."

"Is it too late to make it up to you?"

The question hung between them as she searched his face. There was concern there, affection of some sort, and behind the formal expression, unreadable emotion. Finally she shrugged. "I'm not sure that making up for past pain is any way to run a relationship."

"Do you want a relationship?"

She backed into the counter, pushing him away with an irritated motion. "You can be so maddening sometimes. You want it all from me. I'm supposed to tell you what to do, what to feel. Under those circumstances, no, I do not want a relationship."

"Are we having a fight?" he asked, grasping her hands and covering them firmly with his.

"You can't tell?"

"We never fought when we first met. You were always so yielding, so giving."

"Times have changed. I was so head over heels in love with you then that I'd have jumped off the roof of the law school if you'd told me to. No more of that nonsense." She tried to shake off his hands, but he held them tight.

"Then why did you leave Florida without a word to me about the baby? If you were really so much in love, why in the hell did you just pick up and go? Were you afraid that I'd let you down, leave you to deal with the pregnancy alone?"

"I did deal with the pregnancy alone, Justin. All alone. I worked and I saved and I labored alone. So obviously that couldn't have been my worst fear."

He was hurting her. He could feel the fragile bones in her hands underneath the punishing grip he was inflicting, but he could not let go. "Then why?"

"Are you so out of touch with your own feelings that you can't see why I wouldn't tell you?" There were tears of frustration in her voice.

"Just answer me, please. Why did you leave Tallahassee without telling me you were pregnant?" He recognized his own voice; it was the one he used when cross-examining hostile witnesses.

"Because," she said with the tears finally streaming down her face, "it was apparent you didn't love me. I was not going to chain myself to a man who felt nothing but a brief spurt of desire for me."

"How could you have thought that was all I felt?"

"What evidence did you give me that it was anything more? You left me, wrote me only stiff unfeeling letters, and eventually you allowed even those to trickle off. That was not the behavior of a man desperately in love."

"Bethany..." His answer, whatever it was, was interrupted by the sound of the bedroom door opening.

"I'm ready, mommy." Abby stood in front of them, wearing a thin cotton nightgown, clutching the scraggly cat in front of her like a teddy bear. "Why are you crying?"

Bethany wiped away the tears on her face. "Your daddy and I were just remembering things, and sometimes memories make people feel like crying. It's all right, though. I'm fine now."

"Why did you make my mommy cry?" Abby turned to her father.

"Sometimes mommys need to cry. Even daddys cry sometimes," Justin said evenly.

"Really?" Abby's eyes lit up. "Do you really cry just like mommy and me?"

"Yes, I do. Is that such a surprise?"

"I'd like to see you cry sometime. That would be neat."

It was the longest speech she had ever delivered in her father's presence, and it destroyed the tension in the air like a pin stabbed into a helium balloon. Justin threw back his head and laughed, joined by Bethany and finally Abby. "The next time I cry," he promised the little girl, "I'll come right over and show you."

Bethany found Abby's favorite book and tucked the little girl into the bed, leaving Justin alone with her to begin forming their own nighttime ritual. Completely exhausted from the emotional displays of the past few minutes, she flopped on the couch and lay back to let her weariness wash over her.

It was sometime later that she became conscious of Justin's arm around her and his hard length beside her. "I fell asleep," she mumbled groggily.

"Yes, and I couldn't pass up the chance to hold you like this."

"How long?"

"Who's keeping track? Here, come closer." He buried his nose in her hair. "You feel so good beside me."

There were no lights on in the apartment, only the reflection from streetlamps. Wrapped in the womb of darkness they snuggled closer, with no words to keep them apart. It was a comforting time, a giving of support and encouragement. Tentatively she reached up to stroke his face, her fingers exploring the contours of his cheekbones. She relished the faint rasp of his cheeks and the polished feel of the skin along his nose and under his eyes.

"Have I changed?" he asked softly.

"I'm not sure. I think you have."

"How?"

"Mmm...well, for one thing you play video games. The Justin I knew never would have."

"I'm not sure that video games were the rage five years ago that they are now. In those days I was a secret pinball fanatic."

"Why 'secret'?" she said, giving up the exploration of his face and leaning fully against him. His arms encircled her.

He ignored her question. "Did you also know I'm an obsessed runner? I even compete in marathons now."

"Well, that explains it."

"Explains what?"

"This," she said reaching behind her to poke his abdomen. "There's not an ounce of fat on you anywhere. You have that lean, hungry look now."

"Lean, yes. Hungry? That's becoming more and more true every minute." Holding her firmly, he began to plant nibbling kisses on the back of her neck.

What had been comforting and casual was fast changing into something else. Five years might as well have not passed. Bethany was transformed from the self-assured young artist and mother back into a starry-eyed girl in the arms of her first love. Slowly Justin's hands crept up her sides until they rested on the sides of her breast. Fingers fanning out, he moved to cover the soft pillows of flesh with his hands. She could feel her nipples hardening in response, and she groaned as she realized the signs were there for him to read, too.

"You've always been too good at that, Justin," she said lightly. "Don't you think this is going to complicate our relationship too much?"

"What's one more complication in a relationship fraught with them? I only know that I want you."

"No." She covered his hands with hers, moving them away from the sensitive area they caressed. "I'm sure you have every reason to think I'm a pushover, but I assure you, I'm not."

"You want me, too. Don't tell me you don't. When I touch you, you melt like a snow cone on a New Orleans summer afternoon."

"I don't want another casual fling with you, Justin." She pulled away and stood. "I think you'd better go."

"Not until we settle some things. There are too many issues that need clarifying. We were on our way toward clearing up some misunderstandings earlier when Abby walked in. I want to finish what we started."

"Not tonight," she said firmly. Her heart was pounding from his touch, and she stood on trembling legs. How could her self-control desert her every time this man came near? "I think we should talk when we're calmer."

"I'm never calm around you, Bethany. I want to finish our discussion."

"Well, you can't always have it your own way, though God knows, I'm probably responsible for letting you think you can."

"I'm not quite the selfish egotist you're trying to make me out to be." He stood to face her, hands gripping her shoulders. A faint noise from the bedroom stopped them both. "Did you hear that?" Bethany asked. "I'd better go check on Abby."

"I'll come with you." There was to be no avoiding him tonight. She went without a word to open the bedroom door and peer into the dark room.

"Abby?" she whispered.

"Mommy," said a pathetic little voice. There was a gasping sound, a choke and a wheeze. "Mommy."

"Turn on the light, Justin." Bethany, momentarily blinded by the brightness, stumbled to the bedside, almost tripping over Bum, who leaped off the bed. "Abby? What's wrong?"

Justin was at her side in a moment, taking in the sight of the little girl sitting up in bed, clutching her throat and trying desperately to breathe. In a moment he had picked her up and was headed toward the bathroom. "Turn on the hot water full force, Bethany and leave the shower curtain open. If it's just the croup, then that will help. Shut the door behind you."

The tiny bathroom filled slowly with mist. Too slowly, Bethany agonized, because there was only one hot-water heater shared by the four apartments and the shop. Justin held Abby on his lap, talking calmly to her, but the mist and his patience made no inroads in the little girl's struggles for air.

When it became obvious that no good was coming out of the steam, he stood, gesturing with his head for Bethany to follow. Still talking patiently to Abby, he swept her through the apartment and down the stairs. "Get my keys, Bethany, and unlock the car door." She reached in his pockets, struggling to keep pace with him without running, and managed to extract the keys. They had covered the blocks to his car in record time, and she hurriedly unlocked the door and slid into the seat to receive Abby on her lap.

Expertly Justin swung the car out onto the narrow French Quarter street and guided it through the traffic. Minutes ticked by until he reached an intersection where he could begin to gather some speed. "What hospital does her pediatrician use?" he asked.

"We don't have a pediatrician, Justin. The last time she was in the hospital a general practitioner looked in on her. The emergency-room doctor took care of her treatment."

"Where was that?" he asked tersely, obviously upset by her answer.

She named a hospital and then shook her head. "Don't take her there, Justin. I'm not finished paying the bill, and they might give us trouble about treating her since I don't have insurance."

"Damn," was his answer.

They were at another hospital in minutes, pulling up in the emergency-room parking lot. Justin ran around to open the car door and lift Abby out of Bethany's arms. Inside the nurse on duty took one look at the child and paged the physician on call.

The next hour was a whirlwind of activity. After the briefest of examinations the doctor ordered medication for Abby that had her breathing near normally in minutes. With the worst of the anxiety behind her, Bethany was breathing normally again herself, except when she looked at Justin. Loving and patient with the frightened little girl, he was frozen with Bethany, answering her questions in monosyllables only.

The emergency-room doctor, who was an older man with a forbearing air, asked the two of them to step outside Abby's cubicle after she seemed to have stabilized. "Mrs. Walker. How often has this occurred?"

She shook her head. "Never like this. She's been wheezy from time to time and she's had pneumonia two—no, three times—" she flinched at the look Justin directed toward her "—but she's never had anything like this happen before."

"Mr. Walker, have you ever noticed her wheezing?"

"I'm Justin Dumontier." He held out his hand to the man. "She's my daughter, but I've had no contact with her up till now. Her mother will have to answer all your questions."

The doctor looked perplexed at the unusual relationship, but shrugged his puzzlement off. "Has she had anything major change in her environment in the past week, Mrs., er, Ms Walker?"

Bethany shook her head slowly. "She's been under some stress. Other than that I can't think of anything."

"How about that cat?" Justin asked quietly. "Abby told me tonight that you'd never let her sleep with the cat before this week."

"That's true. It's not even our cat. We're just watching out for him this week. Could that have anything to do with this?"

The doctor nodded, seemingly satisfied by her answer. "I wouldn't be at all surprised. I suspect your daughter has a severe allergy to cat dander. She's probably got other allergies, too, if her respiratory history is any clue."

"What can I do about it?"

The doctor smiled at her, patting her on the shoulder. "It could be a lot worse. If it's allergies, and I feel pretty certain that's what it is, you'll have to make some adjustments in her environment and have her seen by an allergist for a few years."

"What are you going to do with her now, doctor?" Justin asked.

"I'm going to recommend that she stay a few nights. I don't like the way her chest is sounding, and I want to be sure it's clear before I send her home. Besides, this will give you a chance to clean her room thoroughly and get rid of the cat."

"Go ahead and admit her, doctor. I'll be along to take care of the paperwork in a minute," Justin said.

Bethany watched the physician disappear down the hall. "She's going to hate this," she said with a sigh.

"Why didn't you tell me the truth about her health, Bethany?" Justin's voice was deadly.

"I did." Her eyes flickered over the rigid contours of his face. "All right, I didn't go into enough detail. But she's been fine since the last bout of pneumonia. I really didn't think there was anything to worry you about."

"Lady, you shouldn't be allowed to get close enough to people to have a simple conversation. It seems that you can't ever be trusted to tell the truth." He turned on his heel and reentered the emergency room, leaving her to stare helplessly after him.

CHAPTER EIGHT

STANDING IN THE DOORWAY of the hospital room that had been assigned to Abby, Bethany watched Madeline walking through the corridor toward her. Bethany had spent an uncomfortable night sleeping on a foldout chair next to Abby's bed, and Madeline was bringing her a much needed change of clothing and some toys for Abby.

"How is she?" Madeline asked as she gave Bethany a quick hug.

"Doing fine. The doctor was here a little earlier, and he seems to think I can take her home tomorrow or the next day. She's responded very well to everything they've done."

"Is she awake?"

Bethany shook her head. "No, she's been chattering away all afternoon and she just this minute went to sleep. I'm sorry you didn't catch her in between naps."

"How are you doing?"

"I feel like I've been run over by something large and devastating."

"I would imagine so. This was a lot to handle by yourself. I wish you'd called me last night."

"I wasn't alone. Abby's father was with me."

Madeline was surprised at the news and at Bethany's careful tone. "Well," she said cautiously. "I'm glad you had some help."

"Yes, on one level he was a great help." Bethany seemed to sag with the weight of her exhaustion. "On another level? Well, I guess his behavior was to be expected."

"Is the man giving you problems, Beth?"

Bethany was too tired and too depressed to invent a tactful denial. "I have had problems since the first day I met him, although most of them are of my own making. Where Justin Dumontier is concerned, I show no sense at all. I'm afraid last night was no exception."

"Why don't you drive my car back to the apartment, take a shower there and catch a nap? I'll stay with Abby." Madeline gripped Bethany's shoulders as if to make her point more forcefully. "It won't do you any good to make yourself sick, you know."

"I know. But I wouldn't feel right about leaving her. Can you wait here with her while I take a quick shower? The head nurse said it would be all right."

Madeline shrugged. "If you're sure you won't consider my offer."

"I'm sure." She took the overnight case that Madeline handed her. "I'll be back in a few minutes."

Madeline settled herself as comfortably as possible on the chair beside Abby's bed and opened a book. Abby was sleeping peacefully. After finding with relief that the little girl looked like her normal healthy self, Madeline tried to become engrossed in her novel, but her conversation with Bethany haunted her, instead. Staring fixedly at the page, she didn't notice the tall man enter the room and stand at the foot of the bed.

"Excuse me."

Madeline lifted her eyes to see a stranger with the face of Abby. Coolly she examined him, not missing the impact of his virility, the elegant but simple clothing, the confident way he stood. In a flash she understood more about Bethany's unusual spell of moodiness. "You're Justin Dumontier," she said evenly.

"Yes. You must be a friend of Bethany's? Are you baby-sitting so that she could go back to work?"

She was in no hurry to answer him. Continuing to take his measure, she finished her minute inspection. Justin Dumontier, she decided, was a man who was used to respect and used to making decisions. He was also the man who had hurt Beth so badly years ago that the scars were still painfully obvious to those who were close to her. Although Beth had not told her any details of the previous evening's rush to the hospital, Madeline knew that again this Justin Dumontier had hurt the young woman. Champion of the underdog and loyal friend, Madeline seethed with indignation. "You say that as if she had no right to have help."

Justin returned Madeline's stare. "I came to see my daughter. If this is an inconvenient time, I will wait outside."

"I'll wait with you." A flicker of surprise crossed Justin's face as the determined older woman followed him into the corridor.

"Why don't you tell me what's on your mind, Ms—"

"Conroy. I'm Madeline Conroy, Beth's business partner and friend and Abby's godmother."

Justin inclined his head in recognition. "How do you do."

"Right now, Mr. Dumontier, I do angry."

"I'm sorry, Ms Conroy, I have no idea. . . ."

"Then let me fill you in." She watched the handsome face, devoid of any expression except polite interest.

"Beth has given me no details, but I am under the impression that once again, even in the middle of this crisis, you have managed to make her miserable."

With surprise she detected an expression of concern flash over the masculine features. Momentarily taken aback, she waited for him to answer.

"I see."

"I doubt if you do," she said, forcing herself to remain calm. "That girl has had more to deal with in her twenty-six years than most people do in a lifetime. She has had more misery, more heartache, more rejection than any two people I know. Perhaps you should think twice before you add any more to her burdens."

Madeline, being an outspoken, cultivated eccentric, was used to her remarks causing a strong reaction in others. But nothing prepared her for the look of self-condemnation that transformed the man's face. The swift change from self-assured professional to repentant little boy made her want to reach out and reassure him, but she restrained herself. With a sigh at her own audacity, she turned to go back into Abby's room to get her purse and book. When she returned he was leaning against the wall, staring at nothing.

"I'm leaving. Tell Beth I'll come take over for her anytime. She'll be back in a minute. She's just in the shower."

BETHANY LET the sharp needles of hot water pierce the haze of fatigue that enveloped her. There had been too many sleepless nights, too many hours spent worrying. Why did life have to be one series of problems after another, she wondered, her usually positive outlook in danger of collapse.

Toweling her hair dry, she thought, for the first time in years, about a game she had played as a little girl. She had been an only child. A lonely child. When she thought back on images of herself as a little girl, she remembered one very clearly. She had been Abby's age, and she had been invited to the birthday party of a little girl who attended the church where Bethany's mother sporadically took her to Sunday school.

Bethany remembered getting dressed for the party. She had put on a pink taffeta party dress all by herself and pulled on too-small black patent slippers that pinched her feet. She had brushed her long hair until it was no longer tangled. Then she had stood by the dirty plate-glass window in her living room and waited for her mother to return.

"I'm just going to the store, Beth," her mother had said, and Bethany had kissed her goodbye. The little girl did not know that other mothers did not leave their children by themselves. She was used to it, and even at the age of four she knew how to take care of herself.

But she didn't know how to get to the party, and as the long afternoon wore on and her mother did not return for her, she knew she was not going to go. Carefully she had taken off her dress and her too-small shoes and gone into the living room to turn on the television set. Much later, when her mother returned smelling of that strange odor that always meant she would act funny for a while, the little girl was engrossed in one of her favorite television shows.

It was shortly after that that she developed the game. In later years, when she would think about it she would give herself a pat on the back for her own resourceful behavior. But as a child it had been nothing more than an act of desperation. The game had begun as she had watched one of many reruns of a family situation comedy on television. On this show the mother and father loved each other and took care of their children. They didn't go off and leave them alone, and they didn't act funny most of the time.

The mother of this family kept the house clean and baked cookies. She always dressed in high heels and nice dresses. She was never sloppy or loud. The father came home every day after work and kissed his daughter good-night and tucked her into bed. He was not gone all the time, sailing around the world, and the family never moved from base to base, from state to state. They lived in the same house, kept the same friends, and their lives were happy.

There were many hours for the child, Bethany, to engage in fantasy play about the family, and gradually she became a member herself. When her real mother would forget to come home and fix dinner for her, Bethany pretended that her fantasy mother was right there taking care of her. She carried on long conversations with the patient, loving woman as she found something for herself to eat.

Even when she started school the little girl continued the game. It didn't matter where she moved, the family always went with her. And eventually when the show that Bethany had based the game on was finally taken off the air, there were other television families to take their place. From each of them she gleaned information about the ways that people who cared about one another acted. She discovered that not everyone lived the way she did, and she was left with the hope that one day she might also live happily herself.

So the game gave her courage. And with her courage and her big blue eyes, the little girl set out to make adults notice her. Her television families provided her with information on the proper way to behave, and with skill and natural charm the little girl put her information to work.

And work it did. Adults loved Bethany. Teachers sat her in the place of honor in front of their desks. The mothers of school acquaintances used her as an example for their own children to follow. Neighbors waylaid her with candy and with conversation.

Another kind of adult entered her life, too. Social workers, with reports of the shameful way the little girl was being treated, visited her, taking endless social histories and suggesting endless sources of treatment for her mother. They were powerless to do much, because no authority who looked at Bethany could believe she was really mistreated, but their concern and advice was another step up the ladder of her own personal growth.

Even into adolescence, when life would get too painful Bethany would sometimes retreat into the safety and security of her make-believe families. On the night that her mother took a last in the series of one-more-for-the-road drinks and crashed her car into a telephone pole, it was to her fantasy mother that Bethany had turned for comfort. And when the funeral was over, she lifted her pixie-pointed chin and put the game behind her forever. It was no longer necessary.

Now she stood in the hospital shower room, dressing in the clean but wrinkled clothes that Madeline had stuffed into the overnight case and wishing she could still indulge in an escape of some sort. But it was not into the arms of her fantasy mother that she wanted to escape. It was into the arms of a certain Creole man, a man who unfortunately did not have the same fantasy about her.

When she had combed her hair and brushed her teeth she looked at the dejected image in the mirror one last time and headed back to Abby's room. Seeing Justin beside the sleeping child's bed was the last straw; she turned and headed back into the hall.

"Bethany, wait."

"What do you want?" she snapped with the irritability typical of people who have not slept or eaten well in twenty-four hours.

"I want to talk to you."

"I'll just bet you do," she exploded. "I'll just bet you want to tell me what a schmuck you think I am and see what other guilt trips you can lay at my feet."

"No."

"Then I doubt if you have anything else to say to me." She turned on her heel and headed for the elevator. His hand gripped her arm, but she shook it off. "Go away, Justin."

The elevator door opened and she stepped in, followed closely by Justin. The elevator was crowded, and even in her present state of mind she was not up to picking a fight with him in front of so many people. Her arm shot out to push the button of the next floor, and she got off immediately, searching for the stairway.

"Bethany, wait." She tried to shake off the detaining arm again, but his grip was steady and firm, and she was held prisoner against him.

"Go away, Justin," she said again.

"Not until you listen to me."

"I don't want to listen to you." She tried to shake him off again, flailing her arm uselessly.

"Is this man bothering you, miss?" Looking up, she saw a burly security guard complete with uniform and gun, watching them.

The question shocked her back into reality. The man was advancing on them with the suspicious look common to high-school principals, bank loan officers and dental hygienists. "No, he's just trying to help," she said in a deflated tone. "We're on our way to the coffee shop."

"Thank you," said Justin with a trace of irony. He pushed the elevator button, and they waited in strained silence to take the six flights down to the coffee shop.

"What will you have," Justin asked formally after they settled themselves at a small table.

"I don't care. I'm here to listen to you, not to eat."

"She'll have a bacon, lettuce and tomato sandwich on whole wheat, with potato salad on the side and a cup of coffee with lots of milk in it," he told the waitress. "You have to take care of yourself, Bethany. You're going to end up as a patient yourself."

"How nice of you to be concerned," she said with no feeling. "Please get on with whatever you wanted to tell me."

"I wanted to apologize for last night." He watched her expressive face as she struggled to stay angry at him. It was a fascinating display of self-control over feeling. She was managing to remain upset, but only with difficulty. He pressed his advantage. "I thought back over everything you told me about Abby and her health problems. I think you purposely downplayed some of it, but you never really lied to me. I can see that you were just trying to keep me from worrying."

"I was trying to keep you off my back."

"Pardon me?"

"I was trying to keep you from hassling me, Justin."
She sat back, working to harden her heart against the melt-ing feeling inside of her. "From the day you found out you had a daughter, you've been criticizing everything I've done. You've judged me for raising her in the French Quarter, for not having a car, for giving in too easily to her, for not providing adequate medical care. I was tired of being called on the carpet for doing the best I could. So I didn't give you a complete description of her difficulties because I knew you'd criticize my handling of them."

"You've got to admit, you weren't showing good judgment about her health. Look where she's ended up." The minute the words escaped his mouth he knew he had made a mistake.

"I've shown the best judgment I could." She sat stonily, watching the waitress lay flatware on her place mat. When the woman had gone, she continued. "I've raised that child by myself. It's been wonderful, but it's also been difficult. I've raised her on a very limited in-come. Until recently we were lucky if we had two nickels left over after the bills were paid. Abby has always had medical attention when she's needed it. She's never gone without good basic care. But there hasn't been money for specialists. We've frequented clinics, gone to emer-gency rooms. If I'm guilty of anything, it's of listening to overworked, harassed emergency-room doctors more than I should."

Justin's fist hit the table. "I guess that's what makes me angriest, Bethany. You've done all that for no reason. I have money. Lots of it. And you know it. Yet you've let my daughter go without."

"Do you know what else she almost went without, Justin?" For the first time in her life she felt the power of revenge cascade over her. Just once she wanted to hurt him as he was hurting her. "She almost went without a mother. I came this close to giving her up for adoption."

She held her thumb and forefinger an inch apart and waved them in front of his nose. "This close, Justin, because I knew I couldn't afford to raise her alone. That child is a gift from heaven, but Madeline Conroy gave me the gift of raising her when she offered me the apartment you detest so much. Think about it Justin. At least you've been given this chance to know your daughter. If it wasn't for the life-style you hate so, you wouldn't have been given that chance at all." She got up from the table, almost knocking over the waitress who was bringing her her sandwich.

"Excuse me," said the woman hesitantly.

Bethany swept the sandwich off the plate and opened her purse, cramming it inside. "We poor folks don't refuse a free meal." She snapped the purse shut. "Abby gets out tomorrow. Please call Madeline and tell her when you want to see my daughter next. I'm going to have Madeline coordinate your visits." With an angry shove that sent her chair sliding under the table, she stalked out of the room.

Munching on the sandwich later by Abby's bedside, she wondered how much of her tirade had been brought on by low blood sugar and lack of sleep and how much by genuine feelings. She was angry at Justin, and she felt she had a right to be, but never, never did she have the right to say those awful things to him about almost giving Abby up for adoption. She should have spared him that. Now she had utterly, irrevocably pushed him out of her life. Abby slept on, and Bethany's sandwich was baptized with the salt of tears.

"Do poor folks even eat wet sandwiches?" The voice at her side was low and comforting, and with a fresh cycle of sobs, she turned and put her face against Justin's shoulder. He was squatting with his arms outstretched, and he held her gently as the healing sobs washed over her.

"How can you be nice to me after what I said to you?" she gulped, her lower lip trembling with the effort.

"You are not so hard to be nice to. You're very special."

The statement precipitated another wave of tears. Finally drained, she fished around in the nightstand for a tissue and wiped her eyes and nose. "I'm glad you came back."

"I brought you something," he said. He pointed at a vase filled with full-bodied red roses. "Some are for you and some are for Abby..." He hesitated, then smiled slightly as he said, "And some are for Madeline."

"Madeline?"

"Another very special lady," he said cryptically.

"Mommy." The little voice from the bed sounded sleepy but otherwise perfectly normal. "I'm hungry."

"Good, sweetheart. It's almost dinnertime. Look who came to visit while you were asleep."

The little girl studied her father seriously and then gave a tentative smile. "Hi."

"Hello, Abby. You look like you're feeling much better today." Justin sat down on the bed and casually took his daughter's hand. "I am very glad to see you."

Abby looked at the big hand holding hers and then at the man sitting casually on her bed. Bethany held her breath in fear that the little girl would overtly reject his gesture of affection. Instead Abby smiled more broadly. "You carried me here last night. I remember. And the doctor made me better."

"That's right." Justin patted her hand, then released it. "And from now on you're going to be just fine."

"If I'm fine will you still come and see me?"

"I'll come and see you no matter what."

Bethany stood and stretched, running her fingers through her still-damp hair. A yawn matched the stretch, and she closed her eyes momentarily in fatigue. "Well, you two look like you might like to play a game of Go Fish. I'm going for a walk. I'll be back in about half an hour, if that's all right, Justin."

"I'm driving you home," he said in his firmest voice. "I'm staying all night with Abby myself." Her protest was cut off immediately. "No arguments. You're dead on your feet, and I'm not."

"I don't want to leave Abby by herself while you drive me home," she said firmly.

"Neither do I. That's why I called Madeline. She's on her way now to take over while I run you back to the Quarter."

"You called Madeline? What is this, a conspiracy?"

"Let's just say it's two people who are concerned about you organizing your life for your own good."

"Let him stay, mommy." The little girl's eager piping voice was a surprise. "I've never had a daddy stay in my room before."

Nothing more needed to be said.

BRIGHT NEW ORLEANS sunshine the dark-golden color of cane syrup flowed through the windows of the Royal Street apartment. Bethany opened her eyes lazily and propped her arms under her head to stare at the sunbeams dancing in tatted-lace patterns on the ceiling. She had called Abby's room the night before as she was crawling into bed, and as she had expected, everything at the hospital was going well. Talking to Abby, she could sense the little girl's excitement at having her father there to cater to her every whim, and after receiving Justin's reassurance that he would call if there were any changes, she had hung up feeling secure and very sleepy.

She slept better that night than she had in a long time. With a small fan drowning out the noise from the street below, she had opened her windows to let in the cooling breeze, stripping down to nothing but a light sheet between her and the fresh air. Sleeping in the raw was not a luxury she often allowed herself in the small apartment with a young child.

In the middle of the night she awoke suddenly, reaching out in her semiconscious state for Justin. It was a dream she had experienced before. In it Justin was making love to her, slowly bringing her toward the fiery explosion that was their love at its most potent. Suddenly he began to disappear, his body dissolving into the wispy mists of a mirage. She reached out for him and found nothing. Always she awoke at that point, struggling to find him in the covers tangled around her body.

It was an obvious dream. Bethany did not need years of therapy to figure its meaning. After Abby's birth, she had castigated herself for holding on to her memories of her former lover. Telling herself to forget him sometimes worked during the day, but at night she was reminded of her feelings by the fading wispy images.

Time had passed, and the frequency of the dream had diminished. That night she had awakened to find him gone, but she had not felt completely destroyed by his desertion. There had been something different about the dream, something that distinguished it from the others like it. Staring at the ceiling in the morning sunshine, she tried to piece it together.

She skimmed over the painfully erotic beginning, for it had been the same as always, frustrating and unfulfilling. At the place where Justin always dissolved and disappeared she stopped. The difference came sharply into focus. Last night Justin had not left her. He had kissed her slowly with a lingering gentleness and he had whispered something to her. Straining to understand his words, she had come into full consciousness, destroying the dream.

The words still eluded her, but the dream's new message was a surprise. Justin had not left her. For the first time, he had not withdrawn, leaving her to suffer his loss. Bethany realized that she was lying in bed, grinning uncontrollably. His feelings were still unclear to her, evidenced by the words that she could not understand, but he had still been there to touch and to hold.

Swinging her legs over the bedside, she rose, slipping into a flimsy nylon bathrobe, and headed for the bathroom. Halfway across the room the phone stopped her.

"Is everything all right?" she asked, panic seeping through her veins at the sound of Justin's voice.

"Just fine. Abby has evidently inherited her appetite from you. She put away more food this morning than I thought little girls ate in a week."

"Did you see the doctor?"

"Not yet. Why don't you come over in a little while. I've arranged a ride for you."

"Madeline?" she asked with a strong surge of guilt. Her partner really needed to be working this close to Mardi Gras. Even though the shop didn't open until late morning, there were masks to make, accounts to figure. With Bethany out of commission the work load had increased.

"No, one of my mother's staff. In fact, I thought I'd better warn you. Three of them are going to descend on the apartment in about half an hour to clean it thoroughly for you."

There was silence on Bethany's end of the phone line.

"Don't be angry. The doctor said it would have to be scrubbed from top to bottom to rid it of cat dander. You have more important things to do, and I knew you'd want to spend the time with Abby."

It was impossible to be angry in the face of such thoughtful logic. "All right. That was considerate of you." The impact of his statement hit her. "Your 'mother's staff'? Does she know about Abby?"

"She knows that something's up. I promised to fill her in this evening. In the meantime she's doing this on faith alone."

"How's she going to take it, Justin?" Bethany asked in a small voice.

"We'll just have to see. In the meantime, when they arrive, Homer will drive you right over here."

As she hung up the phone it occurred to her that her relationship with Justin had reached a new level. His family, his status would now play a part in decisions about Abby's life, thereby affecting Bethany, too. It was not a comforting thought.

RIDING TO THE HOSPITAL in a sleek black Cadillac with a uniformed driver in the front seat was not an experience that Bethany relished. The old man had been politely formal, as had the two other servants who had shown up at her door with enough mops and equipment to clean the New Orleans Superdome. With strict instructions not to enter her workroom, where Bum had not been allowed, anyway, she had turned over a key and followed Homer to Mrs. Dumontier's car.

Unaccustomed to such luxury, she sat quietly trying to imagine what kind of woman Justin's mother was. If she was half as stiff and formal as the car she owned, Bethany had a sinking feeling they were not going to get along. Somehow the realization that Mrs. Dumontier would have to be told about her granddaughter had not penetrated her consciousness before. It only made sense; it was only fair, but Bethany wished it didn't have to be so.

She thanked Homer and waved goodbye, giving him a bright smile. He rewarded her with a wide grin and a salute. As she passed the hospital gift shop she peeked in the window and then stepped in to buy some variegated ribbon barrettes for Abby. With her purchase in a colorful box tied with a red bow, she headed upstairs to the little girl's room.

"Why sweetheart," she said in surprise, "you're all alone."

"Justin went downstairs to have coffee with a lady," said Abby nonchalantly.

"You're calling him 'Justin' now?"

The little girl nodded. "We 'cided that would be good."

Bethany sat lightly on the bed beside her daughter,

smoothing back Abby's hair. "Tell me, why don't you want to call him 'daddy,' sweetheart?"

The simple question turned the child into a carbon copy of her father, all expression wiped away and replaced with only a polite mask. "Do I have to tell you?"

Obviously the decision was based on some major emotion, not a childish whim. Bethany shook her head. "No, of course not."

"Good." She was silent for a moment, and then, unable to keep the reason to herself, she said with a sigh, "It's because I want to be sure he really is my daddy."

"I see. And you're afraid he might not be?"

"If he goes away again then he won't be. Then I'm going to ask Lamar if he'll be my daddy."

"Abby," Bethany said carefully. "Your father may have to go away again, but he'll always come back to visit you. Sometimes you can go to his house and spend time with him by yourself."

"Not without you," Abby answered with an expression that indicated that the conversation was closed.

"Bethany, you're here already." Justin's voice sounded from the doorway.

"Yes, Homer brought me right over." She patted Abby's hand, turning to see Justin come into the room followed by a young woman.

Wearing a bright smile and a pin identifying her as a member of the volunteer organization that helped staff the hospital, the woman came to stand next to Justin at the foot of the little girl's bed, linking her arm through his as if they were intimate acquaintances. She was dressed in a golden-beige knitted dress that clung everywhere it was supposed to, a raw silk blazer and heels so high she almost tottered. Her hair was long and the same color as her dress exactly, giving the impression it had been dyed to match.

"Bethany, this is a friend of mine, Danielle de Bessonet. Danielle this is my ex-wife, Bethany Walker."

Bethany looked at him incredulously. Ex-wife? The look on his face was enough to convince her that confronting him about the newly bestowed title would best be done at another time.

Danielle held out her hand. "It's so good to meet this sweet little girl's mother," she gushed. "Can you imagine my surprise when I saw 'Abigail Justine Dumontier' on the hospital admission form?"

Bethany took her hand politely. "I think I can," she answered. *Abigail Dumontier?*

"No one even knew this sly rogue had been married. He can certainly keep secrets."

"He certainly can," Bethany agreed ominously.

"And such a lovely child," Danielle continued. "Such a sweet little girl."

Abby made a face, reaching for her mother's hand. "Did you bring me something, mommy?"

Bethany handed her the box with the barrettes. "Yes, I did. Go ahead and open it."

"So did I, Abby," Danielle gushed. "I saw something downstairs that was just right for you. Why it's like Christmas morning." Danielle presented the child with another small box.

Abby opened the barrettes first, fastening them at odd angles in her hair. "Thanks," she said, digging into Danielle's present.

It was a sterling-silver heart on a chain. Engraved on the heart was, "Abigail Dumontier."

"What does it say?"

"It has your name on it, sweetheart," Bethany answered quickly. Abby hadn't noticed when Danielle announced that she had been renamed on her hospital admission form, but she was sure to comment on the incorrect name on the heart.

"Let me help you put it on," said Danielle, taking the heart from the little girl's hand and unfastening the clasp.

"I want to do it."

"Why it's too hard for you, honey." Danielle ignored Abby's outstretched hand. "I'll fix your barrettes, too."

With polite forbearance, Abby lay quietly in the bed, letting Danielle fuss over her, but Bethany could almost see Danielle dropping in Abby's estimation, and the thought gave her secret satisfaction. "Thank you," the little girl said primly when Danielle had finished.

"Well, Justin, I must run. So nice to meet you, Beth. Goodbye Abby. I'll try to stop by tomorrow." Danielle stood on tiptoe and kissed Justin's cheek. "Will I see you at the auditorium tonight for the Pisces Ball?"

"I'm not sure."

"Be sure to find me if you come. I'll save a place on my dance card." She waved goodbye and rustled out of the room.

"'Dance card'? I thought they went out a century ago," Bethany asked casually.

"Actually, women like Danielle went out a century ago. She's something, isn't she?"

"Yes, she's something."

"I think perhaps you and I need to have a talk about a few things she mentioned."

"My thoughts exactly," Bethany answered sweetly.

"Coffee?"

"Will you be all right for a little while by yourself, sweetheart?" Bethany asked Abby.

"Can I turn on television?"

Bethany tuned in "Sesame Street" for her and followed Justin out into the hall. "Let me tell the nurses we'll be gone for a while. This may take you some time to explain. In fact, maybe I should tell them not to expect us before dinner." She marched toward the nurses' station, with Justin close behind.

CHAPTER NINE

"WHAT WILL YOU HAVE, Bethany?" Justin asked cordially after they were seated in the coffee shop.

Bethany eyed the same waitress that she had almost knocked over the previous day and shook her head.

"She'll have two eggs over light, toast and grits. Give her some coffee with lots of milk in it and orange juice on the side," Justin said, ordering for her.

"Grits are kinda hard to shovel into your purse, sweetie. Are you sure?" asked the waitress, addressing Bethany with her lips pulled back in a half grin.

"Maybe you'd better serve them on a plate to go, just in case," Bethany answered in a tone that dripped sweetness. "I have a feeling it may be that kind of a meal."

"You got it," said the woman as she headed behind the counter.

Justin sat back in his chair, making a tent with his long fingers. "Well, you don't look quite as mad as yesterday."

"Looks can be deceiving."

"After you left here yesterday, a man at the next table stopped on his way out the door to give me his opinion of our little scene."

"Oh?" She lifted one eyebrow nonchalantly.

"Yes, he said...let me get this right...he said that you were one foxy chick when you were mad."

"I'll bet!"

"It's true."

"And what did you say?"

Justin smiled, his eyes traveling over the parts of her that were visible above the table edge. "I told him I hadn't failed to notice."

In spite of herself she smiled. "I'm surprised you even know what a foxy chick is."

"We federal attorneys hang out with some pretty cool characters. I have a vocabulary of slang you wouldn't believe."

"Oh, the unplumbed depths of Justin Dumontier," she chanted. "And speaking of unplumbed depths, I'd love to hear about your previous marriage...to me, if I heard Miss de Bessonet correctly."

"It's very simple, Bethany," Justin said, his voice growing serious as he settled down to the discussion. "We have a daughter who, for better or worse, is going to have to grow up in this town. New Orleans is more liberal than many parts of the South, but illegitimacy still has a stigma here, especially in certain social circles. I had to do something to protect her name."

"Justin, no one has ever questioned me about Abby's background. No one I know could care less."

"Unfortunately, almost everyone I know *would* care, at least on some level. They'll feel sorry for Abby, exclude her from certain social groups and pass on their prejudices to their own children, who will be her peers."

Bethany shook her head firmly, her dark hair swishing around her serious face. "I don't want her living a lie."

"Funny you should say that."

"Justin!"

"Here's your breakfast, folks." The waitress eyed them warily. "Shall I put it on the table or in your purse?"

"Thank you," Justin said with a smile. "We'll eat it here."

They ate in silence. Finally Bethany began again. "I guess you'd better tell me our history, so I'll be sure to get it straight if I'm asked."

"Then you'll play along with it?"

"I guess we owe your mother that much. I suspect having an illegitimate grandchild could be a lot to explain."

"I'm going to tell her the truth. But she'll be glad to have a story invented to tell everyone else."

"So what's the scenario?" Bethany sat back, finishing her coffee, which was the only thing left at her place. In spite of her anger she had devoured the breakfast.

"We met five years ago in Florida, fell instantly in love and were married. The marriage was a mistake, and we went our separate ways when I moved back to Chicago. You discovered you were pregnant but didn't want to stop the divorce proceedings, so you didn't tell me."

"I just love being the heartless vixen in this little melodrama," Bethany said acidly.

"Can you think of a way to explain the fact that I have had no contact with my daughter in four years that doesn't hinge on you being the heartless vixen?" He cocked an eyebrow. "I'll be glad to use an alternate explanation if it covers all the bases."

"How about this one," she said after some thought. "We were married. I discovered you were having an affair with every woman on our block. And I left without telling anyone about the baby because I couldn't figure out which house to find you in."

Justin glared at her. "This is serious."

"Why don't we just tell everyone I pleaded with you to take me back after I discovered I was pregnant, but you refused. When you found Abby and me begging in the streets, you relented."

"Why are you doing this?"

"Your story is just about as bad."

"My story is almost true."

"Is that how you saw our relationship, Justin? A failed marriage?"

His forehead was creased into a frown. "What we had was very good, and I didn't see it as a failure at all."

Dropping all pretenses of humor, she shivered inadvertently. "No, failure carries with it the connotation that something was worth working on, at least initially. To fail you have to give something a try. What we had was just a good old-fashioned fling."

"It was never that." The words hung between them like three-dimensional objects. "Someday, when we can get all the ramifications of this situation behind us, I'd like to tell you what I think our relationship was. Right now there is too much between us that needs settling."

"You don't owe me any explanations. It all happened a long time ago." *Then why is my heart pounding like this,* she asked herself.

"We have ghosts that need to be put to rest."

"Well, I'll be happy to take the blame in your little story, so you can put that ghost to rest immediately. I don't really care what people I don't know think of me, but if it's important to you, then I'll go along with it."

She finished her coffee and set the cup down with a bang. "There is the small matter of my daughter's name."

"I want to have it changed legally. I want my name on her birth certificate."

"I thought you might. I have only one condition." She looked him directly in the eye, leaning forward to make her point.

"That is?"

"I want you to sign a statement saying you will never try to take custody away from me."

"Do you really think I'd ever try?" His black eyes searched her face, seeing the vulnerability there.

"We both know that if you tried, with your superior resources you just might be able to manage it."

"I'd never hurt you like that," he said softly.

"Will you put that in writing?"

"Yes, I will, if you'll give me your promise right now that you'll let me have Abby on a regular basis."

"And you would trust my promise?"

"Yes."

"All right."

Neither of them missed the significance of their agreement. The past was being laid to rest and new trust was being established. Bethany reached to cover his dark, strong hands with her soft white ones.

"I think I'm going to like being your friend again," she said with a trace of shyness. Without righteous anger she felt unprotected, but it was a feeling she liked. She had never been the type for defenses and hard shells.

"It's a good place to start," he answered, turning her hand over to run his thumb across her palm.

It was a gesture of friendship, a sign that they were starting a new relationship, but it sent waves of feeling tracing paths through her nervous system. After all those years, Justin Dumontier could still reduce her to shivers. His was a power she could not afford to underestimate.

"One more thing," he said lightly.

"Yes?"

"I'd like to take Abby to see my mother tomorrow."

"All right," she said, pushing her chair back and standing to leave. "If she's out of here by then, you're welcome to come get her."

"I want you to come."

"You're kidding."

"Abby will feel better if you do. And my mother should meet you, under the circumstances."

"She's going to hate me."

Justin pushed his chair back and stood beside her. "No one in their right mind could hate you. I can't guarantee she'll fall at your feet, but she'll be polite to you. She's never impolite—she wouldn't know how to be."

"I feel frozen already."

"Bury your prejudices. Life on St. Charles Avenue is not as stuffy as you might think," he said with a flashing smile. "Give her a chance."

They parted at Abby's door after finding that the little girl was taking a nap. "I'll call you tomorrow to make arrangements," Justin told her.

"I'll let you know what the doctor says when he comes today. Will you be at your office for the rest of the morning?"

"I've got an appointment with a real-estate agent for

the remainder of the day, so I won't be available. I'll check with you when I can get to a phone.''

"Making investments?"

"House shopping for a friend."

Bethany wondered briefly if the friend was Danielle de Bessonet, but discarded the idea. She had a feeling that Danielle would not have failed to let it slip if Justin was spending his afternoon with her. "See you later, then." She turned to go into Abby's room.

"Bethany?"

"Yes?" His hand came under her chin, turning her to face him again. "You really are a foxy chick when you're angry, but you're absolutely breathtaking when you aren't." He bent to press his lips gently to hers. He was down the hall and in the elevator before she turned the knob and entered Abby's room.

"I'M GLAD TO BE HOME, MOMMY." Abby twirled around and around, running from the bedroom back to the living room. "Look, the windows are sparkly."

Bethany looked out the distorted glass panes to see the French Quarter in pristine beauty. Mrs. Dumontier's servants had cleaned the apartment from top to bottom, polishing everything they could reach, scrubbing and vacuuming, cleaning the upholstery on her few pieces of furniture. Although she prided herself on being a neat housekeeper, the apartment had never looked this clean. Even Abby's collection of dolls had been bathed and dressed in newly washed clothes. If there was any cat dander left in the apartment, it was so sanitized it would not have a prayer of affecting the little girl.

"I'm glad you're home, too, I missed you so much

when I wasn't with you." Bethany thought, with a trace of disbelief, that it had only been two weeks since Justin had walked back into her life. It seemed like forever. The changes that had occurred already were startling.

"Can we go to the square today? Maybe Lamar is fiddling."

"No, remember when he visited you last night, he told you he was going to Baton Rouge for the weekend."

Abby's lip stuck out far enough to balance a basketball on. "I want to go somewhere. I've been in bed forever!"

"Two days is not forever. But we are going somewhere. Justin is going to take us to meet his mother, your grandmother." She watched Abby for signs that the importance of this new piece of news had been communicated to the child.

"Does she have anything for kids to do?"

After an internal sigh of relief Bethany nodded. "She has a great big house," she said with forced enthusiasm, "and I'll bet there'll be lots to do and see." Actually, there would probably be lots that Abby wouldn't be allowed to do in the showpiece of St. Charles Avenue, but Bethany wasn't about to tell Abby that. With a sinking heart she envisioned an hour spent drinking tea and trying to keep Abby on her best behavior.

"Let's go."

"No, we're both going to change our clothes first. Your grandmother is sending her car for us in an hour."

"Her car goes by itself?"

"No, that's just an expression. What dress would you like to wear?"

An hour later they were both ready, wearing, at

Abby's insistence, the one mother-daughter outfit they owned. Dressed exactly alike in emerald-green cotton sweaters and matching skirts, the two females looked like a page out of the Spiegel catalog. The effect was a bit much for the occasion, but Abby was so delighted that Bethany had given in. Bethany just hoped that Justin's mother wouldn't think she was trying too hard to make a point about whose child Abby was.

Homer escorted them down to the waiting limousine, and Abby, with a shriek of joy, hurled her little body onto the luxurious seats and bounced for the entire ten-minute drive. It was a sunny day, and New Orleans was beginning to look as though spring were arriving. Since it had been a fairly mild winter, azaleas and camellias were beginning to bloom, sending bright rays of color out to meet the sunshine.

Homer drove the length of St. Charles, taking his time as if he understood that Bethany would be in no hurry to arrive. She sat by the window, gazing at the ornate mansions of Italianate, Victorian, Greek Revival and other architectural styles she couldn't identify but could appreciate.

Finally Homer signaled and pulled the car to the right into a circular driveway in front of a huge Greek Revival mansion. If only, she thought, growing more discouraged by the moment, Mrs. Dumontier could have lived in one of the colorful Victorian houses along the avenue. Dripping gingerbread trim and bright stained-glass windows gave them a warmth and character that was not foreboding, although the houses were obviously worth a great deal. This house, with its pillars and formal design, made her feel she was about to approach a priestess in her temple.

Slipping out of the seat, she saw with relief that Justin was standing on the front steps. After bringing them home from the hospital, he had rushed off to another appointment with his realtor, and Bethany had been afraid she would arrive at his mother's house before he did. During their brief time together in his car that morning she had been unable to find out how his mother had reacted to the news of a four-year-old granddaughter born out of wedlock.

Justin walked down the steps to take her arm and to hold Abby's hand. "Come on, you two. If my mother has to wait any longer to meet Abby, I think she'll pass out from anxiety."

"Justin," Bethany said in a stage whisper, "won't your mother think it's strange that you're holding on to me, too? Aren't I supposed to be the villainess?"

"I'll just tell her I'm holding on in case you try to run away again."

The front entrance took them into a center hall flanked on one side by what Bethany could only guess was a drawing room. The hall itself was painted a Wedgwood blue, with interior millwork that included carved wreaths and "lamb's tongue" molding. A heavy eighteenth-century brass mirror hung to the side of the staircase, bordered by sconces heavily laden with prisms that sent refracted light to dance on the wall. Underneath the mirror was an inlaid chest embellished with a crystal bowl flanked by bronze urns. With a sideways peek into the drawing room Bethany could see heavy mahogany furniture accessorized with carefully chosen antique pieces, including what looked like a Ming vase.

Abby and a Ming vase. Bethany's heart threatened to quit beating. She pulled away from Justin and grabbed

Abby's other hand. "Abby," she whispered. "Be sure you don't touch anything unless I tell you it's all right."

"This is not a museum, Bethany. Don't worry so much." Justin pulled her around to stand beside him again. "Come on."

They followed the long hallway past other rooms, some of which were equally as formal and ornate as the drawing room had been, some of which were surprisingly informal and almost cozy. Without examining them carefully, Bethany could still see that each room seemed to be an entity unto itself. Although Justin had said that the house was not a museum, it was beginning to appear like one. Each room was decorated in a different style, almost as if it were a showcase for a different period of history. They turned a corner, following the hall, and stepped down into a brightly lit sun-room furnished with contemporary furniture covered with rainbow-hued canvas pillows. The room was a mass of tall trees, vines twined around windows and flowering shrubs in huge clay pots.

The contrast to the rest of the house caused Bethany to blink in surprise. Abby let out a whoop and ran toward an antique carved wooden horse straight off of a nineteenth-century carousel. "Justin, can I ride it?" the little girl piped.

"Of course. But first come meet your grandmother."

Bethany had almost forgotten the purpose of their visit, she had been so enchanted with examining the sun-room. She turned to see an older woman with perfectly sculptured silver hair and a lovely patrician face come into the room. The two women stared at each other for a moment until Mrs. Dumontier caught sight of Abby. Bethany watched the woman grow pale, and she waited with real concern as Justin went to his mother to lend support.

"I told you she looked like Marie," he murmured, "but I'm sure you couldn't have imagined how much." Justin put his arm around his mother and she leaned against him briefly.

"Introduce us," Mrs. Dumontier said huskily.

"Abby come here." The little girl walked curiously to her grandmother.

"You're real pretty," she said. "I didn't know grandmothers were s'posed to be real pretty."

Mrs. Dumontier knelt on legs that were visibly shaking. "Hello, Abby." And then, as if she couldn't stop herself, she reached out to trace the little girl's features. "You're real pretty yourself."

"I look like him." Abby pointed to her father. "I didn't even know him, but I still look like him."

"Yes, you certainly do." Louise Dumontier looked straight at Bethany for a moment, examining her. She turned back to her granddaughter. "But you have your mother's lovely skin coloring."

"Can I ride the horse now, Justin?"

Justin picked her up and carried her across the room as the older woman stood and eyed Bethany. Finally she held out her hand. "Thank you for coming, Bethany," she said simply.

There seemed to be no response that was appropriate. Bethany swallowed hard, and the pause lengthened. "I don't know what to say," she said finally, taking Mrs. Dumontier's hand, "except that I'm sorry I've kept you from your granddaughter for so long."

"I think that you had your reasons, and someday perhaps you'll share them with me. For now, I feel as if I've been reborn and there is no place inside me for regrets."

Justin came over to stand beside them, spontaneously putting an arm around each of them. "I think you'll find you have a lot in common. I want you to be friends."

Under the circumstances, it seemed like a lot to ask, but as the afternoon progressed the two women became more and more at ease with each other. With Justin in the lead, Abby and Bethany explored every inch of the gigantic house. Mrs. Dumontier seemed pleased to find that Bethany was well acquainted with antiques, and the two women chatted about interior decorating, which was a passion of Louise's.

"I wanted to open my own shop," the older woman told Bethany, her arm around Abby, who had fallen asleep next to her. "But my husband was against it. He felt it wouldn't give me enough time to fulfill my social obligations. So I took out my frustrations by redecorating the house room by room. When I finished, I'd just start over again. Sometimes I'd forget what was next and redo a room that had been recently renovated, but it kept me busy."

"I like the eclectic feeling. I think I'd grow tired of only one style in a house this large," Bethany sympathized.

"We never had time to grow tired of anything," Justin said with a wry grin. "Just when I'd get used it something it was gone."

"I never even knew you noticed, dear," Louise answered. "You were always upstairs studying or working on some project, and I did leave your room alone."

Bethany stretched lazily and smiled at them both. "I hate to leave, but I'm a working woman who is very far behind in her work. I've got to get home pretty soon and start finishing some masks.''

"Mother, will you keep Abby for a little while? I've got something I want Bethany to see that's not too far from here. We'll be back in about half an hour so I can get her home early enough to get some work done.''

Bethany watched the pleased smile creep over Louise's features. Abby's grandmother was going to be delighted to have her granddaughter to herself. She felt a surge of warmth for the older woman, who had been denied so much and still found it in her heart to forgive. "Will we really be back in a half an hour, Justin? I'm serious about working tonight.''

"I know you are. This shouldn't take long." He stood and Bethany followed him, perplexed by his secretive manner.

"Thank you for watching Abby, Louise.''

"Don't hurry back," Louise said in answer.

"WELL, THIS IS a lovely neighborhood, Justin. I'm impressed with all these glorious houses." Justin had driven her about a mile from his mother's mansion to the Uptown residential section of New Orleans, characterized by gracious old houses in a surprising array of architectural styles. Parking the car on the corner of State Street and St. Charles, they had strolled several blocks to stand in front of a raised Creole cottage with a spacious front gallery.

"Would you like to see this one inside?''

"Well, yes," she said puzzled by his question. "Do you know the owner?''

"Very well. Come on.''

Bethany followed him up the walk, admiring the lush

green grass and spacious yard. The house was set back from the road, a quiet side street with little traffic. Obviously the owners had hired a professional gardener, because the yard was a mass of color and crisply trimmed shrubs. In the side yard was a magnolia tree large enough to tower over the house. "Wouldn't that tree be perfect for a child to climb."

Justin turned and grinned as if he approved of her comment. Pulling a ring of keys from his pocket, he unlocked the door, pocketing his keys and taking her hand. They entered the house through a center hall with cleanly laid out rooms bordering it. "Originally," he said, "this style of house was always small, with four rooms forming a square and no hall. This one was built later, with the six rooms downstairs and the center hall, which my mother says was primarily Georgian in inspiration."

"Justin, this house has no furniture."

"You're right. No one lives here right now."

So this was the piece of real estate he had been looking at. A suspicion began to form. "Justin, what . . ."

"Don't say anything yet. Come look at it with me."

She followed him into each room, admiring the polished floors and cypress woodwork and mantels over the fireplaces. The rooms were painted white or creamy pastel colors and everything about the house was in perfect order. They walked through the kitchen into a tiny room containing a small curving stairway.

"This leads to a dormered attic with two rooms. Come on."

They climbed the stairs to find two perfect little bedrooms side by side. "Originally these were probably servant's quarters, but the previous owner used them for his children."

One of the rooms was papered with beige wallpaper covered with tiny bouquets of multicolored flowers. Curtains of nubby rose cotton still hung at the window. The other was painted an off-white, with a mural of sailing ships on one wall. In what was obviously at one time a large hall closet they found a tiny child-sized bathroom.

"There's a finished playroom downstairs, too," Justin enthused. "It's big enough for an indoor gym."

"Justin. Why are we looking at this house. Why do you have the key?"

"Come see the playroom."

Resigned to his refusal to communicate, she followed him down two sets of stairs. The playroom was large enough for an indoor gym. In fact, it still had pieces of indoor climbing equipment on the plush carpeting. "Did they run a nursery school?"

"No, they had a big family."

Bethany walked over to the mass of wood and metal and sat on the bottom of the little slide, her knees drawn up in front of her. "I'm not moving until you tell me what's going on."

"I bought it. For you and Abby."

She shook her head slowly, the feathery strands of hair tickling her neck. "You'll never believe what I thought you just said. . . ."

"I did. I bought it for you."

"Without checking with me? I could have saved you a lot of money."

"You don't like it?"

"It's wonderful. It's a fairy tale. It's New Orleans architecture at its finest. But you can't just buy me a house, Justin."

"Well, then think of it as an investment in Abby's future. This house will be worth a fortune someday."

"It's worth a fortune right now!"

Justin shrugged. "I can afford it, Bethany." He went on ignoring her protests. "I talked to Abby's doctor at length yesterday. He said that the preliminary allergy testing they did at the hospital indicated that she is allergic to house dust and feathers. It's going to be very difficult to keep her away from either of those elements in your apartment."

" 'Feathers'?"

"Ironic, isn't it? He's not too worried about her—she's not in any danger from her allergies. But she'll be more comfortable here. I'm going to have a new filtering system installed on the heating and cooling equipment. It will filter out lots of the pollution and pollens from outside, and for at least the time she spends indoors she'll be better off."

"I can't afford to live here. I don't have any furniture, I don't have a car."

"You do now. I bought you a Toyota Corolla yesterday. They're going to deliver it on Monday."

"You did what?" She jumped to her feet, almost tripping on the gymnastics mat at the bottom of the sliding board. "You did what?"

"You don't like Toyotas?"

"You're rearranging my life. Who told you to take responsibility for me? I've done just fine without you all these years."

"Damned if you have," he said, advancing on her. "You've managed by scrimping and saving, with hardly any life of your own. Madeline has told me stories of the years you've done without so that you could establish yourself as a mask maker and build up an inventory of materials.''

''‘Madeline’? Madeline?'' She stood aghast, her mouth hanging open in shock and fury. ''What is going on here, Justin!''

His hands locked on her shoulders, pulling her so close that there was no molecule of air between them. ''I won't have it that way anymore, Bethany. Neither you nor Abby is going to go without ever again. Now shut up.'' His mouth covered hers and his arms gripped her resisting body, holding her firmly against him.

The more she fought him, the harder he held her, until she thought she would pass out from lack of oxygen. Gasping for air, she opened her mouth, allowing his searching tongue access. And then she was no longer struggling, but alive in his arms, seeking to be closer, hungry for his touch.

She could feel Justin's lips curve into a smile. He moved a scant inch away, murmuring, ''I'll have to remember that you like aggressive men.'' His mouth took possession again before the angry words bubbling to her lips overflowed to put an end to their contact. His grip relaxed and his fingers began to explore her spine through the emerald sweater.

What had been his statement the night Abby went into the hospital? He had said that when he touched her, she melted like a snow cone on a New Orleans summer afternoon. He was right. She wanted to freeze, to put distance between them, but she was helpless before the need that she felt for him. And it was useless to be angry at herself for her weakness. Her passion for Justin Dumontier was a reality she could not change.

Without knowing how, she could feel his frustration

building at the limited contact. Finally he pushed up the emerald sweater, his hands traveling up her back to communicate his need. Moving apart just enough to cover her breast with his hand, he growled softly, searching for the soft peak and massaging it with his fingers until it was hard and aching for him.

Feeling her was not enough; he wanted to taste her, to savor the sweet aroma of magnolias that hung in the air about her. The token resistance he had felt from her at first was gone, replaced by a response that made him crazy with desire. No one had ever responded the way Bethany did. From the first time that he had taken her innocent and unaware into womanhood she had withheld nothing, given everything. And no one else could force him to replace his own watchful detachment with the piercing brightness of total involvement.

Clasping her to him again, he pushed her to the soft carpet below them, pulling the sweater over her head and leaving the top of her naked except for her bra, transparent in its fragile laciness. Blue veins were visible under the alabaster skin, the rosy peaks of her full breasts excited and tantalizing under the wisp of cloth.

"Justin," she cried as his mouth dipped down to taste the creamy skin whose feel and scent he craved. Made helpless by her own desire, she lay beneath his hard body, her head turning from side to side, making an impression on the long fibers of the carpet. Threading her fingers through his black hair, she held him to her, moving with pleasure underneath his ministrations.

"All these years," he gasped. "I couldn't forget how you tasted, how you smelled. All this time I've wanted you so much I could hardly stand it." His fingers sought the front clasp of her bra, unfastening it to

pull it from her. At the moment he had almost succeeded in covering the bared treasure of her breast with his
mouth, they heard a door slam upstairs.

"Yoo-hoo, Mr. Dumontier! I saw your car outside.
Yoo-hoo!"

With the groan of a dying man, Justin sat up, pushing
his hair off his forehead. Bethany jumped up, searching
frantically for her clothing. "Mrs. Nelson?" Justin
called.

"Where are you, darlin'?"

"I'll be right up, Mrs. Nelson!" He found Bethany's
sweater as she slipped on her bra. "It's the realtor who
sold me the house."

"Terrific," she gasped, her face suffused with color.

"I feel like a kid who's been caught making out with
his date in the back seat of his father's car." He stood,
offering Bethany a hand. She noticed it was trembling
slightly, and that realization gave her enormous pleasure.

"Well, I was almost caught with my pants down,"
she said finally, her tone as cheerful as she could make
it.

"You're awfully chipper about all this," he grunted,
following her to the stairs.

"Neither of us had any business writhing around on
that carpet, Justin. We were acting like irresponsible
idiots."

His tongue found the hollow in the back of her neck,
and she shivered as his arms went around her, settling
on her breasts. "Don't tell me you weren't enjoying it."

"All right, I won't."

"Bethany?"

"Hmm?" His hands were once again causing the

sensations that had led to her loss in control, and she felt powerless to stop him.

"If you remodel the house, don't you dare take up that rug. Someday I intend to finish what we started on that very spot."

"Yoo-hoo, Mr. Dumontier!"

"Damn that woman," he muttered in frustration.

CHAPTER TEN

BETHANY WANDERED THROUGH THE HOUSE while Justin conducted some final contract negotiations with his realtor. Again she followed the curving stairway, to stand in the upstairs hallway gazing at the bedroom with the flowered wallpaper. Their encounter on the floor of the playroom had left her more tremulous than she had let herself appear, and she was glad to have a few moments away from him. The evidence of their mutual desire for each other was a fact that would have to be explored at some other time, however. She was still too shaken to think about it clearly. The only thing she knew for certain was that it was time to see a doctor for birth-control precautions. No matter how their relationship culminated, this time she would be prepared.

"That room would be perfect for Abby, wouldn't it?" Justin's voice came from behind her, and she turned to see him leaning on the banister, watching her.

"Actually, I think Abby would prefer the sailing ships," she said. "But she'll never get a chance to make a choice, Justin. I know you think you're doing what's right for us, but I certainly can't accept a house or a car from you. The roses were almost too much."

"I appreciate your pride, but it's misplaced this time. I'm not trying to buy you, only a place for you to live and raise our daughter. I want to put the house in your name, but if you insist I can put it in Abby's."

"This seems like a pretty casual decision. Have you given it much thought?"

"I've been thinking about it since the first day I saw where you lived." He held up his hand to stop her. "Look, I'm not the prudish aristocrat you try to make me out to be, but environment is important. This house and this neighborhood have so much to offer our daughter."

"Why did you choose this particular house? I'm frankly surprised that you didn't consult me first." The house was not a safe subject, but it was sure to be less volatile than a discussion of their recent behavior à la carpet would be. She was in the peculiar position of being grateful to him for giving them something else to argue about.

"I was sure you'd refuse to come with me." He nodded at her shrug. "But actually, I planned to narrow the decision down to a half-dozen houses and twist your arm to get your cooperation."

Lifting her hand to her hair, she spread her fingers wide, combing it back from her face. "And?"

"Well, I saw this house, and I knew it would be perfect. The owners were on the verge of accepting another bid, and I had to decide right then or risk losing it."

"It's a wonderful house," she said in a noncommittal tone. "But what was it that seemed to make it perfect?"

"Come on, you haven't seen the best yet."

She followed him down the stairs and waited as he unlocked the back door. It opened onto a wide gallery running the length of the house. Bethany could almost see wrought-iron tables holding pitchers of iced tea and

frosty glasses on a hot summer day. Visualizing a bad-
minton net set up next to the rose garden in the spacious
backyard was equally easy.

Justin motioned for her to follow him down the brick
steps and over the patio running beside the gallery. A
small freshly painted white building garlanded with wis-
teria and honeysuckle sat at the back of the lot under the
shade of another giant magnolia. An impressive pad-
lock fastened the door, and Justin tried several small
keys before he found the one that opened it. "See what
you think," he said, standing aside to let her enter.

The building contained one large room with a small
bathroom and what appeared to be a storage room off
it. Carpeted in no-nonsense tones of rust and brown, the
main room was paneled in a light natural wood sealed
with a satiny finish. An elaborate track lighting system
and large windows with miniblinds gave the room
brightness, accented by several domed skylights in the
high ceiling. In one corner was an apartment-sized stove
and a cabinet with a sink. A small-scale refrigerator sat
beside the cabinet.

"Was this their guest house?"

"I gather it's been used for that, but I think it was
also a hobby room of sorts. I thought it would be perfect as a workshop for you."

It would be perfect. The room was a dream for anyone
who made her living creating. It was light and airy and
peaceful. But her answer still had to be no. "Justin..."

"Don't say anything. Give it some thought. The
house has been here for a century. It will be here for a
few more weeks."

"But you might be able to back out of the deal now.
You should try to get your money back while you can."

"Let me worry about that." He looked at his watch. "We'd better get back."

They walked through the side yard under the large magnolia. Bethany noticed with a sinking heart that a child's tree house was built into the sturdy branches. "Are you sure they didn't run a nursery school?"

"No, they just loved children, and this house was made to be loved by a child."

"You're choking me with guilt," she said lightly.

"I'll use what I have to. I want to see you and Abby here as soon as possible." He intercepted her piercing look. "All right, I'll stop... for now."

"I wonder how Abby did with your mother?" Bethany tried for a change of subject as they drove back toward St. Charles.

"They seemed to get along very well. For that matter, you and my mother got along well, too." A smile spread over his face, replacing the strained look acquired during their unsettled dispute over the house.

His obvious pleasure at the relationship she was establishing with his mother surprised her. Certainly it would make life easier for all of them if she and Mrs. Dumontier could be friends, but his pleasure seemed to go deeper. She probed. "I really didn't expect her to like me, Justin. After what I did, and..." She stopped, letting her words trail off.

"And?"

"Well, and because of who I am."

"And who are you?" he asked, glancing at her.

"Well, I'm nobody, really. I mean socially, that is. I've never been the queen of carnival like your friend Danielle."

"Don't exaggerate. Danielle was never queen of

carnival, either. Just queen of one of the krewes and maid in several courts.''

"Well, whatever. I've never even been to a ball.''

"Do you want to go? I'll take you.''

"No." She shuddered lightly. "But that's the point I'm trying to make. I'm not that type at all. You could scratch my pedigree on the head of a pin and still have room for the Declaration of Independence.''

"You're not a poodle, Bethany. Pedigree is not an issue.''

"I thought it might be with your mother. I know that your family is socially prominent, and I figured out a long time ago that my background was probably one of the things that came between us.''

Justin hit the brakes and pulled the car into a parking spot on the side of St. Charles. "Repeat what you just said.''

"Don't worry about it, Justin. I'm not ashamed of myself at all. But I have come to understand that sometimes these things matter.''

He watched the pointed chin come up a few inches and a barrier of iron-clad defenses settle around her. Hands gripping the steering wheel, he turned to stare straight ahead. "How could you possibly have thought that of me?" he asked.

"It was one of many explanations I came up with. And it seemed the most plausible." She tried to smile. "I guess it was the one that didn't reflect on me as a person, too. Since I didn't have anything to do with my own background, then I couldn't be blamed.''

"Bethany, I left New Orleans primarily to get away from just such a mentality." He propped his elbows on the steering wheel and massaged his temples. "Let me tell you a quick story. About thirteen years ago, when I was ready to go off to college, my parents tried very hard to convince me that I should either stay in New Orleans or at least come back for my graduate work here. Even then I knew what a trap it would be. I chose to go to Harvard and to work in Chicago for only one reason. I did not want to be one of the privileged.''

"Harvard is not exactly Poor Folk U."

"But at Harvard being a Dumontier was nothing. I did not want people to think of me as an entity. I wanted them to see me as an ordinary human being. I've always hated the social structure here. I find it stifling and at its worst I find it prejudicial. I grew up going to all the right schools, participating in activities of the right carnival organizations and clubs. I knew that was not what I wanted from life.''

Bethany sat very still, drinking in his words. "Well, I guess that's one myth destroyed." But his words didn't make her feel any better. His withdrawal from her could only be laid at her own personal doorstep now. "I'm sorry I ever thought that you were a snob.''

His hand was under her chin, turning her so that he could stare into her eyes. "And you're still wondering why I lost touch with you, aren't you? I purposely let our correspondence lapse because I needed time to think. I had to withdraw from you and piece my life back together. You didn't fail me. I thought that you were the finest person I had ever known in my life.''

Her eyes widened at his revelation. "What a lovely thing to say," she said in a husky voice.

"I still do," he said as he kissed her gently. "That has never changed.''

They traveled back to his mother's talking only of

inconsequential things. There were too many emotions sealed in the Mercedes with them, and neither Bethany nor Justin was ready to plunge into the charged atmosphere and begin to sort out the complexities of their relationship.

Mrs. Dumontier was in the drawing room, rearranging her collection of Imari porcelain, when Justin returned from delivering Bethany and Abby safely home. Standing in the doorway, he watched her moving the delicate earthenware from mantel to table and back again.

"What did you think of them?" he asked, trying to sound casual.

She looked up with a radiant smile. "I think Abby is wonderful. She's every grandmother's dream. I honestly couldn't ask for a better mother for her, either, although of course I wish all this had come about in a different way."

"Of course, it doesn't hurt that Bethany shares your interest in antiques, does it?"

"It never hurts when two people have something in common to chat about." She recognized Justin's attempt to prolong the conversation, and she obliged him. "But Bethany really is a lovely girl. I'll confess, I spent a major portion of the afternoon wondering how you ever let her get away." She watched Justin stiffen, and she sighed. "When you do that, you're so much like your father I almost believe in reincarnation."

"When I do what?"

"When you straighten up like that and wipe all expression off your face. You learned that at your father's knee. That and a few other irritating mannerisms."

"That's the second time in my life I remember hearing you sound even faintly critical of father."

"I think, perhaps, that I should have let you know many years ago that I disagreed with some of your father's attitudes." She bent to continue rearranging the porcelain pieces and to signal that she was ready for a change of subject. "I know you prepared me, but I wasn't ready to see the likeness of Marie walk through the door."

"She is, isn't she. But very different in personality. I remember Marie as being very quiet, ultrafeminine and obedient."

"Abby is very much like you were as a child. Dramatic, willful, as bright as a copper penny. Altogether charming."

" 'Dramatic and willful'?"

Laughing softly, she straightened and walked to him. "Willful, you still are. The dramatic disappeared years ago, only to crop up again in that wonderful child."

"She gets the willful part from her mother."

Mrs. Dumontier searched his face, settling on the slight frown. "Has Bethany thwarted you somehow?"

"I bought her a house and she refuses to move into it."

"Just like that? You bought her a house?"

Ignoring her incredulity, he shook his head. "I think she wants to stay in the French Quarter. She maintains that she can't take anything from me, but I think it's because of a man there, a fellow named Lamar, who she seems to be very close to."

Watching the troubled frown on her son's face, Mrs. Dumontier experienced a sharp tingle of pleasure. Justin might pretend to be irritated with Bethany for not doing what he wanted her to, but it was apparent that another emotion existed behind his irritation. "You're jealous, aren't you?"

The troubled expression vanished, to be replaced by a blank mask. "I don't know what you mean," he answered stiffly.

The seed had been planted; pointing out the emotion was the best she could do at the moment. Patting his hand as she moved past him, she said in a consoling tone, "Even a Dumontier is allowed to feel jealousy, son. Even a Dumontier."

"I CAN'T BELIEVE it's only three weeks to Mardi Gras, Madeline." Bethany and Madeline were working side by side behind the display case at Life's Illusions. Bethany was sitting on a high stool gluing feathers on a mask, and Madeline was catching up on paperwork that had not got done during Abby's illness.

"How far behind are you on your orders, Beth?"

Bethany made a face and unconsciously began to glue faster as she answered. "So far behind that I'm not sure I'm going to be done by next year's Mardi Gras."

"You always take too many commissions. I keep telling you..."

"I know, I know. Beth," she said in a deep voice that was intended to mimic Madeline, "Beth, you're only human, child. You have to have more time to yourself."

"It caught up to you this time, didn't it?"

"It's been crazy. But I think the worst is over. Now that Abby is better and Justin and I aren't at each other's throats over her welfare, I think I'll be able to settle down and catch up."

"Valerie was invaluable while you were at the hospital with Abby." As if she were waiting for her name to be called, the pretty black girl entered the shop.

"Hi, you all." She honored them with her stunning smile.

"Valerie, I didn't expect to see you today. I thought you were studying for a big test," Madeline said.

"I stayed up late last night to do it. I thought I'd be able to finish the mask I was working on if Beth wasn't using the workroom today."

The three women chatted for a few minutes, until Bethany excused herself to wait on a customer. When she returned Valerie was gone.

"It's a shame Valerie doesn't have a place at home to work," Bethany said, thinking of the small apartment in which Valerie lived with her parents and three younger sisters. The family was long on love and short on room.

Madeline dropped her eyes and busied herself with paperwork. Her tone couldn't have been more unconcerned. "We could really use that studio we're always fantasizing about. Not only could the three of us use it, but we could take on some extra people to help assemble the easier masks. I hate to hire them out as piece work without being there to supervise. What we need is a studio right on the premises."

Bethany's exhalation rivaled the north wind. "Justin's been talking to you, hasn't he."

Madeline's frizzy head bobbed a scant inch.

"What is it between you two?" Bethany asked incredulously. "Justin dropped hints about endless personal conversations yesterday when he was trying to move me lock, stock and barrel into that cozy little cottage he bought for me on a crazy impulse."

"He's worried about Abby, Beth. And I'm afraid I agree with him."

Another customer entered and, after long minutes of debate and indecision, left the shop carrying a papier-mâché mask of an alligator. Two more customers came in and departed with bundles.

"Why?" Bethany asked as if there had been no interruptions.

"Look around, Beth." Madeline gestured at the street in front of the window. "This is a wonderful place to live in many ways. But it's not the proper place to raise a child. She needs a neighborhood with other children to play with. The apartment is fast becoming too small for you both, and even if we could afford to rent a studio and free up your workroom, there's no decent place for her to play."

Bethany whistled softly. "Sounds like you've been giving it some thought."

"I've been worried for some time. I've even looked at some houses in my neighborhood, hoping I could find something that wasn't too expensive for you. But real estate has gone out of sight recently. Unless you take Justin up on his offer, I'm afraid you're going to be here forever." Madeline turned to face her. "It's time to bury your pride. For Abby's sake."

"Did you know he's even bought me a car? A car, for God's sake. I didn't have the heart to tell him I don't even have a Louisiana driver's license." Bethany laughed softly, suddenly free from the conflicting emotions she had been experiencing. She was not going to like having to admit it to Justin, but Madeline was right; it was wrong to let pride stand in Abby's way. She was going to have to move into the house.

"Getting a license won't be a problem." Madeline visibly relaxed at Bethany's laughter.

"I'm not going to let him hand me the car on a silver platter. I'll pay him for it." She still smiled, but her chin shot up a notch. "It will probably take me ten years, but I'll pay him back every nickel."

"Good for you." Madeline clapped. "There's nothing to be gained from putting yourself in his debt."

"And you don't think that's what I'm doing by accepting the house?" A trace of uncertainty remained in Bethany's voice.

"Not at all. The house is for Abby. For that matter, the car is, too, but paying him back will remind him that you're an independent woman," Madeline muttered softly. "As if he's going to be likely to forget."

"He's going to think I'm pretty flighty, changing my mind in less than twenty-four hours."

"He's going to think you've got good common sense."

"Where he's concerned, Madeline, that's probably the last thing I have, good common sense...or moderate self-control."

"He's a charmer, Beth." Madeline stood and began to pile up the papers she had been working on. "I think that if someone like Justin Dumontier showed as much interest in me as he does in you, my common sense and self-control would be put to the test, too."

"That interest got me into trouble once before," Bethany said lightly. "It won't again."

"You're right. But that's because you're much more mature now, much more secure. You don't have to be afraid of your feelings. I'm certain you'll do the right thing when the time comes to make a decision about Justin." Madeline shrugged into an old beat-up cardigan sweater she used when she was making masks and gathered up her purse. "I'm going to see if Valerie needs any help upstairs. Call us if it gets too busy down here."

The homey wisdom could have come directly from the mouth of one of Bethany's television mothers. Not for the first time, Bethany realized just how much she had gained by having the older woman as her friend. Madeline had become the real-life mother she had never had. If indeed Bethany was more mature, more secure now than she had been at age twenty-one, it was because of the warm nurturing and personal attention she had received from Madeline. Madeline's love was a gift freely given, and Bethany was properly grateful. It was a gift to treasure.

"JUSTIN, JUSTIN, JUSTIN..." Abby stood at the front door of Life's Illusions a week later, waiting for her father and chanting his name as if the repeated syllables would make him magically appear.

"He'll be here in about five minutes, Abby. Can you please do that quietly?" Bethany rubbed her temples with her fingertips, trying to dispel the headache that had indisputably settled in to stay until her Mardi Gras orders reached a manageable level. The last week had flown by with each day seeming to have fewer and fewer hours in it. Between working in the shop and spending every spare minute completing masks, Bethany was exhausted.

Her schedule had been so hectic she had gratefully allowed Justin and his mother to spend large portions of each day with Abby. As a consequence of the concentrated attention, Abby had abandoned almost all the suspicious reserve she had shown when she was with her father. The little girl now treated him to displays of the same exuberant affection she gave Lamar. Justin, for all his reticence, had no trouble expressing his feelings for the little girl, sending back a quiet unwavering love that seemed to wrap Abby in a cocoon of security.

"Will the white tiger be there?"

Bethany nodded, absorbed in gluing sequins on a mask she was just completing. She had developed a pattern to her work in the past week, and it was helping her to finish more masks. At night, after Abby fell asleep, Bethany worked on the plaster forms she used to mold the bases of her masks on. Then, during the day when she was behind the counter of the shop, she glued feathers, sequins and other adornments on the bases. Customers liked seeing the masks take shape before their eyes, and she got more masks made.

"Mommy, can't you come?"

Bethany shook her head, continuing to concentrate on her work.

"Mommy, talk to me!"

Flicking the button on the hot-glue machine, Bethany sighed. "No, I can't come, sweetheart. You and your daddy will have to go alone. I have to finish these masks before Mardi Gras."

"Madeline said Mardi Gras starts this weekend."

"Not Mardi Gras, sweetheart. The parades start then. Mardi Gras is just one day. The carnival season really starts twelve days after Christmas. Remember the first night we had king cake?"

Bethany watched Abby lick her lips at the mention of the circular sweetbread decorated with gold, green and purple-colored sugar. Every year the cake was served from Twelfth Night through Fat Tuesday, or Mardi Gras, the day before the beginning of Lent. Each king cake had a tiny plastic baby hidden in it, a symbol of the baby Jesus. The person finding the baby in his piece of cake was obligated to buy the next king cake.

"I had king cake at grandma's house. Mrs. Waters made it herself."

"Let me guess. I'll bet you found the baby, too." Bethany smiled at the little girl's astonished look.

"How did you know?"

Bethany pictured Mrs. Dumontier guiding Abby's hand as she cut the cake. An unspoken part of the local tradition was to be sure that as often as possible children found the baby. "A lucky guess."

"Justin wanted you to come to the zoo with us."

"I know. I wish I could." In the past week, Bethany had seen Justin only long enough to nod her head and exchange a pleasant word with him. There hadn't even been time to tell him of her decision to move into the Uptown house. When he had called, inviting her to go to the zoo with Abby and him today, she had conveniently forgotten to mention her change of heart again. Slightly abashed at her own devious behavior, she was still enjoying the feeling of keeping him hanging.

The shop bell tinkled and Justin walked through the glass door, grabbing Abby and swinging her high over his head. Right behind Justin was Danielle de Bessonet. The young woman was wearing the same tight designer jeans television stations all over the nation had got offended phone calls about after airing a certain sensuous advertisement. And Danielle looked at least as provocative in hers as the famous model in the commercial had. The jeans were topped by a fluffy angora pullover in a becoming shade of coral, and Danielle's hair was tied back from her baby face with a matching ribbon.

"Why Beth, dear, what a charming little shop," she said, following Justin into the store. "I've spent hours in the Quarter, and I've never even noticed this place."

"Hello, Danielle," Bethany said cordially. "Please feel free to look around." *I am not jealous. I am not jealous.* Bethany repeated the litany to herself as she watched the other woman walk from wall to wall of the little shop.

"Bethany, you look tired." Justin was standing in front of her examining her face, as he held Abby.

"I am," she said truthfully. "After Mardi Gras I'll be able to relax, but in the meantime I'm swamped with work."

"Did you do all of these?" Danielle asked with enthusiasm.

"Good heavens, no." Bethany swept her hand toward the far corner, where her feathered masks hung. "I'm the primary feather artist, although there are other people in the city and in California who supply us with some from time to time. The leather masks are done by my friend Madeline, and some of the papier mâché and wood carvings are done by Valerie, another artist who works with us. The rest are done by local people who sell here on consignment."

"I'm really impressed," Danielle said, and Bethany kicked herself for having jumped to the conclusion that the other woman would not be capable of appreciating her handiwork.

"Thank you, Danielle. I'm really glad you like them."

"Do you need more business?"

"We can always use more sales. We advertise by word of mouth, which is cheap, but not always effective."

"My mother's carnival krewe is looking for unique favors for their big spring banquet." Danielle pointed to a simple buckram mask covered with sequins, lace and swirls of feathers. "These would be perfect. Could you handle an order for two hundred of them, each a little different?"

"With enough notice we could."

Justin, watching the two women, stepped forth to interrupt. "Where would you make that many—or store them, for that matter?"

Bethany caught his eye and smiled slightly. "We are going to be using the entire apartment upstairs as a workroom as soon as I move Uptown."

She wondered why she so often thought of Justin's face as lacking in feeling. The warmth of his expression could have lit a Cajun Christmas-eve bonfire. "That's good news," was all he said, but Bethany knew the simple words hid a large helping of relief at her decision.

The shop bell tinkled again, and Bethany waved at Lamar, who, for once, was dressed sensibly in a plain knitted shirt and conservative dark pants. The shirt was pink, and instead of an emblem of an alligator, or even a crawfish, it had a cockroach going after a crumb. It was as Middle American as Lamar would ever get.

"Lamar, come meet Danielle." Bethany waved casually at Danielle and made the introductions. Justin put Abby down, and she promptly ran to Lamar and threw her arms around his legs. It was a measure of the improved relationship between the little girl and her father that Justin did not bat an eye. Instead he motioned Bethany to one side as the two new acquaintances chatted, the little girl wedged between them.

"I've missed not seeing you," Justin said softly, his eyes warm on her face.

"It doesn't look like you've been too lonely."

Justin's face lit with a slow grin. "If I didn't know better I'd think you were..."

"I'm not. Not at all." She met his eyes with a challenge in her own, and then smiled sheepishly at the laughter she saw. "You're absolutely right. Are you having as much trouble as I am figuring out what our relationship is?"

Justin brushed her hair back from her face with his hand, his fingers lingering along her jaw. "You're the most open person I have ever met. Who taught you to be absolutely honest about everything you feel?"

"I spent my life watching adults who were incapable of expressing any honest emotion unless they were drunk or angry," she said flatly. "I decided never to be that way."

"It was a wise decision." And then, in front of Lamar and Danielle, who were still having an animated conversation, judging from the speed with which Lamar's hands flew, Justin bent and brushed a lingering kiss against her lips. "What are you doing tomorrow night?"

"Working," she said softly.

"I'd like to take you to dinner."

She shook her head with genuine regret. "I'm swamped. I can't."

"Tomorrow at 7:00. We can take Abby to my mother's house for the evening. I want you to show me the French Quarter."

"You're making this very difficult."

"I know."

"I'll have to be home early enough to get some work done."

"Whenever you say."

The conversation between Danielle and Lamar was progressing at top speed. It seemed to have something to do with Lamar's music and Danielle's ideas for promoting their band. Far from being offended by Danielle's propensity to want to take over everything she touched, Lamar was delighted in her interest. And Danielle seemed genuinely fascinated by the big Cajun, turning on all her baby-doll charm.

"I wanna go to the zoo." Abby had separated from the animated couple and was pulling at her father's hand and steadily moving him to the door.

"Danielle, are you coming?"

Danielle turned with an expression of regret and nodded. "I'll be right there."

Bethany watched with delight as Lamar and Danielle exchanged phone numbers, and she turned to see Justin's reaction. Her delight was magnified by the benign smile on his face. Far from being upset by Danielle's interest in the other man, Justin didn't even seem to notice. Bethany kissed the green-eyed monster of jealousy goodbye as she blew a kiss to Abby, who finally succeeded in getting Danielle to follow her out the door.

CHAPTER ELEVEN

"I DON'T HAVE THE TIME, but I've got to go buy something to wear tonight. Nothing I have is suitable." Bethany rummaged in the closet she shared with Abby and pulled a wool sweater and skirt from the very back. She stuck out her tongue at the brown outfit that was the precise color of Mississippi mud. "See what I mean?"

Madeline sat on the antique mahogany four-poster bed that was Bethany's pride and joy and watched her friend obsessing about her upcoming dinner with Justin. "I have a feeling Justin will like you in anything you wear, but buying something new sounds like a good idea. When was the last time you shopped for yourself?"

"I'm not sure, but I think B.C. was tacked after the date." Bethany flopped down beside Madeline and picked up one of the two glasses of cinnamon-and-rosehip tea on the night table.

"Buy something bright. You have the coloring to carry it off. Hot pink or bright yellow."

"I was thinking about red." Long ago she had thrown away the red sundress she had been wearing the afternoon Justin had walked into her life. Did he remember anything about that day?

"Red would be beautiful. I've never seen you in red."

"Justin has."

"You're excited about this date, aren't you?"

"I might as well wear a neon sign on my chest. Nothing I feel is ever sacred." She sipped the spicy tea, letting it glide smoothly down her throat. "Sometimes I think that was one of the reasons Justin withdrew from me."

Madeline watched Bethany trying to talk nonchalantly about her feelings. The long fingers raking through her straight silky hair were only one of the signs that betrayed the depth of her emotion. "And what do you think at other times?"

"I think that he just never cared very much. That I was an enticing diversion."

"If I had to make a guess, I'd say it was the former." Madeline rose and took Bethany's glass and her own into the kitchen. Bethany followed her, watching the older woman wash and rinse the dishes.

"What makes you think so?"

"Well, he's a very private person. I think you probably scared him to death. You're so intense, so giving and so open. He probably didn't know what to do with you."

"All he had to do was love me, Madeline. I didn't ask him for anything else."

"To someone like Justin, honey, that's asking for everything."

I would give him everything in a moment, she thought. But that was a fact she didn't need to burden Madeline with. Instead she observed, "Maybe I should withdraw from him, pretend I'm not interested and play hard to get." She pulled herself up to her full five feet four inches and raised both eyebrows in a haughty expression. "Really, Justin," she drawled lazily, "must you be so demonstrative? I'm purrrfectly capable of holding my own hand."

"The real question is whether *you* are interested, isn't it?"

Joking about her feelings was not an art Bethany had developed to perfection. Madeline was ignoring her attempt to be playful and cutting right to the heart of the matter. The question was one that Bethany had been living with since the day Justin had stepped up to her table at the flea market.

And it was a question that had continued to saturate her existence as she and Justin had begun to resolve their differences. At first she had answered it by chastising herself for being so vulnerable as to even ask the question. Later she had stopped flagellating herself for normal feelings, trying to talk sense to her heart like a wise older sister. But the question would not go away. Finally, the night before, when she had awakened once again from the recurring dream of Justin dissolving in her arms, she knew that the answer to the question was a simple yes. She was still totally, completely and dangerously in love with Justin Dumontier.

"I still love him, Madeline. I wish I didn't, because I think I'm heading for heartbreak again." She screwed her face into a contortion usually seen only on the expressive faces of mimes. "That sounds like a country-and-western song title, doesn't it? One more member in that sorority of sentimental women who suffer from the disease of unrequited love."

Madeline watched the kaleidoscope of emotions flashing across Bethany's face, and she wanted to shield her from the pain that she might encounter again. It was difficult not to remember the stricken look that had been Bethany's only expression for the first year after Abby's birth. That heartsick girl had been a shadow of the cheerful, engaging adolescent Madeline had enjoyed teaching so much in high school. The experience with Justin had tamed some of the exuberant joy of living that Bethany had once shown. But in recent years she had developed a quieter maturity that was also appealing and real. "And what will happen to you, Beth, if Justin never returns your love?"

In answer Bethany asked, "Do you remember how completely shattered I was when I came here with Abby?" She watched Madeline. "You don't have to worry." She reached over and squeezed Madeline's hand. "I'll never be that way again."

"And what is the difference now?"

"I've changed, Madeline. I am stronger, more resilient—" she lifted her pointed chin a notch "—and more determined."

" 'Determined'?" Madeline's own face relaxed to light up in a slow grin.

"Determined. In the next few weeks Justin Dumontier isn't going to know what hit him. He may not recognize it yet, but that man is about to fall hard." Bethany polished her nails on the soft white T-shirt she was wearing, blowing on them once in imitation of someone who had just won a major battle. "I will not come out of this fight a loser. And you can quote me on that."

"I DON'T SEE WHY I can't go with you and Justin." Abby sat cross-legged on the bed, watching her mother dress in the red crepe dress she had bought that afternoon. The dress was such a major success on Bethany's petite figure that she was almost afraid to wear it. The silky material clung where it was supposed to cling, fell in folds where it was supposed to fold and dipped provocatively where it was supposed to provoke. Since it was still early enough in the year to be chilly at nighttime, Bethany had splurged on an embroidered Mexican shawl that picked up the bright red of the dress and added subtler shades of gold and green.

"I told you, you're going to your grandmother's house. She's cooking a special meal for you herself."

"Does she cook?"

"Yes, and Mrs. Waters is not going to be there tonight, so she's going to make everything herself."

"You and Justin don't want me."

Bethany remembered reading somewhere in one of the many parenting books she had digested early in her career as a mother that four was "an age of disequilibrium." It was a scientific way of saying that four-year-olds were very difficult to live with. Silently she counted the months to Abby's next birthday. Five was supposed to be a more balanced, cheerful age. "Go wash your face and hands, sweetheart. Even if you're not happy about it, your father and I are going out by ourselves. And you will be clean before you go to your grandmother's!"

Fortunately the apartment was so small that even with Abby dragging her feet, the little girl was not capable of delaying the four-yard walk to the bathroom long enough to keep them from getting ready on time. When Justin buzzed and Bethany pressed the button to let him into the courtyard, she and Abby were both waiting.

Justin's eyes traveled over Bethany slowly as he held out his arms to his daughter. Bethany had chosen to carry the shawl, a rather daring decision, considering that she felt exposed in the red dress. Modest enough on the hanger, on her slender body the dress revealed every asset she had to offer. Since the vivid coloring of her outfit required some additional color of her own to off-set it, her makeup was more dramatic, too. She had fastened her shining hair back on one side with a cloisonné comb, and she wore golden hoops in her ears. A spot check in the mirror before joining Justin in the courtyard had assured her that she looked her best. Justin's expression assured her of the same thing.

"You're more beautiful than any carnival queen I have ever known," he murmured, obviously referring to their conversation about social standing. It was like him to want to reassure her, and she felt a wave of love for this careful man who was so filled with feeling under-neath his elegant, formal manners.

"What about me?" said Abby with the unmistakable ring of jealousy in her high voice.

Far from being upset by the little girl's petulant tone, Justin focused his gaze on her with a wide smile. "You are absolutely gorgeous, just like you always are." Bethany could tell he was delighted that Abby wanted his undivided attention. It was one of many signs that their daughter was beginning to care deeply about her father.

"Can I go with you and mommy tonight, Justin?" Abby batted her long eyelashes at her father in an un-conscious imitation of a soap-opera vamp.

Before Bethany could reiterate that Abby was going to her grandmother's house, Justin was shaking his head firmly. "No, your grandmother would be very dis-appointed, and your mother and I need some time alone together tonight." He looked at Bethany as if he were afraid she had promised the little girl she could accompany them.

"Abby, I already told you that," Bethany admonished.

"Your grandmother is making red beans and rice with sausage just for you," Justin announced, tickling Abby under the chin.

"Hot sausage?"

Justin nodded.

"Okay, I guess I'll go. I like hot sausage."

"You're raising a real native, Bethany," Justin said with a laugh as the three of them walked toward Justin's car.

"You say that with a trace of concern, native."

The drive to St. Charles was short and lively, with Abby contentedly bouncing on the seat behind them. For once Mrs. Dumontier was the picture of a storybook grandmother, with an apron and a trace of flour on her nose. Abby immediately forgot to look disgruntled, and ran off through the big house with her proud grandmother close behind.

Justin turned the car back toward the Quarter, and they parked on a quiet side street just off of Royal. Taking Bethany's hand, he strolled leisurely with her toward the Restaurant Antoine, a spot that he had selected. It had rained earlier in the afternoon, and the setting sun caught the little puddles of water in the nooks and crannies of the old buildings, creating the sparkle of a thousand brilliant diamonds. Bethany squeezed Justin's hand with a shiver of appreciation. When they reached the restaurant they bypassed the line standing in the street, to be ushered in immediately by the maître d', who obviously was expecting them.

"I've never been here before, Justin." Bethany looked through the gracious old rooms with delight. They were seated in one of the interior dining rooms, and Bethany reveled in the atmosphere of dark wood, muted lighting and exquisite service. This was Antoine's, where secrets had been told, business had been conducted, presidents had dined and promises had been sealed for over a century and a half.

"I thought you were going to give me a French Quarter tour, not vice versa." Justin had chosen to sit beside her, not across the table, and his proximity added the correct touch of intimacy to the atmosphere.

"My tour wouldn't cost you a thing," she joked, "and it's strictly a daytime affair. I hardly venture out at nighttime."

"How do you spend your evenings?" he asked casually, looking up from the menu to watch her face.

"The way most single parents do. I take care of Abby. Or working. Occasionally Madeline relieves me and I go out to dinner with friends or go to the club where Lamar plays."

"Abby really destroyed your freedom, didn't she?" He was looking at his menu again, and Bethany could not discern what emotion lay behind the question.

"Everything in life is a trade-off. I've never regretted having her." *She's part of us both,* she thought, *how could I ever wish she hadn't been born.*

"It sounds like having any personal life has been difficult." The tone was again noncommittal, but charged with some hidden question.

" 'Personal life'?"

This time he lifted his head and met her eyes, his statement clear and to the point. "It sounds like it's been very difficult to become involved with any men.''

The personal nature of the statement startled her. She tried to imagine the Justin from her past saying such a thing. Hedging, she said simply, ''Well, it hasn't made it too easy.''

A waiter appeared at their table to take their order. Bethany remembered enough French from college to decipher the elaborate menu, but the choices were too varied for her to make an easy decision. ''I'll never decide. You order for us, please.''

In flawless French Justin ordered a full array from the menu, choosing a variety of well-known and more obscure dishes. He included Oysters Rockefeller, Restaurant Antoine's own original creation and enough other seafood dishes, including alligator soup with sherry, to make the meal a New Orleans extravaganza.

''Is someone else joining us?'' Bethany asked after the waiter disappeared.

''Not unless you invited them.'' Casually he took her hand, lacing his fingers with hers. ''It may sound like a lot of food, but I seem to remember that you could eat any two-hundred-pound athlete under the table.''

With awe she realized that every place each of his fingers touched seemed to have a life of its own. His hand was a conduit of electricity, stimulating each cell it explored. If she had any doubts about her recent decision to go after Justin, they were wiped away like chalk drawings in a rainstorm. The years of separation had done nothing to her basic feelings of love and desire for this man. No one had ever affected her the way that he did, and she knew instinctively that no one ever would.

''Is something wrong? Am I hurting you?''

She realized that she had been staring, entranced, at their entwined hands. "No," she said softly. "The only time you ever hurt me was when you stopped holding me."

"I never meant to hurt you." Raising her hand to his lips, he kissed each fingertip in a public demonstration of emotion that confounded her. Never in those weeks long ago when they had been together almost constantly had he ever shown his desire for her in front of others. Except for the time he had kissed her under the mimosa tree on the Florida State campus, he had never done anything more overt in public than hold her hand.

"I believe you. I never felt that you set out to bring me pain. In your way, I think you tried to let me down easy." An involuntary shiver coursed through her as he kissed the sensitive skin of her palm before he lowered her hand to the table. "We never talked about commitment. I had no reason to expect anything permanent from you. I was just very naive."

"Innocent, would be a better choice of words. Beautiful, desirable, incredibly warm, you were everything any man would want." His voice was low, and the faint Southern accent she always found to be so charming became stronger as he talked while staring at their hands on the table. "I had never met anyone like you. You were like a potent drug I couldn't get enough of. At first I thought that my fascination would wear off after we spent more time together. Instead it increased. When I was with you I felt out of control and vulnerable. For the first time I knew what it was like to be bewitched."

Like boxers slowly circling a well-lit ring, they were getting closer to revealing their feelings and establishing motives for their behavior of half a decade ago. But the effort was costing them both something, and Bethany could feel her heart beating unevenly. Hearing Justin's explanation was not going to be easy. In fact she wondered, in a flash of insight, if she had left Tallahassee without confronting him with the reality of her pregnancy because she had been terrified to hear what he really felt for her. "You don't have to go on, Justin. It was a long time ago," she said at the same time that she chastised herself for her lack of courage.

Their appetizers arrived: Oysters Rockefeller and Shrimp Remoulade. They were two of her favorites, but she found that her appetite was on hold for the moment. She took a deep breath and said evenly, "I was wrong. You do have to go on. I need to know why you distanced yourself from me. Was it something I did?"

"In a way it was. You made me feel things I didn't want to feel. I had my life planned out in detail and it didn't include what was happening." The food sat in front of them, but he continued to hold her hand, gripping it tighter than before.

"What was happening? I need to know."

"For a long time I couldn't identify what I felt. I knew I wanted you, that I couldn't get enough of being with you. When I left Tallahassee, I told myself that after a time I'd be able to put it all in perspective. I was sure that once I could think clearly again, once you weren't around to touch and to hold, I could make the right decision for both of us. Instead being away from you made me realize my true feelings."

The image of a fisherman trying to open an oyster on the chance that it might contain a pearl came into her mind. Justin was not having an easy time letting go of his thoughts, and Bethany staunchly fought back the desire to pry them out of him. Completely eloquent in debate or ordinary conversation, he was extraordinarily uncomfortable talking about his feelings and she suffered silently at the pain it was costing them both.

"When I realized that I loved you you were gone," he said finally.

A shudder went through her, and she knew that it had been communicated to Justin. She, who had learned to be patient in all the difficult years with her mother, had not been patient enough. She, who had learned to have faith in others despite the absence of people to have faith in within her own life, had not had enough faith. Five years ago when they truly needed each other, when their baby daughter had been growing slowly inside her womb, she had given up on love and disappeared from Justin's life. "I always thought you loved me. I was just in too much pain to wait any longer to find out."

"You must think I'm an emotional zombie, an unfeeling corpse ripe for a little New Orleans voodoo." Perhaps his words were intended to be light, but pain was rampant beneath them.

"I think," she said carefully, swallowing the lump in her throat that was condensed tears, "that perhaps neither of us was mature enough to deserve the love we had for each other. I had so many needs of my own, and you evidently had so many concerns to overcome, that perhaps all the love in the world wouldn't have made the difference for us."

"I told myself the same thing when I discovered that you had left Tallahassee." He relaxed his grip on her hand, pulling his fingers from hers to make a tent beneath his chin. "I went to Hawaii for a conference. I had been attempting for weeks to pull back from you and from our relationship in order to try and see everything more clearly, and I remember being grateful to the conference for providing me with a diversion.''

''That must have been about the time you stopped writing.''

''I didn't even want to sit down and think about you long enough to put pen to paper, I was so confused. When I got to Honolulu I threw myself into the tourist routine, thinking that would help. But everywhere I went I kept seeing these gorgeous women with waist-length black hair, and I could only think of you.'' Justin's voice was strained, as if his look into the past were cutting away a part of him. ''Finally, one night I took a walk along the beach, trying to come to terms with myself and with you. I walked for hours, and when I realized the sun was coming up, I knew what I'd been fighting all along.''

''That's when you realized you loved me?'' she said in a tiny voice she almost didn't recognize.

He nodded. ''I went back to my hotel and called you, but there was no answer. I tried all day, and finally I changed my reservation and took the next plane I could get to Florida. Before I left I went to a tourist-trap gift shop and bought you a red muumuu. I remember I was going to tell you that you'd look wonderful barefoot and pregnant in it. Pretty ironic,'' he choked, lapsing into silence.

''I was gone when you got to Tallahassee.''

He nodded again. ''Yes, you were. Gone without a trace. I checked with everybody that I remembered you knew. I haunted the art building, talking to professors, but no one had any idea where you'd gone. You shocked everybody when you withdrew from school, throwing away your scholarship. Finally I managed to find out your father's address."

"And he didn't tell you what had happened?" Bethany couldn't believe that her father would have kept the news a secret from her baby's father. Chief Petty Officer Walker was much more the type to enforce a shotgun wedding.

"He was gone. Off to sea when I finally tracked him down."

"I was so ashamed," she said in the tiny voice. "Not of being pregnant, but of falling for a man I thought didn't really care for me. Instead of a scarlet A I felt I deserved an F for foolish."

"I was the fool," he said. "I thought I had all the time in the world to make decisions about our relationship. Can you imagine my conceit? I was so sure of you that I didn't even bother to express what I was feeling. If I had just told you that I cared about you but that I thought we ought to spend some time apart to think about our future, you would never have left Tallahassee without telling me about the baby."

Bethany's hair swirled around her face, threatening to dislodge the comb she had so carefully placed there. "We can't second-guess now, Justin. Neither of us will ever know how things would have turned out had either of us been more honest."

They had chosen the perfect place for their discussion. Their waiter seemed to be perfectly attuned to their mood, and they had suffered no disturbances as they'd bared their souls. Now, however, the young man came to their table with a concerned expression.

"May I get you something else? Perhaps you would like to try a different appetizer?" Justin and Bethany looked at the plates in front of them filled with untouched food.

Justin shook his head, and as if on signal, they began to eat in silence. The food was marvelous, with all the subtle flavors of fine Creole cuisine. Here, as in the other famous and not-so-famous restaurants of the cosmopolitan city, the food was a blend of French, Spanish, and African, and native foods and spices. It was uniquely New Orleans. They finished the first course, sharing tidbits from each other's plates, still without talking. For the first time in the history of their relationship, they had been completely honest about their feelings, and the experience seemed to have opened up new and subtler avenues of communication for them.

"There's one more thing I'd like to know," Bethany asked as they waited for their soup to arrive. "When you discovered I was gone, what did you think was my reason for leaving?"

"I thought you had probably got involved with someone else and that you didn't tell me because you were embarrassed."

"And that's why you didn't make more of an effort to track me down." All the pieces of the puzzle were complete. He had been in love with her, but his own pride had kept him from doing more to find her.

"If I had even suspected that the person you were involved with was my baby," he said in a voice heavy with emotion, "then I would have torn the country apart to find you. But I never thought of that as a possibility."

Their soup was set in front of them, and as before, they ate in silence, assimilating the story of their past with each spoonful of the well-seasoned liquid. Finishing first, Bethany watched him abstractedly finishing his. This man, the only man she had ever loved, had once felt the same wonderful feeling for her. It was like him to choose this time and place to tell her that. The atmosphere precluded any emotional displays on either of their parts; no hand wringing, floods of tears, or temper tantrums would be appropriate at Restaurant Antoine. Only quiet explanations, careful expression of feeling was acceptable here.

The choice of this time and this place to set the record straight was a signal of something more, too. Bethany knew instinctively that in this safe place it would be impossible to carry the conversation one step further. This was not the right moment to discuss what their present feelings for each other were. And she was absolutely sure that Justin had planned it that way. The careful, dignified atmosphere surrounding them was the perfect extension of Justin Dumontier's own privacy.

"Is our past really behind us now?" It was as close as she could come to signaling that she wanted to deal with more than the past from now on. "I'd like it to be finished."

"I would, too." And then he looked at her in such a way as to make her heart drop to her toes. "It's been between us too long," he said, his midnight eyes flashing messages she was afraid to read. "I don't want anything between us anymore."

His words were a magic incantation, a charm that seemed to set them free. Bethany felt a giddiness akin to emotional hang gliding. They were free, free from the haunting memories, the pain of rejection, the tenseness of unrevealed emotions. They had come out the other side of the experience older, wiser and together.

The rest of the sumptuous meal passed quickly, for

with the benediction to the pain of their past came the beginning of a return to the easy, natural relationship they had once had together. For the first time they both felt free to ask questions and to share information about the ordinary details of the past five years. Bethany questioned Justin about his life in Chicago and about the job he had left to come back to New Orleans.

"At first," he said, his eyes warm and relaxed, "I just planned to come back and close out my father's share of the practice. But there was a lot more to do than I had anticipated, and I finally had to make a commitment to stay for several months. Luckily I had all kinds of vacation time coming to me in Chicago and I wasn't in the middle of something so big that it couldn't be turned over to another attorney. I'm scheduled to go back next month."

"You miss it, don't you?" Thrilled to see him without his guard up, she was reveling in the chance to make just casual conversation with him.

"I haven't had time to miss it. I've been too busy with the firm and with you and Abby."

"I remember how much you liked being involved in all those big cases, though. Didn't you tell me once you thought you'd die if all you had to do all day were real-estate transactions and tax law?"

"Actually, my father's firm has just begun to get involved in some pretty interesting cases. They've done very little criminal law, but one of the junior partners has taken some cases recently. The firm is trying to make it worth my while to stay and take charge of an important client they've been asked to defend."

Bethany's heart missed a beat. Justin in New Orleans longer? The idea was so appealing she had to use every bit of willpower to appear casual. "Would one case be interesting enough?"

"Actually, I'm finding some of the more mundane cases interesting, too. I always thought that divorce and custody cases were so much grist for the mill. But now I have a new empathy for what my clients are going through."

"I can understand that."

He smiled warmly. "I've needed to sensitize myself to the pains of everyday existence. There may not be anything earthshaking about this kind of law practice, but it feels important to me when I do it. I never would have thought that was possible."

"I feel so frivolous in comparison." The combination of the good food, the one glass of wine she had allowed herself and a large dose of peace of mind ran through her in a burst of happiness, and she was sure that she was lit up like the sky on the Fourth of July. "Making masks feels important. I love what I do, but it certainly isn't contributing anything to society."

"I suspect that it contributes a great deal. Beauty, gaiety, drama—they're all important. It suits you to be a mask maker, and from what I can tell, you put yourself into everything you make."

The unfished-for compliment was the grand finale of her fireworks display; she couldn't hold back her exuberance another moment. Leaning toward him, she ran her finger down the side of his face and followed it with a kiss on his clean-shaven cheek. The touch and smell of his warm, spicy skin sent a shimmering rush of blood through her body. "You've always known just how to make me feel good," she said more breathlessly than she had intended.

"Let's get out of here," he said, dropping some bills on the table and taking her hand.

The night was star sprinkled, with the old-fashioned lamps in the street sending out a smooth golden glow to surround them as they walked for blocks along the flag-stone sidewalks. Justin held her close to him, his arm around her waist as they drifted from street to street, en-joying the warm sweet-smelling air and the crowds of merrymakers who were beginning to come out to cele-brate the Mardi Gras season.

Banners of green, gold and purple, the official New Orleans Mardi Gras colors, hung from balconies and doorways, and shop windows were decorated with bal-loons and clowns, beads and doubloons. There were masks displayed, too—rubber masks from Taiwan, cer-amic masks of clowns and masks on sticks to be held up as temporary disguises. Occasionally there were handmade masks, and Bethany proudly showed Justin a display win-dow with masks she had made and sold the year before.

"I love this time of year," she said, her happiness reflected in her voice. "The rest of the world has no idea what it is missing."

"You almost convince me that I could learn to like carnival," Justin answered, settling her in the crook of his arm on a bench overlooking the Mississippi River. They had drifted to the Moonwalk across from Jackson Square and were sitting peacefully watching the lights glimmering across from them on the west bank of the river.

"I can't believe it. Don't tell me you're one of those native New Orleanians who would fly to Timbuktu every year on Twelfth Night and return on Ash Wednes-day if they could."

"I moved to Chicago, didn't I?"

"Mmm.... You need carnival, Justin. It's just what the doctor ordered." She was only half joking. The freedom to let go and celebrate with few inhibitions was foreign to Justin's nature, even though it was an integral part of the culture he had grown up in. Somehow she knew that if he could learn to be less careful, his life would be happier.

"Analysis from the beautiful, mask maker?"

"Before I can make the masks, I have to understand what goes on underneath them. I'm just presenting you with valuable insight." She turned her head toward him, to discover that he was looking at her. Their faces were inches apart, and she held her breath as his mouth descended to meet hers. Justin's kiss was hungry, slowly devouring her with a steady aching pressure that threatened to eat into her very soul. Her hands tangled in his black hair, and she fingered the silky strands as he deepened the kiss.

Finally he pulled away just far enough to ask, "And what do you need?"

It was the perfect time to tell him that she needed only him to make her life complete. The confessions of the evening had convinced her that secrets between them could only be destructive. But taking the ultimate step and admitting to him that she still loved him was one confession too many to make. "I think I need another kiss," she said, instead. And he complied with her request, holding her tightly against his chest until she could feel the warmth of him burning through the thin material of her dress.

The walk back to her apartment was long and purposely slow, as if they could draw the evening out into infinity by their reluctant pace. Bethany quietly basked in the glow of Justin's kisses and his revelation of the love he had once felt for her. Silently they climbed into the Mercedes parked in front of Life's Illusions to drive to Justin's house to pick up their daughter.

"You know this is not how I want the evening to end, don't you?" Justin said with husky promise in his voice.

"I think there will be other evenings," she said carefully. And she knew that if they could strengthen the tentative bonds they were forming, that someday there might be even more than that.

CHAPTER TWELVE

THE POUNDING THAT ECHOED through the tiny apartment did not stop when Bethany pulled the pillow over her head sleepily. The bed springs creaked with a vengeance and the unmistakable jolt of a small body on top of hers forced her to reluctantly remove the pillow. "What is going on, Abby? It's the middle of the night."

"It's not. Lamar is at the door."

Yawning, Bethany began the slow process of sitting up and stretching. When one eye was wide open and the second was on its way, she realized that Abby was right. Sunlight streamed in through the large windows, filtered only by sheer curtains, and Lamar's voice at the door sounded entirely too cheerful to be anything other than a good-morning greeting. "Let him in, sweetheart." She followed Abby to the bedroom door, closing it behind the little girl, and pulled on softly faded jeans and her white T-shirt. Running a comb through her hair, she crept into the living room, still blinking sleepily.

"*Cherie,* why are you so tired, you?"

"I stayed up late last night finishing masks. Why are you here so early, you?" she responded in her best imitation of his Cajun speech.

"I bring an invitation from *maman* and the rest of the family, particularly my adoring brother Celin."

Bethany waved him toward the sofa and stumbled

into the kitchen. "Considering that Celin is only sixteen, I guess it's safe to ask what the invitation is for."

"*Maman* is tired of not seeing me, she says. Everyone is coming up for a crawfish boil today, and you and Abby are to be the guests of honor." Lamar stood in the kitchen door, watching her make the coffee, while he leisurely ate a banana from the fruit bowl in front of him.

"Where on earth are you going to have a crawfish boil? Your apartment is only large enough to hold you, and if you eat any more of those bananas, possibly not even you."

Lamar grinned as he reached for another banana. "The park. They're going over to Audubon Park to set up now. *Maman*, Celin, my brother Aldus and his wife, Celestine, and their three children are already here. More will come later. You will come, heh?"

"When?" Mentally she ticked off all the things that needed to be done that day. Masks that needed to be completed, a trip to the grocery store to stock up for the week and to replace the bananas, a two-hour shift at Life's Illusions until Valerie could come and take over. There might be room for some fun, too.

"Come anytime. We'll eat around three o'clock or so. *Réellement*, we will eat all day—the crawfish, they will be eaten at four."

"We'll walk down to canal and catch the streetcar as soon as I can get finished here. I can't wait to see your family again."

Lamar finished off the last banana with a flourish. "Perhaps your Justin would like to come, heh?"

"Lamar, he is not my Justin," she said too quickly, and then blushed at Lamar's laughter.

"I see the way he looks at you. Justin Dumontier would like to be your Justin."

"And how about you and Danielle de Bessonet? I've never seen two people get along better and faster than you did," she retorted.

"Judge for yourself. She is coming to meet *maman* today."

Bethany looked at the big Cajun man. As much as she teased him about his appetite, he was solid muscle, a veritable giant. She noticed that for the first time since she had known him, the long beard had been trimmed so that it was no longer scraggly. His hair was still long, but neatly so, and his face radiated the glow of a man with someone special on his mind. Pierced by the sweet pain of concern, she stood on tiptoe and kissed him on his lips, which were now much easier to find. "You watch out, you. Make sure she is special enough."

"*Mais, non,* Beth. Choosing is for robots. Falling? Falling is for lovers."

He reached out for her and she snuggled against him. It had always been this way between them. Friends, confidants, givers of comfort, neither had ever expected anything else from their relationship. Perhaps if she had never met Justin Dumontier she would have had a different place in her heart for Lamar, but Justin had firmly occupied the place she had reserved for love. Lamar, perhaps sensing this from the first, had asked for nothing more than friendship.

"Of course you're right. If I could have chosen with my eyes open I would have married you myself. Danielle is a lucky woman. I hope she'll let us continue to be friends."

"Danielle will learn that a Cajun man does what he wants."

"Just the way your brother Aldus does what he wants? Only as long as Celestine tells him he's allowed."

"Ah, that one," he said, his hands cutting through the air in an arc. "He is still so in love that he would tie her shoes every morning if she asked him to."

"I'll be sure to tell Danielle not to buy any sneakers," she teased.

Abby, who had escaped to the courtyard looking for Bum, came running back into the apartment. "Bum is out there with a skinny black cat and they were kissing. Yuck!"

"Ah, springtime," said Lamar, kissing his fingers in a classic Maurice Chevalier gesture. With a crushing hug to Abby and a quick wave to Bethany, he was gone.

"I love Lamar, mommy," Abby said, watching from the tall windows as the big man disappeared down the sidewalk. "When I grow up I'm going to marry him."

"I love him, too. And I think you're the only person I know who is special enough for him," Bethany said, coming up behind the little girl to give her a hug.

"Bethany?" A deep voice sounded behind her from the door, which Lamar had left open.

"Justin," she said, feeling a gush of warmth bubble like a natural heated spring inside her. "Please come in."

"Was I interrupting anything?" She detected a stiffness in his tone that she couldn't identify, and she straightened and turned toward him.

"No, of course not. Come have some coffee and cereal with us."

Justin stepped inside, carrying a large box that he set down with a bang on the counter. "No, thank you," he said formally.

Wrinkling her brow, she stood, hands on hips, trying

to figure out what was wrong. There had been so many times that she had tried to understand what he was feeling and so many times that she had failed. "Would you please tell me what the problem is?" she asked with a hint of exasperation. "It's definitely too early in the morning to be reading your mind."

The expression on his strong features changed to one of mocking surprise. "I feel as though I interrupted something I shouldn't have interrupted."

It was an answer, albeit not a very clear one. "Sometimes, Justin Dumontier, I feel as if I'm trying to transcribe a foreign language when I talk to you. What did you interrupt?"

"A rather touching scene where you and my daughter proclaimed your love for that Cajun Goliath, whom I saw leaving your apartment at this tender hour."

"What's a Goliath, mommy?" asked Abby with interest.

"You can see I've been neglecting her religious training, as well as compromising her innocent morals by allowing Lamar to visit with us while I made coffee," she said dryly. Turning to Abby, she answered the little girl's question. "Goliath is a giant from the Bible."

"Like Jean Lafitte?"

"Sort of. Do you suppose that Bum still has his girlfriend here?" Bethany asked.

"I'll go see. How long do I have to be gone?"

Justin and Bethany burst into uneasy laughter at the little girl's wisdom. "Not very long, sweetheart." *Just long enough for me to tell your daddy where he can put his sanctimonious attitude,* Bethany steamed.

"I'm sorry, Bethany. I had no right to be upset about who you have in your apartment," Justin said after

Abby disappeared down the steps. "I've got no claims on you, do I?"

And if you don't, it's your own fault. "That's right," she answered out loud. "And I won't have you ruining Abby's relationship with Lamar, either. She's crazy about him, and there's nothing in the world that's wrong with that."

"And you? Are you crazy about him, too? Do you really love him?" His eyes were cold.

For a moment she was tempted to say that she was hopelessly in love with Lamar. It was a childish flash of anger at the question he had no business asking. But the only lies she had ever told him had brought her untold misery. "I love him, yes. Lamar is the brother I never had. Lamar's family has helped fill the place inside me that my own family was never capable of filling. From Lamar and the rest of the Robicheaux clan I have received the gift of being loved just because I am me." The entire panorama of her miserable childhood lay before her as she tried to make him understand. There was no pleading in her tone, only facts that needed to be stated.

"When I was a kid, Justin, nobody ever loved me with that unqualified emotion parents are supposed to feel for their children. I spent my childhood by myself or taking care of my mother, who was totally incapable of giving me anything in return. I figured out early that the only way to get others to pay attention to me was to give and to give and to give." She watched his eyes cloud over, revealing, not hiding, his concern for her, but she went on.

"I don't mean to make it sound as if it were all bad. Lots of people did notice me, and some of them gave me what they could, like Madeline and like the family who took me in so I could finish high school after my mother died. But it's taken me all these years to discover that I'm intrinsically worthwhile. Lamar and the Robicheaux family have helped me see that. They like me because I'm me. And I love them for that.''

"I always felt that about you," he said softly as he moved toward her, enfolding her in his arms and massaging the stiffness from her neck. "I wanted to tell you so many times that you didn't have to work for my love, that you had it without even lifting a finger.''

The anger drained out of her like a tidal wave rushing out to sea, leaving her poised on shifting sands. "I'm not sure I can stand any more revelations right now. I still haven't adjusted to last night's." She could feel Justin's lips in her hair and his thumbs caressing the back of her neck as his fingers entwined in her hair. He murmured something that she was certain she was not supposed to interpret, and finally he released her.

"No more revelations, then." His smile was disarming with its relaxed openness.

"I love it when I can figure you out," she said impulsively. "When you're not hiding your feelings behind an impassive mask." She pulled back and looked at him with a calculating eye. "I'm going to make you something for Mardi Gras. Something secretive and mysterious, dignified and elegant, the epitome of Justin Dumontier.''

"It's been years since I participated in Mardi Gras, and I never went in costume, not even as a child.''

"The Creole Spirit," she continued as if she hadn't heard. "I'm going to make you a mask and a costume, too.''

"But you can't make me wear them," he teased,

reaching out to smooth a strand of her hair back from her face.

"It will be so wonderful you won't be able to resist."

"Well, I have something you won't be able to resist, either, although it's not for Mardi Gras." Walking to the doorway, he called to Abby. When she arrived he motioned to the box on the counter. "This is for you and your mother. Go ahead and open it."

The little girl struggled with the string tied around the large rectangular box, finally slipping it off the edges. Inside, nestled in white tissue paper, were two burgundy running suits trimmed in charcoal gray. There were soft charcoal T-shirts to wear with them. Abby pulled hers out and pushed the box to Bethany, who held hers up to her cheek. The material was thick and fleecy and as soft as velvet. "They're beautiful, Justin. There's just one problem. We don't run."

"That oversight can be remedied. Why don't you both go put them on?"

"I'll wear it, but you can't make me run in it," she teased.

"You won't be able to resist."

"I don't have any running shoes," she shot back as she closed the bedroom door.

"That's only because I have to take you both with me to fit you for the shoes." Clearly, he wasn't going to give up.

They emerged a few minutes later looking like marathon finalists. Justin nodded in approval. "They will do very nicely," he said as his eyes lingered on the soft curves under Bethany's T-shirt. "Shall we go for the shoes now?"

"Oh, I can't Justin. I've got to finish masks, go to the

grocery store, work downstairs for a couple of hours.'' She remembered Lamar's invitation. ''And then we're all invited to a crawfish boil at Audubon Park with the Robicheaux family.''

''I'm invited, too?'' he asked in surprise.

''Absolutely. The Cajun Goliath requested that I bring you.''

''What time is this party?''

''We can get there anytime before four.''

Justin ruffled Abby's hair as she wrapped herself around his legs. ''I'll pick you up at two to go shopping for groceries and shoes. Will that give you enough time to do everything else?''

''Why don't you eat breakfast here before you leave,'' she said, nodding her answer.

Only Justin didn't leave. As the morning slipped by they both seemed to find excuses to prolong his stay. Bethany introduced him to the art of mask making and the hot-glue machine, and Justin practiced with leftover feathers, creating a collage of mismatched colors and textures on a plaster gauze form she had decided not to use. In an attempt to hide blobs of glue that had landed in the wrong place, Justin had added great clumps of sequins everywhere he could. The result was hideously gaudy, but Abby fell in love with the mask and demanded that it be given to her.

When it was time for Bethany to open the shop, Justin insisted on coming down to help her, and the three of them stood behind the counter, scaring all the less-confident customers away. Seeing the problem, Justin pretended to be a customer himself, complimenting Bethany on everything about the shop each time someone came through the door.

A pair of old ladies came in to buy masks for their grandchildren, and were so impressed with Justin's enthusiasm they bought masks for themselves, too. One of the women caught sight of Justin's creation behind the counter, where Abby had insisted on placing it, and tried to buy it for a friend who lived out of state. Abby refused to part with it, and Bethany had to bite her lip not to laugh at the disappointment on Justin's face at missing his first sale.

By far the most enjoyable part of the morning was watching Justin, relaxed and humorous, having such a good time. His face was unlined, mobile with expression and smiling. His powerful body, often reminiscent of a tightly coiled spring, was loose and liquid in its athletic grace. When Valerie came in to relieve them, it was with genuine regret that Bethany realized the morning had ended.

Motioning Bethany back into the shop as the three of them left by the back door, Valerie rolled her eyes at Justin's back. "If we were fishin', girl, I'd say that one was a keeper." She laughed at Bethany's contented grin. "Looks like I'm not the only one who noticed, huh?"

They stopped by the apartment long enough to snack. Abby and Bethany cleaned up as Justin brought the Mercedes to the front of the shop. Their trip to the grocery store was uneventful, except that two attractive female acquaintances of Justin's stopped to exclaim over Abby and look curiously at Bethany. The shoe store was so crowded that Justin himself ended up fitting them for shoes, tying Bethany's himself to be sure they were the correct size. Her tinkling laughter as she silently recalled Lamar's joke about his brother Aldus obviously mystified him, but for once she was in no hurry to explain.

Since they had to pass Justin's house to get to Audubon Park, Justin insisted on stopping and changing into his running suit and shoes. When he emerged to join them in the sun-room, where they were sitting with Mrs. Dumontier, Bethany was struck with an overwhelming awareness of his masculinity. The slate-gray suit clung to his firm, muscular body, emphasizing his long strong legs and muscled thighs. The vee-neck black T-shirt he wore with it stretched tightly across his broad chest, revealing his well-shaped torso. Her impressions weren't lost on him, and he laughed and teased her for gawking. Mrs. Dumontier just smiled and commented on how much hotter it seemed all of a sudden.

"What's your mother going to think after your comment about my professional artistic appraisal of your body?" Bethany chastised him when they were on their way again.

"I guess she'll think that neither one of us is oblivious to the other." He turned for a second and flashed her one of his rare grins. "What did you want her to think?"

"You're impossible."

"She knows that better than anyone."

Audubon Park was 240 acres of green grass, huge trees and blue water inhabited by indulged ducks. Unfortunately Bethany had neglected to find out what section of the sprawling acreage was hosting the Robicheaux crawfish boil, and they drove the entire perimeter of the park before discovering the Cajun encampment on the shores of a lagoon nestled in the center. Parking as close as they could, Justin helped

Bethany out of the car, and they both jumped back as Abby sped past them on her way to the lively gathering.

"I thought you said she didn't run. That child should be in the Crescent City Classic," Justin said as he casually locked hands with Bethany.

If they had expected a small family gathering with only Lamar's closest relatives, they were completely mistaken. To Bethany it seemed that the entire Robicheaux clan from little towns up and down Bayou Lafourche, southwest of New Orleans, were there to celebrate. In fact, there were relatives she had never met in her own frequent travels to the bayou to visit with Lamar's family.

There were tiny Robicheaux in playpens under the spreading oak trees. There were slightly larger Robicheaux, who immediately captured Abby and added her to their frantic games. There were teenage Robicheaux, teasing and flirting with one another, distant cousins that they were. And there were adult Robicheaux, drinking, playing the Cajun card game *bourée* at card tables and gossiping. Of course, not all of them were Robicheaux. In fact, Bethany had a sneaking suspicion that some of the people there weren't even from Bayou Lafourche, but instead were onlookers who had been invited to join in the fun.

Lamar's mother, Vertalée Robicheaux, who was never called anything except *maman*, even by nonfamily members, came forth to greet them. A tall, dark-haired woman with just a touch of silver in her long coiled hair, *maman* was the prototype of the Gallic matriarch. Her face was wreathed in smiles as she said, "Ah, Beth. You come as I knew you would." The two women hugged affectionately. "I tell Lamar not to come unless he gets you to say yes."

"I would never miss a chance to see you." Bethany

stretched her hand to Justin and pulled him forward to introduce him. Mrs. Robicheaux's snapping black eyes made a thorough sweep of him from toes to hair before nodding her approval.

"I see now why Lamar brings that other woman with him today. You will be married soon, heh?"

Bethany laughed shakily. "I'm afraid not. Justin is Abby's father, and we are..." She searched helplessly for a word. "We are friends."

"Yes, it is easy to tell he is Abby's father, him. But friends?" She laughed good-naturedly. "Friends do not make babies together. When the time comes to marry, you come to my church. We have a wedding you will never forget."

There was no time to gauge Justin's reaction to the woman's words. They were caught up in a melee of introductions that soon separated them. Picnic tables groaned with mountains of food, a prelude only to the crawfish that were to be served soon. Bethany found herself eating *boudin*, a sausage containing pork, pork liver and rice, which was a Cajun specialty. There were mountains of raw oysters and pink spicy shrimp. A kettle with only a trace of thick brown-and-green soup testified that once seafood gumbo had also been available.

The Cajuns, or Acadians as they were officially referred to, had come to Louisiana after their expulsion from their colony in Nova Scotia in 1755. A hearty people well-known for their endurance under the worst of circumstances, they thrived along the bayous of Louisiana, absorbing other ethnic groups, who became "Cajun," too. When they discovered that apples, from which they made hard cider, would not bear fruit in the semitropical climate of their new home, they embraced beer as a substitute. Today the beer flowed freely, washing down the spicy food.

"Hello, Beth." Bethany, who had been having a spirited conversation with Lamar's brother Celin, an adolescent with a flattering crush on her, turned to see Danielle. She was dressed in a simple buttercup-yellow dress with sensible shoes, and her blond hair was pulled back in a braid. Nothing could disguise the woman's delicate loveliness, but today she looked very much as if she belonged in the group of picnickers.

"Well, hello, Danielle. Are you having a good time?" At Bethany's words, Celin, used to gossiping women, rolled his eyes and edged away toward a group of teenagers lounging beside the lagoon.

"I'm having a wonderful time. Everyone here is so nice. Imagine coming from a family like this." Danielle looked around wistfully.

"They really are something, aren't they?" Bethany mused out loud. "But you have lots of family, too, don't you?"

Danielle nodded, seemingly lost in thought. "My family isn't the same, though. They expect so much out of me. I was always supposed to be something. Do you know what I mean?"

Bethany was surprised at Danielle's honesty. "I think I do. The Robicheaux are easy just to be yourself with."

"My father is a lot like Justin's was." She turned to Bethany. "Did you ever get to know Mr. Dumontier very well?"

Bethany realized that Danielle wasn't aware she had never had any contact with Justin's family. "I didn't know him at all," she said carefully.

"He was a real bear, or so I've heard. I didn't know

him very well myself. But after he and Louise lost their daughter, he went on some kind of campaign to make Justin into the perfect son. He was always after him to achieve this, achieve that. I guess Justin finally rebelled and left home to get away from all that pressure."

"I wasn't aware of any of that," Bethany said, shocked by the revelation.

"My father's not that bad. Both my parents have pushed me very hard to be a social success, sort of the stereotyped society debutante. It's been hard to have any life of my own, but I plan to make up for that." Bethany watched Danielle's eyes search for Lamar in the crowd.

"Danielle," she said impulsively, "don't make Lamar a test case for your independence. He's too special to be used like that."

To her credit, Danielle didn't even flinch. "I can see why you might be worried," she said, turning her attention to Bethany's face. "But you don't have to be concerned. If my parents made Lamar king of carnival and they were serving him on a silver platter with their best china, I'd still be crazy about him. He is very special."

She meant it, and Bethany knew it. Pointing toward the pond, Bethany gave her blessing to the strange union when she said, "Then go get him. He's right over there."

Danielle walked toward the lagoon, and Bethany turned to find herself face to face with Justin. "I missed you," he murmured against her ear. "What were you and Danielle gossiping about so seriously?"

"Love, parents, silver platters. What have you been doing?"

"Playing *bourée* with Uncle Cyprien and friends."

He gestured to a card table surrounded with rowdy old men. "I barely escaped with my life."

"Let's go for a walk," she said, taking his arm.

"No, for a run," he advised her. "There's a track that runs all the way around this pond. I'll see if Abby wants to come, too."

Abby didn't. With the promise that if Bethany ran she'd be able to eat at least an extra pound of crawfish, Justin persuaded her to make a lap around the pond with him. They jogged very slowly, with Justin managing to look as if he were taking a nap, so little did the exertion disturb him. Bethany was panting before they had even got halfway around.

"I have to stop," she groaned. "I'm dying." They slowed down a little more so that their pace resembled a walk, and Bethany made it to the halfway point. "Go on without me," she gasped, hanging on to an oak tree as if she were afraid he would pull her around the second half of the track.

"I'll stay, and we can walk back." He dragged her away from the tree to lounge on the grass by the pond. Her head was in his lap before she knew what had happened, and she lay catching her breath.

"I don't understand the glamour of running," she said finally when her heart and breathing had slowed considerably.

"Well, it prolongs your life, keeps you thin, slows down the aging process."

"Is that why you run, Justin?"

"I started running to forget. Now I run because I love it."

What had he needed to forget? His father and the pressures that had driven him north? The girl from Tallahassee he claimed to have loved? Whatever had been his reason, it fitted the pattern that was Justin Dumontier. Running was a solitary experience that was under the sole control of the runner, dependent on nothing but a pair of running shoes to make it successful. Only now he was asking her to share that experience with him. What seemed like a casual gesture was really a symbol of his reaching out to her. Her exhaustion vanished, and she sat up.

"I think I'm going to learn to love it, too. Have I said thank you for the suit and the shoes?"

"Not properly," he answered, his large brown hand fondling the velvety material of her jacket as he pulled her toward him.

She ran her hands over the material of the faintly damp T-shirt as he kissed her, tracing the separate muscles with her fingertips. Abandoning the pretense of casual interest in his kiss, she ran her hands up under the soft shirt to feel the slippery skin beneath. The skin-to-skin contact was unbearably sweet, and sweeter yet when his hands took the same paths up her spine.

The soft chiming of his alarm watch broke into their explorations. "It's four o'clock. Crawfish time," he whispered in her ear, still holding her tightly against him.

"Let's be a little bit late. I hate to watch them get cooked." She rested her head against his shirt, inhaling the sweaty aroma, preferring it to any men's cologne.

"I have a feeling that if we're too late, there will be nothing left to eat. Are you willing to risk it?" He nuzzled her ear with his nose, punctuating his sentence with his tongue.

"Mmm...I'm beginning to think the bigger risk is

staying here with you.'' Gently she pushed him away and stood on shaky legs, offering him a hand.

They walked back in silence, their arms wrapped tightly around each other.

To Bethany's relief, the first few batches of crawfish had been cooked in her absence. Picnic tables were spread with newspaper, and kettles full of the small red crustaceans had been dumped in piles in the center of each table. To a New Englander it would have resembled a feast of miniature lobster, but to a Louisiana native, it was better than that.

The crawfish had been cooked in water with great handfuls of spices, as well as lots of red pepper and garlic. Whole onions, corn on the cob, new potatoes and chunks of andouille sausage were thrown in for flavor and dumped on the table with the crawfish. The entire meal was to be eaten with the fingers, with the delicious juices unashamedly licked off of them when necessary. Separating the authentic natives from the less experienced crawfish eaters was easy. All an observer had to do was measure the pile of shells on the table in front of each.

Bethany, who placed somewhere between the natives and the initiates, took slightly longer to peel her crawfish than some, but unabashedly put the crawfish head in her mouth and sucked the spicy juices with the best of the natives. Justin, for all his elegant manners, peeled crawfish like a Cajun.

Great quantities of cold beer washed down the eye-watering food, and people got merrier accordingly. There were people at the tables who could eat their weight in crawfish, and there were people like Bethany who groaned after a pound or two that they would never eat another thing. Still, the meal seemed to go on forever, with laughter, telling of tall tales, gossiping and—more crawfish. It was no matter that some portion of the conversation was in Cajun French, a language Bethany had not learned to understand. The spirit could be absorbed easily, anyway.

"When you come see us again, you?" Maman Robicheaux asked Bethany as her long nimble fingers popped meat out of the crawfish tails faster than Abby, who was sitting next to her, could eat it.

"After Mardi Gras. Then I can take some time off to relax and visit."

"You should come visit us some year for the Mardi Gras. We have a *fais dodo* that night like in the old days," *maman* answered. Lamar had often told Abby and Bethany stories of the Cajun Mardi Gras celebrations throughout Louisiana. An old Cajun custom called for bands of masked riders on horseback to go through the countryside looking for chickens, rice and other provisions for the gumbo pot. Often the bands would dress as clowns, and their horses would be decorated, too. The farms that they visited would donate food, and the gumbo ingredients would then be taken to the dance hall, where huge kettles of gumbo were made to be served at the big *fais dodo* or community dance that night. Although the custom had died out in most places, it had experienced a revival in others, along with additional traditions peculiar to Cajun life. Lamar and others like him were determined to see that the great melting pot did not destroy the best of what their unique culture had to offer.

"I'll come to Bayou Lafourche if you'll come walk through the French Quarter with me on Mardi Gras Day," Bethany teased.

"The things I've heard about your Mardi Gras," *maman* said, fanning herself with her napkin.

A burst of music from the shore of the little pond had Abby scrambling to her feet. "Look, mommy, Lamar is fiddling."

Stretching and groaning simultaneously, Bethany took the little girl's hand and allowed herself to be pulled toward the raucous sound. Lamar was playing his fiddle, accompanied by his brother Aldus on the accordion and another man on an unplugged electric guitar. Celin was beside Lamar with a metal triangle for emphasis. Although not nearly as polished as the band Lamar performed with regularly, the little group embodied Cajun soul.

Cajun music was meant to be danced to, and Abby began her own impromptu routine, joined by other children. Eventually some of the adults began to drift toward the sound, pairing off to do a graceful, old-fashioned two-step or, music permitting, a rather bumpy outdoor waltz.

"Would the lovely mask maker like to try this one?" Justin's voice stroked her ear with its husky whisper.

"I'd love to," she answered, snuggling against him. Lamar was singing a plaintive ballad, "La Délaissée," a folk song she had heard him sing many times before. It was not really meant to be danced to, but that suited Bethany just fine. Justin took her in his arms and they moved slowly to the music, lost in thought. "Lamar refuses to translate this for me," she murmured against his chest. "Is it such a naughty song?"

Justin had been concentrating on the words, and he pulled her closer. "No, not at all."

"Tell me, then."

"I'm afraid that Lamar was just trying to protect you. The song is about a young girl, pretty as a flower, who falls under the spell of an unfaithful man who seduces her and leaves her pregnant."

"I'm sorry I asked."

"She gets her retribution, though. She murders him."

"Why didn't I think of that?" she said sweetly.

The next song was livelier, since it was the song sung by Mardi Gras bands out on the road looking for food for their gumbo pot. Others followed, and more couples joined Bethany and Justin. The sun set over the tall oaks, leaving a sky streaked with purple and orange. "It's a Mardi Gras sky," Bethany crowed enthusiastically. "Even the sun king is celebrating carnival."

It was with regret and the realization that she had a very tired little girl that Bethany found Maman Robicheaux to say their goodbyes. Most of the Robicheaux family was going in to the French Quarter to see Lamar perform before driving back to Bayou Lafourche late that night. Bethany, taking one look at Abby, had discarded that option for herself.

"I promise," she told the older woman, "that I'll come see you as soon as I can."

"Bring your man," *maman* said knowingly. "I will set him on the right path for you."

Heaven help Justin if he ever had to tangle with Maman Robicheaux. "I'll keep that in mind," Bethany answered as she gave her a goodbye hug. When all her other farewells had been said, she found Justin leaning against an enormous oak tree, holding a sleeping Abby against his chest. Bethany followed him back to the car caught in an iridescent bubble of happiness.

CHAPTER THIRTEEN

"WHERE DO I put her," Justin whispered as he followed Bethany into the little apartment, carrying Abby. "She must have eaten her weight in crawfish. She's twice as heavy as usual."

"She's also completely dead to the world, poor thing. All the excitement completely exhausted her." Bethany stroked Abby's hair, but the little girl slept on. "Let me pull the sofa bed out. That's where she usually sleeps." Carefully piling the sofa cushions on the floor, Bethany tugged the hidden mattress into place. The sofa was now a comfortable double bed, complete with pink sheets and lightweight patchwork quilt. Mistaking Justin's pained expression for a condemnation of the sleeping arrangements, she tried to placate him. "We won't be sleeping this way much longer, Justin. I think we should be able to begin moving right after Mardi Gras, if you've closed on the house by then."

"You don't have to apologize." He carefully laid Abby on the sheets and silently fingered the embroidered pillowcases as Bethany undressed the sleeping child. "This is beautiful. Did you do it?"

She nodded. The design was a collage of tiny animals chasing one another across the hem of the pillowcase. The patchwork quilt featured the same animals, one to a square. Justin's unexpected compliment when she had expected criticism filled her with warmth.

"Everything you do reflects who you are," he went on. "When I was busy finding fault with the way you were raising our daughter, I should have been more aware of all that you have done so well."

"If you don't stop," she said carefully, "all these kind words might cause me to explode. I'm too full of happiness to hold much more."

She felt his eyes on her, but she busied herself smoothing the sheet and tucking the quilt around Abby to avoid looking at him. The intimacy of the two of them standing over the bed of their child suddenly seemed too great to bear thinking about. For someone who prided herself on the honest expression of her feelings, she felt strangely tongue-tied and uneasy.

The apartment was dim, lit only by a bedside lamp that Bethany had left burning in her room. The faint light filtering through the tall windows cast distorted shadows on the walls and ceiling, creating a fantasy universe complete within the narrow confines of the apartment. With a sense of awe Bethany realized that she and Justin were completely alone except for the sleeping child and that the barriers of the past weeks were no longer between them. She straightened, trying to cast off the simultaneous fear and longing that went with her realization. There was nothing to be gained from allowing the magic of the place and the magic of the day to rule her emotions.

Her eyes sought Justin's, and the sense of wonder grew and burst into a million pieces inside her. Justin was watching her, and his eyes were filled with hunger and with happiness. He and Bethany stood on opposite sides of Abby's bed with no need to verbally communicate what was happening between them. They waited for long minutes, as if afraid that any movement would break the spell that bound them to each other. And finally Justin extended his hand across the bed, and she saw that he trembled slightly. That small weakness gave her the courage to take a step in his direction. Grasping his hand firmly, she ran her thumb along the back of his hand as he pulled her to stand at the end of the bed.

They faced each other, only their hands touching, and Bethany felt as though she were being slowly devoured by his hunger for her. If his eyes alone could cause these spiraling explosions inside her, she trembled at the thought of what his touch and his kiss would do. Always before there had been a wall of problems between them, effectively curtailing the powerful magnetism that had pulled at them since their beginnings. She was vulnerable now, even more vulnerable than she had been when he had made love to her the first time. For now she understood what pleasure and what pain the act could cause them both.

"I want you the way I've never wanted anything in my life," he said huskily. "But if you tell me to go away I'll understand. Perhaps it's too soon...or too late for us."

It was both. It was too soon and it was too late, and when those two impossible entities were added together the summation of them was "now." She was a fool to be adding up the decisions of a lifetime like a third-grade math problem, but she knew that no matter how foolish her calculations, the answer was the right one for her.

"I want you, too. I could no more tell you to go away

than I could cut out my heart. But you must know something first," she said as she withdrew her hand to face him without the anchor of his touch. "I love you, Justin. I've never stopped, although I tried very hard for five years to cut you out of my heart and out of my life. You need to know that, and if it makes a difference, then I'll understand."

"After all that has passed between us," he said with a catch in his voice, "and with all that must still pass between us, you stand there and proclaim your love like a priestess chanting the holiest of holies. Tell me, are you flesh and blood like the rest of us?"

"I am a woman in love, nothing more," she said, taking a step closer to him. "Perhaps now is the time to find out if I'm truly made of flesh and blood."

If she had expected Justin to scoop her up and carry her to the four-poster bed in a passionate display of his need for her, she was wrong. He was strangely gentle, as if he were afraid she might be hurt by the fire she saw reflected in his eyes. With his arm lightly around her shoulders he led her into the bedroom, closing the louvered French doors behind them. A slow insidious heat burned in her veins, igniting in a series of passionate explosions each time he touched her. But Justin was in no hurry, and guided her to the windows, looking over the balcony to the street below and away from the bed.

Gently, almost reverently, his hands touched her hair, stroking it away from her forehead, running his fingers through the straight silky strands that clung to his wrist like jasmine vines on a trellis. Her eyes were closed as he explored her face, slowly tracing each inch of soft skin, covering her eyelids with the delicate pressure of his thumbs. His lips lightly kissed a whispering path down her nose, stopping before he reached her mouth to explore the rest of her face first.

She tried to respond, to explore him in the same way, but she wasn't allowed. "No," he murmured as he continued his sweet torture. His lips found her ear and he discovered each secret crevice, until she was shivering before him. With his thumbs on her collarbone, his fingers softly tickled the back of her neck, finding the sweet hollow under the wealth of her hair. He bent over to find it with his tongue, pulling her to stand against him as his hands sweetly stroked her back.

Her arms crept around him and under his T-shirt to feel the rippling muscles of his torso and to give him back some of the pleasure that raced through her body. "No," he said. "Let me do it all."

With wild gratitude she felt his hands under her T-shirt and his fingers unhooking the delicate lace bra that she wore. She stepped back only far enough to help him in his attempt to remove the shirt and jacket that she wore over it, but he would not rush, and pulled her close again. His hands played slowly down each vertebra of her spine like a musician on a xylophone. And then, when she had despaired of him ever escalating their contact, he began to stroke her breasts with his thumbs. The movement was only a fluttering, a shimmering sensation she wasn't even sure existed, except that she was so alive to the nuances of his touch she thought she could feel his heart beat in his fingers.

Finally he pushed her away and brought his hands up to cup the rounded thrusting mounds, using his thumbs to create peaks of arousal. Her legs were weak with excitement and she knew what it meant to have her knees knock. Just when she thought she would collapse he led her to the bed, sitting on the side and pulling her to stand between his thighs. He slipped the burgundy jacket off, and the T-shirt and bra after it. His movements were slow, with teasing flourishes, and she groaned in anticipation as his mouth finally sought the treasure he had bared.

That a tongue could create such an effect on the human body was a glorious mystery, and she collapsed against him, almost sobbing her need. But still he moved slowly, continuing his exploration of her upper body with his mouth as he began to inch off the soft pants of her running suit. He cuddled her close as he slipped off the still-tied shoes and finally the wisp of silky panties. She lay naked in his arms, and yet he didn't hurry, his fingers exploring her smooth stomach, pausing to rest on the delicately etched silver stretch marks, an honor badge of her pregnancy.

Standing, he turned and lay her against the quilt covering her bed, and then bending over, he began to undress before her. She watched in fascination as each part of his body came into view. His chest was covered with fine curly hair, tapering on to his stomach and below. His legs and arms were powerful, and each part of him was hard and finely built, like a statue carved from smooth cypress. When he was finally naked before her, the evidence of his desire put to rest any fears she had entertained of his lack of excitement. It was exquisite control, not disinterest that had allowed him to take such pains in arousing her.

When he stretched out beside her she tried to melt into his strong body, aching to merge with him in a fierce bonding of spirit and of flesh. But he held her off as he had before. "Wait," he said. "Let me."

His hand began a heated exploration of her most inti-mate space. Without knowing what she was doing, she writhed against him, all thought suspended. His palm rode her soft, wet warmth, gently but with sufficient pressure to send waves of longing crashing on the shores of her consciousness. She tried to pull him to her, to give him back some of the pleasure he was bestowing on her like a fabulous gift, but he wouldn't allow it. "Let me give to you," he whispered in her ear as his tongue began to explore again.

The place she was trying to reach seemed unobtain-able, a beach that she must swim to through dangerous waters, but this realization could not stop her striving. For the first time since he had begun to make love to her, Justin kissed her mouth, his tongue tracing paths on the inner surface of her top lip, finally thrusting into her mouth to find the wet warmth there for him. The kiss shot her over the edge and onto the impossible beach. She lay in his arms, shuddering against him as he held her securely. Her arms were around him in a death grip with the fear that he would disappear, dis-solve into nothingness, as he had so many times in her dreams.

Although he could not know of the recurring night-mare, he whispered over and over again, "It's all right. I'm right here." Finally she lay quietly, spent emo-tionally and physically from the force of his lovemaking and from the overwhelming response of her body. But peace was not to be hers.

Again his hands began to travel the sensitive paths of her body, until she was sure she had imagined her first release. With the determination of a man who knew what he was capable of doing, Justin again brought her body to such a state of excitement that she could not keep silent, and she poured out her love and need for him.

It seemed to be all he wanted. With his powerful body poised above, he entered her slowly, savoring each millimeter of contact with constraint that seemed almost demonic to her. When he was fully inside of her he stopped, waiting for her to accustom herself to the feel of him. Tentatively she moved beneath him, and with a rush of relief she realized that his control was not so strong to make him unaffected by her. He groaned and wrapped his arms around her back, beginning slow sure thrusts that bound her to him with the certainty of his desire for her.

Still his control was extraordinary, giving her all the time she needed to climb the ladder of ecstasy with him. And when she could finally hold nothing back in that excruciating second filled with fear and anticipation, he too held nothing back, filling her with passion and with the certainty of his own needs.

Afterward he held her tightly again, rubbing her back and crooning soft words of gratitude and affection. If there were no words of love, it was only what she expected. Justin was still Justin, and love, if it came again, would only happen gradually. For now, their mutual bond of ecstasy and affection was almost enough.

He let her go only long enough to pull the patchwork quilt from beneath them, covering them both as protection against the night's humid chill. But wrapped securely in his arms, with her head on his shoulder and the musky smell of their lovemaking surrounding them, she was anything but chilled. They drifted off to sleep in a warm cocoon entirely of their own making.

She had no idea how tired she was, or how deeply she slept, until a tentative tapping on the French doors awakened her, and she realized that sun was streaming through the windows. "Just a minute, Abby," she said with a yawn. Her hand thrown out in a stretch contacted empty space, and she remembered the details of the night before. Eyes wide open, she looked up to see Justin standing over her with her T-shirt and panties in his hands.

"Better put these on before I let her in." He grinned, his eyes traveling the curves exposed by the forgotten quilt. He was wearing only the pants of his running suit, and she felt a familiar warmth course through her at the sight of his muscular chest. But now was not the right time for the thoughts she was cultivating. The pounding on the door increased as she jumped up and threw on the clothes Justin had dropped into her lap.

"I thought I heard you talking, Justin." The little girl looked at her parents, who were both sitting with pretended nonchalance on the bed. Bethany was frantically trying to recall what the women's magazines she occasionally read advised their readers to do in a situation like this. But before she could venture an explanation, Abby leaped across the room and jumped on the bed between them. "This is neat. Mommy's never had a man in her bed before."

Bethany sputtered helplessly at the revelation, while Justin roared with laughter. "Out of the mouths of babes," she muttered finally, picking the burgundy running suit off the floor and pulling on the pants. "I'm going to take a shower!"

For once the water was hot, and the cascading warmth washed away all traces of her embarrassment at the same time that it washed away the signs of the night's lovemaking. She lathered her hair with shampoo, letting the water complete her journey into wakefulness. When she was finished she toweled off, taking special care of the part of her that was newly tender from their passion. After wrapping herself in a blue chenille robe with the determination of a knight donning a suit of armor, she shouted for Justin to come take advantage of the hot water.

"Was Abby right?" he asked with a smile as they passed in the doorway. "Was that the first time a man has ever been in your bed?"

"You should know the answer to that one," she said with her pointed chin in the air. "And you'd better be careful, or I'm going to start asking you about your love life."

"Enough said," he conceded with a grin. "Case closed."

The morning was entirely too much of a landmark to celebrate with cold cereal. With Abby's help, Bethany chopped enough onions, green pepper, tomatoes and boiled shrimp to fill a large omelet. She set water on the stove to boil for the mandatory grits and measured coffee with chicory into her coffeepot. When Justin emerged from the shower a few minutes later, it was to the smell of a luscious Creole breakfast.

Justin, with his hair damp and tiny droplets of water clinging to his bare chest, was more devastatingly virile than she had ever seen him. Her tongue flickered lightly over her lips, and she wanted to bury her face in the curly hair and savor each diamond drop of water. Instead she asked him casually, "Will you take milk in your coffee?"

"Are you going to live here now, Justin?" Abby asked as they lingered over breakfast.

Bethany watched him through lowered lashes. For once it was nice to have Abby address her embarrassing questions to someone else. Let Justin explain his presence there.

"I can't, honey. This place isn't big enough for another person."

"Maybe if you were smaller," Abby said with a sigh. She brightened up noticeably as she thought of a new possibility. "Maybe we could all move. Then you could live with us like a real daddy does."

There had been no point before now in informing the little girl of the impending move. Suddenly Bethany realized that she had waited too long. If she told Abby now, the little girl would assume that Justin was going to live with them, too. "Abby," she began with a sense of dread, "your daddy has to live in another part of the country because that's where his job is. He will have to go back there soon, but you'll be able to visit him sometimes, and he'll visit you here when he can."

"No," Abby answered firmly, her eyes impassive. "If he goes away, I'm not going to visit him. Not ever."

Bethany tried for a change of subject. "Let's talk about what we're going to do today...."

"Bethany," Justin silenced her. His head swiveled to face Abby, and he placed his fingers firmly under the little girl's chin. "Now listen," he said in a soft voice that even the child could tell meant business. "I am your father. Do you understand what that means? It means that you will do exactly what I tell you to. I am not going to let you go out of my life again. Whether you like it or not, you are my daughter and you will not be allowed to forget that."

It was the first time in Abby's life that anyone had spoken to her in such an uncompromising fashion, and she was absolutely speechless. Finally two big tears trickled down her face, and her mouth, which had been open in an incredulous moue, snapped shut. A heavy silence hung over the table as Bethany rose to begin clearing off the plates. Abby's words stopped her.

"I guess you really are my daddy," she said with a lingering trace of defiance. "Only daddies are that mean."

Bethany gasped softly, but Justin understood and he held out his arms to his daughter, who came into them with no reluctance. "A real daddy has to be mean sometimes," he acknowledged. "But I love you very much."

"As much as you love mommy?" she wheedled.

"Different," he said without missing a beat. "Very different."

The little girl needed some time to think about that, and she sat quietly for a few minutes. "Justin, maybe I can call you daddy someday," she said finally, seemingly satisfied with his reply.

Bethany, with tears spilling over onto her pink cheeks, carried the dishes into the kitchen and spent twice as long as usual washing them to give the two most important people in her life a chance to be alone.

As if understanding intuitively that Bethany, Justin and their daughter needed time together that day, Madeline banged on the apartment door later in the morning and announced that she and Valerie would mind the store. Although the rest of New Orleans was restricted under the blue laws, the French Quarter shops were exempt, and Life's Illusions was kept open on the Sundays through the carnival season. It was an extra burden, but the income from some of the thousands of tourists who flocked into town made it worthwhile. Today it was a treat for Bethany to not have to stand behind the counter.

"Let's take that French Quarter tour today," Justin suggested. "When was the last time you two rode in a buggy?"

"Never," Abby shouted. It had been one luxury they hadn't been able to afford, and the little girl had always eyed with longing the fringed buggies pulled by mules or horses with absurdly decorated hats.

"I told you, Justin," Bethany said wryly. "My tour was free."

"I'd like to take you to St. Louis Cathedral for mass first thing, if you'll come," he suggested.

"I'm not sure they'll let you in in that get up," she answered, lamenting that the drops of water had dried now and all there was to stare at was richly tanned male skin and rippling muscles.

Justin left to drive home and change his clothes, and Bethany donned a blue silk blouse and matching skirt she had bought along with the red dress. The color matched her eyes exactly and she had been embarrassed by her attack of vanity, but it hadn't stopped her from buying the outfit. Abby wore a hand-smocked pinafore of white batiste that Madeline had put many loving hours into and that Bethany planned to have professionally wrapped as an heirloom when the little girl outgrew it.

When Justin arrived she saw that he had changed into

a softly striped gray suit, made less formal by a pale-yellow shirt and no tie. His tanned throat and curling chest hair were visible under the two buttonholes he had left undone, and Bethany was entranced by the casualness of the attire.

She had forgotten head coverings, and the breathtakingly beautiful cathedral, the oldest cathedral in North America, deserved them. They walked across Jackson Square, and Justin, signaling one of the pushcart vendors plying his wares, bought headbands of silk and dried flowers for both females. They slipped silently into a pew in the back, and Bethany watched with awe as the timeless drama of the Roman Catholic mass unfolded before them.

It was a revelation of sorts to see Justin caught up in his own unabashed participation. Bethany knew, as she watched him, that when the inevitable decision about Abby's religious training surfaced, she would let Justin have his way.

Afterward they walked across the square again, stopping to look at the portrait artists. As they watched a particularly good one put the finishing touches on her work, Justin pulled a bill from his pocket and insisted that Bethany and Abby pose for the woman.

"It will take too long," Bethany remonstrated.

"Do it for me," he answered.

The woman worked quickly, and Abby, fascinated by the thought of having her image unfold on the sheet of gray paper, sat as still as a New Orleans summer afternoon. By the time they were finally allowed to move, a crowd had gathered to ooh and ahh over the finished work, which had managed to capture Abby's vitality and Bethany's fragile loveliness.

"It reminds me of the one you did for me in Tallahassee," was Justin's only comment as he carefully carried the portrait, encased in cardboard.

"Do you still remember that?" she asked softly.

"I still have it," he corrected her. "It hangs on my bedroom wall in Chicago."

Nothing he had said or done in their weeks together had touched her more. She envisioned the new portrait hanging beside the old one, and she wondered fleetingly how the images would make his Chicago women feel. With a twinge of spite she hoped solemnly that it would make them feel terrible.

The buggy trip was lively as Abby made best friends with their driver, a N'Awlins native who told them tales about the city that were so farfetched they had to be true. After they drew up in front of Jackson Square, they crossed the street for coffee and *beignets* at the famous Café du Monde, an open-air restaurant that served that specialty twenty-four hours a day. They climbed onto the Moonwalk again, this time to watch the riverboats with their cheerfully out-of-tune calliopes, and Justin promised Abby that someday soon he would take her on a steamboat ride.

When they stopped to buy po'boys to go at a hole-in-the-wall restaurant on St. Ann Street as they walked back toward the apartment, Bethany assumed they would be eating lunch in her tiny living room. But Justin had other ideas.

"It's time to show Abby the house," he said quietly to Bethany as Abby skipped ahead of them.

"I guess you're right, but I'm not sure she'll understand," she warned.

"Let's take her over there and have a picnic in the backyard. I'll explain then."

"I wish the house didn't look quite so empty. Four-year-olds have a difficult time envisioning changes," Bethany lamented, picturing the spacious lonely rooms.

"I've been meaning to talk to you about that..." Justin's voice trailed off.

She shook her head firmly. "I know we won't have much to put in it at first, but I'll be darned if I'm going to let you buy me furniture, too." He had bought her a house and he claimed to have bought her a car, although she had yet to see it. Her pride stopped dead in its tracks at the thought of being even more obligated to him.

"You don't have to worry about that. The furniture won't cost either of us a cent." And that's all he would say about it.

The ride to the house was pleasant, even with Abby's insistence that they beep their horn at the antiquated green streetcar that ran down the St. Charles median, or neutral ground, as it was called in New Orleans. When they pulled up in front of the "cottage," Abby was already pressing her nose against the car window, eyeing the group of little girls in a neighboring yard playing with a soccer ball.

Justin had yet to have his talk with their daughter, and Bethany fully expected Abby to seem bewildered over the trip, but with the magic acceptance of all pre-schoolers, she didn't appear to give it a thought. Bethany, however, was astounded. When Abby unlocked the front door, the formerly empty house was filled with furniture.

Wandering through the rooms in a daze, she ran her fingertips over the finely polished wood of antique tables, a contemporary sofa, comfortable overstuffed chairs and a cherry rolltop desk that just ached for an old-fashioned inkwell and quill. There was a mixture of different furniture styles in each room, but interestingly enough, everything fitted together in an eclectic harmony. "Your mother has been here," she said finally, after touring most of the downstairs in silence.

"You don't have to keep anything, Bethany. But it's something to start with. Some of these things have been in my family for generations, and I wanted you to have them. We have lots more up in the attic, too, and my mother is aching to have you come and choose some more things. She just put the bare bones in as a start."

To Bethany, it was already more furniture than she had expected to acquire in a lifetime. "I should be angry," she said thoughtfully, "but I'll bet your mother had a wonderful time doing this. How can I be a spoilsport?"

"Still, if you don't like some of the things..."

"I love it all. It's just that you keep doing things for me—for us," she said, changing in midstream, "and I feel like it's too much."

"Not nearly enough," he said firmly. "Come see the bedroom." They walked through the hallway, empty of all decoration, and Justin stopped. "My mother thought this would be a wonderful place to hang masks. Sort of a gallery effect." They passed on, Justin guiding her with his arm around her waist, until they came to the bedroom. Abby followed behind, exploring with delight, although she was still oblivious to whose house it was.

The master bedroom was large enough to hold Bethany's entire apartment. There was no bed visible, and obviously Justin had told his mother that Bethany had a bed she would want to keep. But the best surprise was that he had apparently described the bed in detail, for all the furnishings in the bedroom were made from the same dark mahogany and were suited to go with it. It was all so much to her liking that she could not even attempt to hold back her delight. "It's beautiful."

"This room doesn't have a bed, Justin. Where do these people sleep?" Abby was beginning to notice the peculiarities of the house.

"There will be a bed soon, honey. Come on, there's another room I want you to see especially."

They followed him up the stairs to the two smaller bedrooms, and Bethany smiled to see that Justin had taken her advice and furnished the room with the sailing ships for Abby. There was a heavy oak double bed with matching chest and vanity that was wonderfully old-fashioned and in keeping with the simple nautical theme. Bright-red curtains hung at the window, and a red plush throw rug covered the shining wood floor. A toy shelf had been installed against one wall, and on one shelf was a beautiful china doll that was probably as old as anything else in the house. Bethany knew instinctively that the doll had once belonged to Louise and later to Marie.

"Do you like it, Abby?"

The little girl nodded solemnly, eyes wide with longing. "Does somebody live in this room?"

"Somebody is going to." Justin explained very carefully that the house now belonged to Abby's mommy and that after Mardi Gras, Abby and Bethany would be moving there to live.

"Is that when you go away, Justin?" Even the happiness of the new house could not erase the lingering question from the little girl's mind.

"I'm not sure," he said, and Bethany knew he was trying to preserve the moment's happy aura. There would be better times to tell Abby the truth.

It would be very easy to forget, as they sat in the shady backyard eating their picnic lunch, that Justin was going away, for his presence there was completely natural and fitting. It would be very easy to ignore the truth, as they watched Abby climb up the ladder into the tree house in the huge magnolia, for Justin seemed to have become an integral part of their lives. And when he ran his hands down the smooth skin of her forearms, pulling her close with gentle pressure as Abby explored the new blue Toyota waiting patiently in the garage, it would be very easy to forget, for just a moment, that the happiness of that day and the rapture of the night were not just lovely dreams fated to be obscured by the clouds of reality.

CHAPTER FOURTEEN

LOUISE DUMONTIER SAT in her drawing room, surrounded by sheets of paper torn from yellow legal pads. In frustration she ripped the latest list she had been working on into dozens of tiny pieces. There was no point in continuing to try to deal with the last-minute details that surrounded the Mardi Gras ball her church was giving as a fund-raising event. With the unexpected death of her husband and the surprise arrival of an unknown granddaughter, the past months had left her unable to concentrate on anything the least bit superfluous. For once someone else would have to take charge, and Father Grinnell would just have to understand.

She was sure he would, for in an uncharacteristic display of emotion, she had poured out her heart to him when he had dropped in for a visit the week before. Now he knew about Justin and Bethany and about the little girl who was her grandchild. He had urged her to be cautious and to pray for guidance, but that advice was fast becoming impossible to follow. Quite simply, Louise Dumontier saw happiness slipping out of Justin's grasp again, and that awareness was making her impatient.

With a toss she threw the tiny pieces of yellow paper over her head like so much confetti and watched them settle around her on the heavy, formal furniture.

"Is this a private party, or can anybody come?" Justin stood in the doorway, dressed in sleek nylon shorts, mopping his face and chest with a thick terry-cloth towel.

"Come in, dear," she said sheepishly. "I didn't hear you come back from your run."

"You were a million miles away." He pointed to the little scraps of paper. "Are you making decorations for the parish ball?"

She made a wry face as she began to scoop up her mess. "No, I decided to forget about the ball. I just don't seem to be able to concentrate."

"What's bothering you, mother? You seem so preoccupied."

There was no time to pray for guidance, and caution flew out the window. "I was worrying about you," she said. Now that she had leaped into the breach there was no turning back. "I know you're still planning to go back to Chicago, and I'll be damned if I can figure out why." As soon as the totally foreign curse word escaped her lips, she clamped them shut. What on earth was wrong with her? What business did she have interfering in Justin's life, anyway? It was just such interference from his father that had driven him away in the first place.

Justin sank into a Regency open armchair, oblivious to the marks his sweaty body was making on the upholstery. "I assume you mean Abby and Bethany." His mouth thinned into a grim line as she nodded. "I thought so."

"How can you leave them here? They are your family, even if you aren't married to Bethany. And she is so obviously in love with you, Justin. If you're not in love

with her, couldn't you learn to love her eventually?'
Astonished that she was continuing to interfere, she
clamped her mouth shut again.

"I asked Bethany to marry me and she refused."

The words, matter-of-fact and said with surprising
nonchalance, did not fool her. Justin, when nonchalant,
was at his most emotional. Something was not right. "
can't believe she would have refused a warm, sincere
proposal," she said softly.

Justin sat silently, his arms folded, and stared across
the room at an empty space on the wall. Bethany had
refused his proposal, but only because she thought it
had been issued without love. She had no idea that his
feelings for her had never really changed, that all those
years they had been apart he had been obsessed with
finding her. Each time a woman with long dark hair or a
sweetly sensual walk mirroring hers had come into his
life he had found it necessary to remind himself to
breathe. Each time he had seen a woman run her fingers
through her hair in that unaffected gesture of thoughtfulness he had died a little inside.

Bethany had no idea that he loved her and that he still
felt completely inadequate to provide her with what she
needed. She had always needed so much. Unloved and
uncared for as a child, she reached out for love, for
touching and for healing. He was Justin Dumontier, a
man frozen inside by formality, by internal and external
demands for perfection. A man doomed to spend his
life alone. Once on a long night on a faraway beach he
had come to terms with that part of himself. He had
flung that image aside, and he had committed himself to
following the path his emotions had set before him.

But that was a long time ago, and that path had led

him back into loneliness, to casual relationships that satisfied physically but not spiritually. And now, like a starving man being tantalized with a banquet, he was being offered another chance. The hardest thing to come to terms with was the realization that all he had to do was tell Bethany how he felt, and she would be his. But would she grow and expand with his love, or would she wither and die like honeysuckle in winter if he took her away from all those who loved her and from the place that was the only home she had ever really known? And if he took her away, what did he have inside himself to offer her?

That night on a Honolulu beach he had been courageous and confident. But it was five years later, and the Chicago winds and lonely nights had worn away his belief in his abilities. At times like these, he knew himself to be an empty shell, filled only by her love. And what was left to fill her with in return?

"Son?"

"I don't know what's going to happen, mother. I just don't know."

"Don't let your pride stand in the way of a happy ending, Justin."

He uttered a harsh, derisive laugh as he stood and walked to the door. "It's anything but that, mother. If only it were that simple."

BETHANY'S EYES stole to the hands of her watch, and she fidgeted nervously as the young couple tried on mask after mask. Justin had been invited for lunch, and she was anxious to finish this sale so she could go upstairs and check on the jambalaya simmering in her apartment.

It was only a little over a week until Mardi Gras, and the extra burden of work was beginning to take its toll. Madeline had finally hired another worker, a mask maker who sometimes sold on consignment for them, to help mind the store. Bethany had worked ten hours at the shop every day and long hours afterward, finishing masks. She was taking the rest of the day off as a reward. Perhaps if Justin weren't still in New Orleans, she wouldn't have felt the need for the free time, but his presence made it difficult to be so caught up in her work. Sometimes she could almost hear the minutes ticking by, reminding her that soon he would be gone.

"Do you have another mask like that one?" Bethany looked up to see Justin smiling in a businesslike manner at her as he pointed to the mask the young man she had been waiting on held in his hand.

"I'm sorry, I don't," she said with feigned regret, but with secret delight at his appearance. "We're completely out of sea serpents. That's probably the last one in the city."

"I was so hoping—" he started again.

"Here, mister, if you want it that badly..." The young man pushed the mask at Justin. "We might be back later, but we've got a couple of other places to look first," he finished, taking his girl's arm.

Justin grinned sheepishly as Bethany faced him with her hands on her hips. "Now was that being helpful?" she scolded.

"My knowledge of psychology is such that I was sure he'd jump at the chance to buy it if I wanted it," he explained.

"Justin, as a psychologist you make a terrific lawyer." Leaning over the counter, she brushed her lips against his, the mandatory shiver coursing through her body at even that casual touch. "And as a lawyer you make an even more terrific lover," she said boldly, running the tips of her fingers down the side of his face.

"Mmm...mmm!" Valerie leaned on the doorframe. "I can see I'm just in time."

"Just in time to take over here," Bethany echoed in gratitude.

Never one to miss an opportunity for big tourist money, Lamar had taken Abby to Jackson Square to collect tips as he fiddled. Bethany suspected that his actions had more to do with her casual announcement that Justin was coming to lunch than with any real desire to have Abby help. Mardi Gras spirit saturated the very air they breathed, and in the lively chaotic French Quarter energy and enthusiasm were running high. Bethany was not oblivious to the way her friends were making a special effort to give her time with Justin, as if they too had been stung by the carnival love bug.

"Are you hungry, Justin?" she asked nervously as they climbed the steps to her apartment. "I made jambalaya, and we can eat now or sit and talk awhile first."

Justin felt the tension, too. Without their daughter there to keep them otherwise occupied, their attention was focused solely on each other. There was time now to say all the things that needed to be said. And yet he had no idea how to begin to explain himself.

"Let's eat," he said finally.

The jambalaya was hot, and Bethany, who still lived with the nightmare of what alcohol had done to her mother, had actually relaxed her restrictions enough to buy a bottle of white wine to go with it. But something was wrong, and they were both aware of it as they toyed with the delicious food, picking pieces of shrimp out of the rice and then reburying them.

"I guess I'm not hungry," she said finally, pushing her plate back and sipping her wine.

"We're both hungry for something else," Justin said in a low tone as he stood and pulled her up beside him. "We always are when we're together, and denying it is hell."

The big bed sagged under their combined weight, but neither of them noticed as they struggled to help each other undress—which made the job more difficult, because they refused to allow the necessary space between them for pulling clothes off. Their lovemaking was as furious as it had been slow and careful the night of the crawfish boil. They reached for each other with the intensity felt only by those threatened by the future. When they were satiated, they lay face to face, finally allowing themselves the luxury of tender caresses.

"Abby is going to be back in fifteen minutes," Bethany said as her eyes traveled to the bedside alarm clock. "Lamar was very specific about when he was returning with her."

"And to think I was jealous of that man," Justin said, his hand brushing her hair back from her pale face, which was still tinged with the passion of their lovemaking.

She was pleased by the admission, and she put her fingertips against his lips to be kissed. "We'd better shower and dress," she said with a sigh. "Unless you think there's time..."

"Insatiable wench," he teased, ruffling her hair. "I wish I could provide you with the attention you desire, but if Lamar walks in even one minute early, we might cause our daughter a trauma that could last a lifetime."

"Did you have plans for the afternoon, Justin?" She indulged herself in a quick hug as he stepped out of the bathroom after his shower, a skimpy towel wrapped around his waist.

"Not really. Did you have something you'd like to do?" he answered as he began to dress.

"As a matter of fact," she said, watching his face for signs of apoplexy, "I'd like to go to the Sheba Krewe's parade this afternoon out in the suburbs. Those parades are usually less crowded, and I think it would be a fun one for Abby to see. It's really the first big one of the season."

"I hate parades. The last time I went to one willingly was when I was eight years old, and even then I had the good sense to realize that it was noisy nonsense."

"But you've never gone to a parade with me or with the right attitude," she coaxed. "I think you'll like it. It's like nothing else in the world to be there watching that incredible pageantry, with everyone shouting and competing for throws."

"I will never understand why anyone would want all those plastic beads and fake doubloons."

"I will never understand why anyone would want to be so deadly serious all the time," she responded with a gleam in her eye. "I'm going to loosen you up. By the time this week is over you will have become a Mardi Gras fanatic, too."

"Hell will freeze over first," he snorted with cynicism.

"I've heard another ice age is predicted," she said sweetly as she padded to the door to let Abby and Lamar into the apartment. "Better send to Chicago for your down jacket."

Abby was ecstatic when she learned they were going to a parade. At four, she had only vague memories of the parades the year before, and she had been looking forward to this season's carnival. Bethany's work kept the excitement of Mardi Gras in front of them all year, but the actual season was something to joyfully anticipate.

With a tote bag of drinks and snacks, bags for the throws they would catch, sweaters and camera, they drove to the parade route. Because it was a suburban parade there was plenty of parking available nearby, and Justin, with analytical zeal, parked in a spot from which they could make a quick getaway.

"A woman's krewe puts this one on," Bethany said with a straight face. "If you'd like to stand in front of me with Abby on your shoulders, you'll get lots of throws. I'll stand behind you to pick up your castoffs."

"Is that because Justin is so beautiful?" piped Abby.

"It works every time, or so I hear," Bethany said smugly.

"And at the men's parades, do you stand in front?" Justin asked wryly.

"Absolutely."

The parade was several blocks away, and they could see the first float in the distance. Abby was so excited she could hardly stand still. Bethany handed the child a handmade drawstring bag made from purple cotton, with "Mardi Gras" in gold-and-green appliqué. New Orleans parades were invariably accompanied by the throwing of favors from the floats. Most of the time the throws were beads and specially manufactured doubloons that were in great favor by collectors. But some parades also threw stuffed toys, plastic tumblers with emblems of the krewe sponsoring the parade, candy, plastic spears and even bikini panties. On St. Patrick's Day, the New Orleans parades threw cabbages to the waiting crowds. Nobody in New Orleans went to any parade just to watch.

"Remember, sweetheart, don't reach down to pick anything up off the ground. Cover it with your foot first, then reach for it." Bethany cautioned Abby just as other mothers up and down the parade route were cautioning their children.

"I know, mommy."

"And don't run out in the street."

"I know, mommy."

They could hear the music from the first marching band, and the truck that checked for overhead clearance rolled by. Although some parades closer to Mardi Gras day had spectators lined up ten or more deep, this parade was less crowded, and their view was unimpeded as the small floats carrying the maids and finally the queen of the court came by. The women were dressed in elaborate costumes of gold and silver sequins, with white ostrich plumes on elaborate headdresses. In this parade the court wore tiny sequined masks, not to hide their identity from their friends but to add a touch of mystery.

The court, with royal dignity, did not throw anything, and by the time the first large float filled with a dozen women dressed as mermaids rolled by, Abby was at fever pitch. "Justin, hold me up!"

With a long-suffering expression that made Bethany chuckle, Justin put the little girl on his shoulders and prepared himself to tolerate the raucous display that was fast approaching. In a minute the air around them was raining doubloons and beads. Bethany scooped the throws off the ground that Abby had missed catching in midair. Sneaking a look at Justin's face, she was overcome with laughter. He resembled a shell-shocked survivor of a major battle.

"They loved you, Justin. I'm not sure I've seen so many doubloons thrown at one person before."

He shot her an irritated glance as Abby began to bounce on his shoulders. "Throw me something, throw me something," the little girl shouted.

After three more storms of doubloons, Abby begged to get down. Although she could not see as well on the ground, she was able to pick up more of the throws that came her way, and after watching a little boy make off with a cup that had been tossed in her direction, the fearless child was ready to get down and join the skirmish.

The bands marching in between the intricately decorated floats added an audibly cheerful note, and the bright colors and holiday atmosphere of the crowd couldn't help but work their wonderful magic on Justin. Bethany first noticed the change when she saw that his foot was tapping in time to the music. The band passing by at that moment was playing a recent Michael Jackson hit, and a crowd of young teenagers across the street from them were break dancing in response.

Although Justin still wasn't actively catching throws, he didn't protest when Bethany slipped several beaded necklaces over his head. "You look more festive now," she whispered in his ear. And he looked even more festive when the next float came by and threw a cup directly at him. Justin, with all his wealth, couldn't resist the lure of the plastic tumbler, and before Bethany knew what was happening—and probably before he did, too—he was out in the street, diving for it.

After that it was every man, woman and child for himself. Justin, Abby and Bethany scrambled for every throw that came their way. Doubloons were covered by dancing feet; beads were snatched from the reach of other bystanders. And the special prize of a stuffed unicorn, which was presented to Abby by a float rider of a temporarily halted float, was gloated over as if it were pirate booty.

When the last float had gone with its traditional blitz of throws, the three weary parade-goers headed back to the car. "I don't know, Justin," Bethany said with tongue in cheek, "you didn't look like you hated parades to me."

"Mass hysteria," he grumbled.

"You loved it," she said smugly.

"Mommy, did you see Justin grab that doubloon from the old lady in back of us?"

"Abby, I did not grab that doubloon from her. I merely caught it before it got to her."

"Her fingers were on it." Bethany giggled helplessly, remembering the picture of the formal Mr. Dumontier and the exquisitely groomed old lady arguing over ownership of the piece of thin aluminum.

"I gave it back to her before we left."

"I'm sure she enjoyed the fight as much as the doubloon," Bethany said, trying to soothe his feelings. But the grin he shot her allayed her fears. He had enjoyed the parade and the chance to let go at least temporarily. Like others in the crowd who lived completely conventional lives year round, Justin had allowed the secret of Mardi Gras to creep inside him. The harmless, good-natured fun was a release valve for the tensions of the city for those who allowed themselves to participate fully in the experience. Those who refused to join in the fun and those who took it too seriously were missing the whole point. Bethany was delighted to see that Justin was not one of them.

Abby and Bethany allowed Justin to persuade them to jog with him at Audubon Park, and they made a short stop at the apartment first for their running clothes. The giant oaks cast lazy shadows over the path around the lagoons as they circled slowly around. Bethany and Abby watched in dazed awe as Justin made the circle again and again. They bought Popeye's spicy chicken and ate it under the branches laced with hanging Spanish moss. Abby fed pieces of biscuit to the ducks as Bethany and Justin watched in satiated silence.

What should have been a short drive home was not. By the time they left the park, crowds had formed up and down St. Charles. "I'm sorry, Justin. I forgot there was a parade on St. Charles tonight." Teaching Justin to like parades and making him stand through more than one on the same day were two different things.

"I live here. I'm supposed to remember myself," he ground out as he pulled the car over into a No Parking zone.

"But we can get around it with a little maneuvering, can't we?"

"I want to see the parade!" Abby's voice cut through their conversation.

"Did you honestly think she'd let us avoid it?" Justin locked the car behind them as they found a spot in the crowd to watch the commotion. Since this parade was uptown, it had many more people attending, and different people had come up with ingenious ways to ensure good places. Fathers had built seats on tops of ladders and chained them to signs, and little children perching in the seats had views of everything without being in any danger of getting too close to the floats. Almost every Mardi Gras had its share of tragic accidents, and parents were naturally cautious. Some families had arrived early enough to set up chairs on the curb, and some just made sure to bring enough strong men to the parade to give their children access to sturdy shoulders.

Justin found a spot for them on the steps of a church, and they watched the spectacle unfold much as it had that afternoon. The main differences were that the floats were lit by running electric lights, and that throughout the parade black men dressed in ragged white sheets carried flambeaux, torches fueled by an oil product perched atop wooden poles. The men strutted and danced, stooping to scoop up coins thrown from the crowd. The flambeaux carriers were a holdover from the night parades of the previous century and a popular part of a half-dozen parades.

Although standing back from the curb, Abby still managed to catch her share of throws, and satisfied with her collection of carnival junk, she followed them back to the car at the parade's conclusion.

"There's a whole week of parades to go, Justin," Bethany said, snuggling next to him on the sofa after tucking Abby in for the night in the four-poster. "Do you think you can make it?"

"Are you going to drag me to every one?"

"If I don't your daughter will."

"She gets the love of this kind of thing from you."

"You know," she said seriously, "when you let go

the way you did today at the parade you're a totally different person. Under that dignified exterior lurks a little boy who just loves to be playful." She wrapped her fingers around the plastic beads decorating the neckline of his jogging suit.

His fingers, spanning her waist, began a sensual ascent toward her breasts, and she could feel her nipples hardening in response. "Bethany, when I'm with you I feel freer, more alive than I thought possible. You've always done that for me."

She caught her breath as his fingers began to tease her breasts gently, and his words sparkled in the air between them. "Do I really do that to you?"

He stopped short at the longing apparent in her voice. "Of course you do. Didn't you know?"

"I always wondered if..." The words wouldn't come.

"Tell me," he demanded softly. "What did you wonder?"

"I always wondered if I really gave you anything at all." She rushed on to cover the sound of the shocked protest forming in his throat. "I always knew you wanted me—desired me, I mean. But I sometimes wondered if that was all our relationship was based on. I never thought I really had anything to give you."

The words had been wrenched from somewhere deep inside her, and he could not miss the self-conscious pain behind them. Bethany, who had done nothing but make his life brighter from the moment she had come into it, had never realized her effect on him. "If you thought it was just desire I felt for you, weren't you selling yourself cheaply?" His voice was harsh with emotion. "Why have you let yourself become involved with me again?"

"Because you give me everything I need," she said in a whisper. "I can't help myself. When I'm with you I'm whole."

"What have I ever given you except heartbreak." He pushed her to one side and then pulled her to face him. "I'm not good for you. I never have been. And yet knowing that, I can't stay away."

"Not good for me?" She was bewildered by his response.

"You're so full of life. I feel as if I'm encased in ice in comparison. You give and give, and I take."

"Justin, that's not true." She was outraged at his perception of their relationship. "I won't have you saying that." She pushed his hands away. "What do you think I want from you, anyway, to be treated like some sort of missionary who goes through life taking care of the needy? I'm not a saint. I'm just as selfish as the next person. You have exactly what I have always needed and wanted—quiet strength, wisdom, a deep caring about life around you. And I only give what I can to you in exchange for what I've got."

"You deserve more than I can give. You always have, and you've never realized it. But I know it." The words were said with heavy finality—a final chapter, the coda of a symphony, the concluding stanza of an epic poem. Justin's face took on the rigid lines of a man suffering alone.

"I see," Bethany said, drawing out the words as she worked to phrase her thoughts. So this was where matters stood between them. She had thought she had only to be patient again, but she hadn't known what she was dealing with.

How could she ever have thought that patience was

going to change the inevitable? Perhaps she did make Justin's life brighter, as he claimed. Perhaps her dark hair and pale skin captivated him in a way that no other woman had before. But good looks and brief surges of joy faded, and Justin, with his analytical mind and controlled emotions had decided there had to be more for him. Once again their relationship was ending almost before it had a chance to begin. Again she had given her body, her heart, and this man had taken them, only to discard them. And this time he had done it in the name of charity.

Justin had used her. Although he accused her of being too unselfish, too giving, he was using the same ploy to end their relationship. He was telling her to go and making it sound as though it were all for her benefit. Justin, the supreme benefactor.

"Sometimes, Justin, people pretend they're doing something for someone else's good when in reality they just want out of a bad situation. You've never promised me anything, and I don't expect anything." She stood and motioned to the door. "I'd appreciate it if you'd leave now. This time I've got your message loud and clear." Her voice was vibrant and steady, but the hand pointing to the door was visibly shaking, and in irritation at showing her feelings, she ran her fingers furiously through her hair.

Justin was bewildered by her emotional display. "What message?" he said standing in front of her.

"Don't play games with me, counselor."

"What games?" he asked softly.

"I think it's called the 'royal kissoff,'" she said, biting off the words like a tenor in a Gilbert and Sullivan operetta.

"Would you explain yourself, please?" His voice was getting steadily softer, but Bethany was beyond caring.

"You pretend that what you really want is my happiness, so you assume the role of the white knight, savior of all befuddled maidens. You tell me you don't want to hurt me—after all, I deserve so-o-o much better. I'm probably supposed to fall swooning at your feet in gratitude for your concern, leaving you free to go your merry way. Only I don't swoon, mister. I'm not an innocent maiden anymore."

"You're all wrong."

"Justin," she said wearily, "you're just looking for excuses to be done with me again. It's all right. I didn't expect a happy ending. Snow White has grown up right along with the little girl lying in there in my bed."

"Bethany," he reached for her, but she skillfully avoided his hand.

"Go home, Justin." Turning, she walked to the French doors leading to her bedroom and opened them. "Call when you want to see your daughter. I'll be glad to arrange visits at your convenience." The doors closed firmly behind her.

She was gone. Only this time she hadn't run away; she hadn't avoided confronting him with the truth. She had faced him with her interpretation of events and tried to set him free.

For a moment he considered throwing open the louvered doors and scooping her up out of the bedroom. But such a sweeping entrance would certainly wake up Abby and frighten her. And what would he say? He was still too confused, too inarticulate to explain himself any further that night.

He locked the door behind him, walked across the

courtyard and through the gate. The quarter was filled with revelers celebrating the carnival season, and he let himself be pulled in the direction of the crowd. Nothing could have been more inappropriate for his mood, but at the same time, the hilarity was vaguely comforting. He was anonymous, but he was also part of something.

Drifting through the streets, he relived the scene with Bethany. She had been so filled with righteous anger, so strong and sure of herself. She was no longer the insecure, sweet young woman he had known in Florida. She no longer leaned toward him for strength, seeking the affection he felt unqualified to give. If he walked out of her life she would survive. This new Bethany was resilient, capable of making her way alone in the world. He was filled with pride at her maturity and with sorrow at the way it had come about.

He sought comfort in a courtyard bar, sitting on a stool to order a warming drink. They had both suffered. Love had caused pain, and the pain was too high a price to pay for the moments of joy.

Or was it? No matter what happened in the future, would he trade the moments he had shared with Bethany and with Abby for a comfortable emptiness? Would Bethany, who had suffered most of all, say that her child and her love for Justin were not worth what she had been through? Justin, staring into whiskey-laced coffee, realized that he had been horribly wrong all along.

Bethany had needed him, just as he had always needed her. Not to survive, not even so that she could grow, but because he completed her. She had said that he filled in the circle of her life and added a needed dimension to her existence. He could see for the first time that it was true.

What was also painfully clear was that he had been using his own incompleteness as a rationalization for not breaking through his walls of reserve to reach out and claim her. His fears had almost cost him the most important thing in his life.

During the five years they had been apart they had grown and changed. They could continue that way—they could manage apart. But life didn't need to be that mundane, that pedestrian. Life should be a celebration, a Mardi Gras. Only love could make that happen.

And Justin Dumontier, the man who for five years had existed in a battle zone between his heart and his head, was suddenly sure that the war had ended. There was no longer a need for armor; there was no longer a place inside him for doubt. With a grin at the bartender, he slapped a large bill on the counter.

"A very happy Mardi Gras," Justin called to the startled little man as he strode out the door.

CHAPTER FIFTEEN

BETHANY SUCCESSFULLY AVOIDED JUSTIN for the next week. Life's Illusions and the finishing touches on the Mardi Gras costumes she had designed for the big day kept her busy enough to warrant the polite excuses she used when he called, inviting her to attend parades or other carnival festivities. She saw him only once. He had come to pick up Abby; the little girl wasn't too busy to want to see every parade she could.

On that occasion Bethany had pasted a casual smile on her face, straining to be distantly friendly for Abby's sake. She had nodded and shaken her head at appropriate intervals during the informal chatter, only to discover at the end of the conversation that she had unknowingly agreed to spend Mardi Gras morning at Justin's house. Busy assessing his calm, open manner and the incredibly attractive walking shorts that revealed so much of his long, muscled thighs, she had not even realized what she was doing. Trying to extricate herself from her own carelessness was impossible. She had been caught off guard, and there was no way to explain to him that she couldn't concentrate in his presence.

On the Monday evening before Mardi Gras Day, she stood in the shop, dazed by the waves of customers who stomped in and out, buying everything in sight. Al-

hough there were those who grumbled that business
vas not as good as it usually was, Life's Illusions had
lone better than anyone had expected. And waiting in
he wings was an order from Danielle de Bessonet's
nother for two hundred masks to be used as party
avors in the spring. The slow years of building up
nventory and customers were over, and Madeline and
3ethany both felt they could safely ask Valerie to join
'eir venture as a partner when summer came. Her tal-
·nted input would make all of their jobs easier.

At ten o'clock, Madeline joined Bethany to help close
ιp the shop. "Well, kiddo, it's over for another year,"
she crowed as she fastened the series of locks on the
front door.

"I'm delighted. And we did so well." Most of their
:ash had already been taken care of earlier, and Bethany
:ounted what was left in the cash register, entering her
figures in their account book. "Things will seem so slow
after carnival, but I can use some peace and quiet for a
while."

"You'll have more time to spend with Abby...and
Justin." Madeline leaned on the display case, watching
Bethany unfasten the lock on the small safe they kept
for petty cash.

"Not Justin," Bethany answered, her voice even.
"I'm not going to be spending anymore time with him—
ever." She straightened up after relocking the safe.
"Justin and I are through for good."

Madeline seemed unconcerned by the bombshell.
"Oh, really? Whose idea was that?"

"It was a mutual agreement. Justin explained to me
that I deserved better, and I decided he was right."

"If you want better, you're going to have to go knock

on St. Peter's gate to find it," Madeline said with a yawn. "It seems to me that Justin Dumontier has everything any woman in her right mind would want."

"Everything except love."

"Especially that. The man's completely, totally, one hundred percent crazy about you." Madeline watched Bethany's expression with a practiced eye. "And that feeling is mutual, as anyone could see."

"I spent a lot of my life giving love to people who didn't want it, Madeline. I don't want to live that way anymore." Bethany sighed and rubbed her eyes with the palms of her hands. "I want to be loved, too."

"What makes you think that Justin doesn't love you?"

"Madeline, he practically came out and told me he doesn't want me. He says I'm too good for him, that he has nothing inside himself to give."

Madeline moved across the room to flick off the overhead light, leaving the room illuminated only by the streetlamps and the small lights in the display windows. The masks left on the wall grinned and stared at the two women like the chorus of a Greek drama.

"It seems to me," Madeline said after a minute of silence, "that neither one of you has quite caught on to the flow of giving and receiving. The two of you are such incredible perfectionists that you truly deserve each other."

"'Perfectionists'? When have I ever demanded perfection?" Bethany's voice was a startled rasp.

"You've always expected Justin to make the first move, to understand your needs. You even denied him his daughter because he didn't. Really, Beth, for someone who grew up viewing the darker side of human nature, you have a most unrealistic view of people. I think you expect Justin to act like the hero in a novel or a television show."

Bethany could feel the color draining from her face. "'A television show,'" she whispered. She thought of her television family, and the time when she had first discovered there could be more to life than what she was experiencing.

"And now," Madeline went on, "now you can't forgive him for his fears, for his lack of self-esteem."

"Justin? Lack of self-esteem? Justin is the most poised man I have ever seen!" Madeline's criticism pierced Bethany to the core. Madeline, who had always been supportive, who had always been there for her when she needed it, apparently had absolutely no sympathy for her now.

"Justin doesn't feel that he's good for you, and you'd see it if you just opened your eyes. Frankly, I wonder if either one of you is even capable of seeing what's right in front of your faces."

Bethany heard the click of the back door leading into the courtyard, and Madeline was gone. The headlight of a police car passing by the shop caught one of the masks as if in a spotlight. It was a flamboyant papier-mâché mask of a sun with a human face and a permanent flirtatious wink. "What are you leering at, you old fool?" Bethany said darkly as she followed Madeline's path out the door.

"STAND STILL, ABBY, or I won't be able to fasten the headdress." Asking a child to stand still on Mardi Gras morning before the sun had risen was unfair, and Bethany knew it. But on Mardi Gras anything was possible, even the impossible. She picked up the satin headband with peacock feathers sewn to it and carefully fastened it with hairpins to Abby's flowing hair. "Do you have your mask, sweetheart?"

Abby ran to her drawer in their shared dresser and found the soft-sculptured mask Bethany had made for her months before. "Here," she said excitedly.

"Well, you'll finally get to wear it," Bethany said. "And you'll look wonderful. Even Justin won't know who you are," she teased.

"I already told daddy what I'd be wearing."

"'Daddy'?" Bethany sat down on the bed, staring at the little girl. "You're calling him 'daddy' now?" she tried to ask nonchalantly.

"Well, he is my daddy," Abby replied with the inflection of one who thinks she is talking to a simpleton.

"Yes, he certainly is," Bethany agreed.

"Aren't you going to wear your costume?" Abby asked, closing the subject.

"Yes." Bethany rose and walked to the closet to pull out her own disguise. After much thought, she had decided to go as the spirit of Mardi Gras. She had sewn a flowing robe of purple voile that was slit up each side to well above her knees, exposing tempting views of creamy flesh. Draped in folds at different angles were yards and yards of gold lamé and emerald-green chiffon, spotted with clusters of tiny sequins and rhinestones. The costume had taken her the better part of a month to finish, which was nothing compared to the time that many people in New Orleans, and especially in the French Quarter, spent on theirs. There were some who started on their costumes on Ash Wednesday and worked steadily for an entire year to complete them.

To complement the robe Bethany had splurged on supplies for a two-tiered mask of golden dyed ostrich plumes and elaborate beadwork. Experimenting with the design, she had rationalized the time spent as development of her art. But the reality was that she wanted Justin to remember her this way: proud, dramatic and absolutely beautiful. She had designed the mask to sweep around each eye, leaving the rest of her face completely bare. And she had cut the eyeholes large enough to clearly reveal her enormous blue eyes. The mask hid nothing and accentuated everything.

Her buzzer sounded, and she pushed the button to allow Justin access to her courtyard. *Why is my hand shaking,* she wondered. Her decision had been made, and she had only the task of learning to live with it ahead of her. Attempting to deaden her responses to his presence was one of the first steps she had to take. She swung the mask up on her head, smoothing her dark hair around it. It was easier somehow to face him with her mask on.

"You're both stunning," he murmured as he stepped into the apartment. Abby in her royal-blue satin pajamas decorated with gold-and-green embroidery and rhinestones and Bethany in Mardi Gras colors with the feathered mask that clearly showed the lovely face beneath, were creatures from another, more gracious and exotic planet. He was bewitched.

"Where's your costume, daddy?"

Bethany saw Justin's quick grin at his new title, and she was glad for him, even though she was still trying hard to harden her heart. "Your mommy hasn't given it to me yet."

She had thought that Justin would forget her promise

of a special costume, and after she made the decision to put him out of her life, she had put the partially completed costume in the back of her closet. But the only projects she ever left unfinished were those that were bad ideas in the first place, and the costume had been taking shape so beautifully that she had finally taken it from the closet and finished it.

"Come with me. I'll get it for you," she said with little enthusiasm. Justin would be very difficult to resist in his new finery. She lay the costume on the bed and left the room, waiting while he dressed. Her heart sank a few minutes later when he stepped into the living room.

His torso was covered by a white satin shirt, neckline bared almost to his waist, clearly revealing his broad chest. The flowing sleeves were caught at the wrist by narrow bands that called attention to his strong slender hands. With artistic precision, she had trailed embroidery down the neckline of the shirt using gold and silver thread in designs that she repeated on the cuffs. The black velvet trousers were cuffed at the knees and worn over black tights that hugged the strong legs under them. But the truly exceptional thing about the costume was the cape—silky black velvet lined with shimmering silver-shot white satin. Yards wide, it swirled around him as he walked, reaching almost to the middle of his thighs.

Swallowing hard, she tried to ignore the sinking sensation she was experiencing. No one should be allowed to look that spectacular. "Here's your mask," she croaked, handing him a black coque-feather creation, designed to hide the upper half of his face, leaving the sensual mouth free to tantalize. When donned, the feathers stood about his face in spikes and trailed down

o the neckline of his cape and over his shoulders. The
ntire costume was simple, with graceful yet masculine
ines, and Justin, in it, was superb.

"What do you think?" he asked, feet wide apart and
hands clasped behind his back like a pirate on the deck
of the *Jolly Roger*.

"I think it's something else," she said in the under-
statement of the year.

"I think we make quite a pair," he said in a voice of
silky elegance.

"Yes, well..." She picked up her tote bag of Mardi
Gras necessities and swung it over her shoulder. "Let's
go." They started out the door, when she remembered
she had forgotten something. Returning to the apartment, she opened the door to her workroom and disappeared, coming back with the white mask decorated
with tiny crystals that she had dubbed the "Snow
Queen." "It's for your mother," she explained as she
hurried back to join them. "It will look perfect with her
silver hair."

Justin blocked her way, raising his hand to her face to
trace an unhurried line around the edges of her mask.
"Have I told you lately what you mean to me?" he said
in his silky voice.

Caught completely unawares, she just stared at him,
speechless and mystified. Finally she sniffed in an attempt to reset the atmosphere. "Not in the past five
years," she responded with intended sarcasm. But the
voice she heard did not quite make the sought after impression; the wobble in it was entirely too vulnerable.

"Remind me to tell you later on," he promised,
reaching to place his fingers possessively in the small of
her back to help guide her down the stairs.

Justin's house lay directly along the parade route, and although it was only seven o'clock in the morning, crowds were already lining the streets. "I hope we can save a place in front of your house from which Abby can see the parade," Bethany mused out loud. She and Justin had removed their masks, and the feathered creations sat between them, along with Mrs. Dumontier's mask, like jungle birds on a tree limb.

"Homer and Mrs. Waters have been taking care of that chore since well before dawn. You'll love what we've rigged up."

What they had "rigged up" was a high platform painted gold, with Mardi Gras banners decorating it. Complete with railing, deck chairs and a small table, the platform had been assembled directly in front of the huge house, creating an ideal spot to see the parade from and to beg for trinkets. "I'm having trouble believing this, Justin," Bethany hooted as she watched Abby climb the step ladder to the platform. "How long did they work on it?"

"Actually, I built it. It's put together in sections, and Mrs. Waters staked out the territory while Homer and I assembled it. I thought Abby should see the parades in style and I knew she'd want to be closer than our front steps." Justin's matter-of-fact tone was belied by what appeared to be a blush under his dark skin. Justin blushing? Bethany was completely entranced.

"Look at her. She loves it, Justin. She'll never forget this Mardi Gras. But you know she'll be spoiled for all the others."

"Well, I hope she'll be using it every year."

"I don't think I'm going to be up to helping Homer assemble it next year," she speculated. "You may have o fly back from Chicago just to show us how." It was nly seven o'clock in the morning and already she was sking him to come back. What had happened to her irm resolve to put him out of her life?

"Oh, I don't expect to be flying anywhere next Mardi Gras. I have my plans for that week made already."

Thanks, but, no thanks, she translated with a mental hrug. Justin was playing the game better than she was. At least he was being honest about his intentions to keep listance between them.

She watched him stride to the platform and lift Abby o the ground. The three of them walked to the house, where Louise had an elaborate breakfast waiting.

"Did you see what daddy built?" Abby lifted her rms to be picked up by her obliging grandmother. Kissng the child, Louise extended an arm to Bethany for a quick hug.

"Happy Mardi Gras, dear," she crowed happily.

"I brought you a present," Bethany said, presenting Louise with the snow-queen mask.

"It's sensational," Louise crooned happily. "I've never had anything so lovely." And she obviously was lelighted, because no one saw her without the mask for he remainder of the day.

Inside they found a table groaning with the weight of lish after dish of mouth-watering food. "I've invited ome others in to eat throughout the morning. I hope ou don't mind," Louise apologized to Bethany.

"Lamar and Danielle among them," Justin added to eassure her.

They filled their plates with croissants, scrambled ·ggs, grits and grillades, which were pieces of veal in a .picy tomato gravy to serve over the grits. For Abby

there was the ever-present king cake, since Mardi Gra
Day was the last day it was served until Twelfth Night o
the following year. Mimosas with French champagn
flowed freely.

Abby flew around the table, taking bits and pieces t
snack on, but she was too excited to sit still. "Aren't w
missing a parade?"

"The Zulu parade is going on right now," Bethan
explained between mouthfuls, "but we're going to hav
to miss it this year. It doesn't come by the house." A
Abby's face fell in disappointment, Bethany added th
ultimate New Orleans bribe. "Besides, Valerie is goin
to try to get you a Zulu coconut. Her uncle is in th
parade." The Zulu Krewe was one of the two blac
krewes that paraded for carnival, and was famous fo
the hand-decorated coconuts that were handed out to
select few during their parade. People had been know
to do almost anything to get one.

"You'll see plenty of floats, darling," Louise inserte
tactfully. "Do you have your bag ready?" Abby pulle
her grandmother into the drawing room, where thei
Mardi Gras supplies had been stored.

"Living right on the parade route, Justin," Bethan
asked with curiosity when she found they were alone
"and having a mother who obviously loves this sort o
thing, how did you miss the parades when you wer
growing up?"

"My father saw to it. After Marie died, my fathe
became very protective and very rigid. Mardi Gras wa
strictly a social obligation to him, not a time to enjo
oneself. I think his intention was to see that I grew u
very fast, and he succeeded quite well."

"It's funny," she mused out loud. "That's somethin

we have in common, and I never realized it before. We both grew up too fast.''

"I think we have much more in common than you've realized," he said softly, and she saw that he was smiling.

"Madeline says we're both perfectionists."

"Yes, she's told me that, too."

"Not only have you gained a daughter, but it looks like you gained a mentor, too."

"I could have done much worse." He shrugged. 'Maybe we should both have spent more time listening to Madeline's thoughts these past few weeks."

There was no time to explore the meaning of his words. Abby could contain herself no longer and insisted on being taken out to the crowded sidewalk to look at costumes. A family of tacos were strolling down the street, complete with a walking jar of hot sauce in their midst. The main characters from the *Wizard of Oz* were standing in a group around a ladder they had set up on the neutral ground next to a bunch of Indians who had erected a small tepee for shelter. All up and down the avenue a fantasy land held sway.

Whole families had coordinated costumes, with everything imaginable from rollicking clowns to fruit salad with grapes made from dozens of purple balloons. Walking clubs in elaborate dress strutted up and down in front of the expanding crowds, and everywhere that a few feet of ground existed were blankets, ladders, chairs and picnic baskets. There was so much to see that no one was in a particular hurry for the parade to arrive.

Arrive it did, however, and a cheer went up, along with concerted scurrying to gain inches closer to the curb. Justin's platform was a deserted island, in contrast, with enough room for the whole family and th last-minute guests who arrived bringing a little gir Abby's age.

The next hour was filled with laughter as people u and down St. Charles vied for throws and greeted car nival's royalty. The Dumontier platform was weighte down with Rex medallions and doubloons. Unlike othe parts of the parade routes, the St. Charles section wa populated by family groups, and the spirit was slightl less raucous then in other areas of the city. Still, ther was enough excitement to last a lifetime on the usuall sedate avenue. The phenomenon was known locally a the two-mile-long family picnic, and the scene trul fitted the description.

Following the Rex parade came the largest paradin organizations of all: the truck parades. Composed o groups of people who rented huge platform trucks an decorated them to their own liking, the truck parader were notoriously generous. The Dumontier platform and the surrounding area received a veritable hurrican of throws, and Abby and her new friend ran out o room in their bags quickly, resorting instead to shop ping bags contributed by Mrs. Waters.

"I'm not sure I can stand anymore of this," Bethan finally confessed to Justin, "but I think Abby plans t stay here until the last truck rolls by." A stuffed plai dog landed at the little girl's feet, and she squealed wit delight as if her shopping bag weren't already half full "See what I mean?"

"My mother has volunteered to stay with her. Hov would you like to spend some time in the Quarter befor all the good costumes disappear?"

It was the kind of invitation she had planned to re

use, and yet the magic of the day had wound itself around her heart, too. "What about Lamar and Danielle?" was as close to saying no as she could come.

"My mother will take care of them if they ever arrive. I have a feeling they may be celebrating Mardi Gras in their own fashion." His hand snaked under the cascading feathers covering the nape of her neck and gently massaged the tight muscles. "Come with me, Bethany. I want to spend the rest of the day with you."

It seemed easier to agree than to make a fuss. Or at least that's what she told herself. They said their goodbyes, thanking Louise, who asked Bethany's permission to allow Abby to spend the night. Since the French Quarter was at its wildest on Mardi Gras Day, Bethany readily agreed, glad to have Abby out of the melee.

Homer had parked his own car on a side street, and he dropped them off as close to the French Quarter as he could get. They walked the rest of the way, holding hands to keep from being separated in the teeming crowds. On Canal Street they saw the same floats that had already chugged down St. Charles. Stepping on discarded beads and ignoring the pushing, shoving bystanders, they wove their way to the Quarter in silence punctuated only by warnings to each other.

The Quarter had gone crazy. On Bourbon Street, every square inch was populated by screaming, laughing, merrymakers. Elaborate costumes abounded, more intricate and costly than the homier ones found on St. Charles. Costume contests were held each year, sponsored by several of the local gay bars, and participants specialized in the outrageous. On Mardi Gras Day, the obscene was acceptable in a way that normally would be

frowned upon, and the costumes, or lack of them,
would make a Bourbon Street stripper blush.

Justin and Bethany wandered arm in arm through the
crushing throngs, at times not able to move anywhere
except where the crowds led them. She proudly pointed
out people wearing masks she had designed, and he
pointed out people who would probably need his legal
services the next day. They caught beads tossed off of
balconies above them and added them to the heavy collection of necklaces that each one sported. Finally
Justin guided Bethany down a less crowded side street,
nudging her to stand against a brick wall as he pinned
her there with a hand on each side of her masked face.

"Let's go to your place." Removing his mask, he
reached toward her and lifted hers off her shining hair.
"It's time we talked."

She was exhausted, and it seemed the simplest thing
to do. Justin guided her through the throngs that crowded Royal Street, and she unlocked the iron gate to her
courtyard. Inside, her apartment was a quiet oasis away
from the rowdy crowds.

"Let me fix you something to drink," she said politely.

"Make it something strong."

The strongest thing she had was wine left over from
their jambalaya luncheon, and she brought him a glass,
choosing iced tea for herself. Leaning against the window, she waited for him to begin.

He finished the wine in silence, getting up to pour
himself another glass before he spoke. "I thought this
would be easier, but I've never been good at expressing
my feelings."

She couldn't resist. "I've noticed."

Her answer was greeted with a wry grin. "I'm sure you have. Anyway, it would be easier if you'd come over here and sit next to me."

Not wanting to appear frightened of his proximity, she moved to the sofa and sat on the edge away from him. "Better?" she asked coolly.

Warm hands found their way around her waist, and he pulled her back to rest against his bared chest. The position was entirely too intimate and she struggled to move away, but Justin's grip was firm. "Please stay here," he murmured in her hair. She went limp against him, knowing that a struggle would seem ridiculous, and she waited for him to continue. "I suppose passive resistance is better than active," he said with a sigh. "This will have to do for a start."

"What do you want to tell me, Justin?" She could feel his lips in her hair, and his arms tightened around her as if he were afraid she might struggle again when she heard his words.

"Something I've wanted to tell you for a long time. That I want you, that I need you, that I love you and want to spend the rest of my life with you." His head was buried in her hair and his hands stroked soft caresses under the fabric of her costume.

The words were not what she had expected to hear. She had been certain that Justin, in his analytical manner, was going to explain why they were a mistake together. She had thought that with concerned formality he would list the reasons they should not continue the hazardous intimacy they were reestablishing. Disoriented by the impact of his words, she was unable to put them into clear focus. It was as if she had awakened at midnight to find the sun shining brightly. She could not form an answer.

"I guess you need some time to think," he said after a long silence. Formality was beginning to creep into the voice that had been so tender and full of promise. "Perhaps I've misunderstood the love you say you feel for me." His hands slid from her thighs, and he loosened the grip he had held her in. "Would you like me to leave?"

Where was her tongue when she needed it most? She could only manage one word. "Never."

His hands caught in her hair and he turned her to face him. "Tell me you love me, that you'll marry me."

"I do, I will."

His kisses had never felt so glorious; for the first time, they were sharing love with no fears, no barriers. Salty tears mixed with lingering kisses, and Bethany knew there had been no finer moment in her entire life. Without exchanging a word, they stood, and Justin carried her to the bed to seal the bargain they had made.

If their lovemaking had been wonderful before, it was perfect now. Their communication was complete, each able to anticipate the other's needs and fulfill them instinctively. Finally, when they lay entwined with hardly a heartbeat between them, they practiced saying the words that had made the difference.

"I love you," Justin told her over and over. "I almost let my own concerns ruin the best thing in my life."

"What were you afraid of?"

"I really was afraid of hurting us both. I didn't want to choke the life out of you the way my father did with my mother. She was so vibrant, brimming with love and excitement. Little by little my father killed that in her. He took who she was and molded her into his own image. And he did the same with me, until I was afraid I'd never be able to give the wholehearted affection and response I knew you needed.''

"You really were afraid for me?" Bethany asked, stroking the hair back from his forehead.

"Right from the beginning. I felt you needed someone more carefree, someone younger and more spontaneous, who could give you the love you seemed to need so badly. You were always giving, but I sensed a need inside you that I didn't feel capable of filling, no matter how much I might want to.'' He trailed tiny kisses down her nose.

"You left me for my own good. All of this was for my good?'' She was silent for a minute. Finally she choked out a request. "Please, Justin. Please don't ever be that considerate again. I don't know if I could live through it if you were.''

His chest rumbled with bittersweet laughter, and she joined him. "Bethany,'' he said when they were quiet again, "don't ever keep anything from me again, either. You were protecting me when you thought you might be pregnant, just as I was protecting you from a relationship I didn't think would be right for you. I know now that love doesn't grow when lovers try to shield each other. It grows when they stand with eyes wide open and face their problems together.''

Their lips met and caught fire, and for a while they were silent again.

"What changed your mind, Justin,'' she whispered later in a lazy voice.

"I got selfish. I decided to risk the future and take a chance on what I felt. And I began to see that you weren't as fragile as I had thought. Last week I finally realized that you could take care of yourself. If you thought we could make it, then you were probably right.''

"We're two parts of a whole, Justin. Together we add so much to each other. Our differences are strengths.'' She lay across his chest, watching with fascination the expressions in his unguarded eyes. "Our life in Chicago is going to be so good.''

"A correction, my love. Our life here is going to be so good. I've quit my job in Chicago. I'm staying with my father's firm.'' He marked a trail up and down her spine with his fingertips, smiling at her astonishment.

"You're not . . . we're not leaving?''

"No. I'm back home for good.''

A suspicious twinkle leaped into her eyes. "Does Abby know?''

"I told her, yes.''

"That's why she's calling you daddy now. I wonder why she didn't tell me?''

"I asked her to keep it a secret. I'm amazed that she succeeded.''

"She has her father's ways.''

"Our next one can be just like you to even the score.''

She pillowed her head in his shoulder, sighing as his hands stroked her back. "Are you sure about quitting your job?''

"I've been running all these years. From now on I'm going to save my running for races and for trips around Audubon Park with you.''

"But you loved your job so much.''

"I'll be a full partner at the firm and I can make sure my job there is interesting.'' His voice took on a note of pride. "I've been offered a seat on a crime commission that the mayor's office is organizing, and I'll finally have a chance to put the Dumontier name to good use.''

"Everyone is going to be so surprised," she murmured sleepily.

"No one is going to be surprised at all. Everyone else saw the handwriting on the wall a long time ago. My mother has probably already asked her priest to perform the wedding. Madeline has probably started making plans to ease your workload. Danielle is undoubtedly planning our reception. And Lamar has most likely booked his band to play, and invited the entire population of Bayou Lafourche to attend. I wouldn't even be surprised if Abby is checking up on the correct etiquette for four-year-old flower girls."

The sun was setting in a spectacular display of Mardi Gras glory by the time they roused themselves to dress and raise the windows to step on to Bethany's balcony. The streets were still crowded, as they would be until midnight, and with enthusiasm Justin and Bethany tossed beads to the costumed throngs below.

"What do you think about Mardi Gras now?" Bethany asked after all their beads had been thrown. "Are you still a skeptic?"

His answer was a lingering kiss, punctuated by cheers from the crowd. "I still think it's noisy nonsense, but I hope I never miss another one as long as I live."

"There's a lot we've both missed, my love, that we will never be missing again." And the words, spoken under the streaked canopy of the New Orleans sky, held the ring of bright promise and unquenchable hope for the future.

ANNE MATHER

Anne Mather, one of Harlequin's leading romance authors, has published more than 100 million copies worldwide, including **Wild Concerto,** a *New York Times* best-seller.

Catherine Loring was an innocent in a South American country beset by civil war. Doctor Armand Alvares was arrogant yet compassionate. They could not ignore the flame of love igniting within them...whatever the cost.

HIDDEN IN THE FLAME

WORLDWIDE LIBRARY IS YOUR TICKET TO ROMANCE, ADVENTURE AND EXCITEMENT

**Experience it all in these big, bold Bestsellers—
Yours exclusively from WORLDWIDE LIBRARY
WHILE QUANTITIES LAST**

To receive these Bestsellers, complete the order form, detach an
send together with your check or money order (include 75¢ postag
and handling), payable to WORLDWIDE LIBRARY, to:

In the U.S.
WORLDWIDE LIBRARY
Box 52040
Phoenix, AZ
85072-2040

In Canada
WORLDWIDE LIBRARY
P.O. Box 2800, 5170 Yonge Street
Postal Station A, Willowdale, Ontari
M2N 6J3

Quant.	Title	Price
_____	**ANTIGUA KISS**, Anne Weale	$2.95
_____	**WILD CONCERTO**, Anne Mather	$2.95
_____	**STORMSPELL**, Anne Mather	$2.95
_____	**A VIOLATION**, Charlotte Lamb	$3.50
_____	**LEGACY OF PASSION**, Catherine Kay	$3.50
_____	**SECRETS**, Sheila Holland	$3.50
_____	**SWEET MEMORIES**, LaVyrle Spencer	$3.50
_____	**FLORA**, Anne Weale	$3.50
_____	**SUMMER'S AWAKENING**, Anne Weale	$3.50
_____	**FINGER PRINTS**, Barbara Delinsky	$3.50
_____	**DREAMWEAVER** Felicia Gallant/Rebecca Flanders	$3.50
_____	**EYE OF THE STORM**, Maura Seger	$3.50
_____	**HIDDEN IN THE FLAME**, Anne Mather	$3.50
	YOUR ORDER TOTAL	$___
	New York and Arizona residents add appropriate sales tax	$___
	Postage and Handling	$___
	I enclose	$___

NAME _____

ADDRESS _____ APT.# ____

CITY _____

STATE/PROV. _____ ZIP/POSTAL CODE ____
WW2

You're invited to accept 4 books and a surprise gift **Free!**

Acceptance Card

Mail to: **Harlequin Reader Service®**

In the U.S.
2504 West Southern Ave.
Tempe, AZ 85282

In Canada
P.O. Box 2800, Postal Station A
5170 Yonge Street
Willowdale, Ontario M2N 6J3

YES! Please send me 4 free Harlequin Superromance® novels and my free surprise gift. Then send me 4 brand new novels every month as they come off the presses. Bill me at the low price of $2.50 each—a 10% saving off the retail price. There are no shipping, handling or other hidden costs. There is no minimum number of books I must purchase. I can always return a shipment and cancel at any time. Even if I never buy another book from Harlequin, the 4 free novels and the surprise gift are mine to keep forever.

134 BPS-BPGE

Name	(PLEASE PRINT)

Address	Apt. No.

City	State/Prov.	Zip/Postal Code

This offer is limited to one order per household and not valid to present subscribers. Price is subject to change.

ACSR-SUB-1